W9-CEK-564

Brooke blinked and focused on him. "Dr. Porter needs to keep Archie at least another night. But he's stable. Sophie called about Rex."

Dan stumbled over his relief for a cat. Who was Rex? He had an image of a dog curled in the back of the kennel, more eyes than body.

Ben jumped up, worry flashing across the seven-year-old's face. "What happened to Rex?"

"He isn't doing well." Brooke touched Ben's shoulder. "Sophie had several more arrivals last night. Dr. Porter and Sophie think Rex needs to be someplace quieter where he'll feel safe."

"He'll feel safe here." Confidence puffed Ben's chest out.

Ben's absolute certainty softened Dan. That was all he'd ever wanted to give Ben: a safe home. One without chaos. One with stability and love.

Brooke shifted to look at Dan.

Again, her dark brown gaze pulled him in. Her wide soulful eyes called to him. Made him want to learn everything about her. Made him want...

Dear Reader,

I'm blessed to have dear friends, lifelong ones and others that feel as if they've always been in my life. These are the friends that might be three thousand miles away and yet you feel so close. The friends that know all your backstory— the good, bad and gray areas—and love you anyway. These friends become family and make life more balanced and so much richer.

Family and friends are a large part of the community in my City by the Bay Stories. Fortunately, this community helps my heroine, Brooke Ellis, rediscover the power of love and friendship. Brooke finally starts to heal from a painful past. My hero, Dan Sawyer, has been surrounded by his family and friends, yet he has learned to guard his heart. But love—and guidance from those who know Dan best— opens Dan's eyes to a fulfilling life he only ever imagined. Together, Brooke and Dan learn that love can be even more precious the second time around.

I love to connect with readers. Check out my website to learn more about my upcoming books, sign up for email book announcements, or chat with me on Facebook (carilynnwebb) or Twitter (@carilynnwebb). Remember to hug your friends and family then thank them for making life special.

Happy reading!

Cari Lynn Webb

HEARTWARMING

Single Dad to the Rescue

—

USA TODAY Bestselling Author

Cari Lynn Webb

⟨H⟩ **HARLEQUIN**®HEARTWARMING™

If you purchased this book without a cover you should be aware that this book is stolen property. It was reported as "unsold and destroyed" to the publisher, and neither the author nor the publisher has received any payment for this "stripped book."

Recycling programs
for this product may
not exist in your area.

ISBN-13: 978-1-335-51078-5

Single Dad to the Rescue

Copyright © 2019 by Cari Lynn Webb

All rights reserved. Except for use in any review, the reproduction or utilization of this work in whole or in part in any form by any electronic, mechanical or other means, now known or hereafter invented, including xerography, photocopying and recording, or in any information storage or retrieval system, is forbidden without the written permission of the publisher, Harlequin Enterprises Limited, 22 Adelaide St. West, 40th Floor, Toronto, Ontario M5H 4E3, Canada.

This is a work of fiction. Names, characters, places and incidents are either the product of the author's imagination or are used fictitiously, and any resemblance to actual persons, living or dead, business establishments, events or locales is entirely coincidental.

This edition published by arrangement with Harlequin Books S.A.

For questions and comments about the quality of this book, please contact us at CustomerService@Harlequin.com.

® and TM are trademarks of Harlequin Enterprises Limited or its corporate affiliates. Trademarks indicated with ® are registered in the United States Patent and Trademark Office, the Canadian Intellectual Property Office and in other countries.

Printed in U.S.A.

www.Harlequin.com

Cari Lynn Webb lives in South Carolina with her husband, daughters and assorted four-legged family members. She's been blessed to see the power of true love in her grandparents' seventy-year marriage and her parents' marriage of over fifty years. She knows love isn't always sweet and perfect—it can be challenging, complicated and risky. But she believes happily-ever-afters are worth fighting for. She loves to connect with readers. Please visit her website, carilynnwebb.com.

Books by Cari Lynn Webb

Harlequin Heartwarming

City by the Bay Stories

The Charm Offensive
The Doctor's Recovery
Ava's Prize
A Heartwarming Thanksgiving
"Wedding of His Dreams"
Make Me a Match
"The Matchmaker Wore Skates"

Visit the Author Profile page
at Harlequin.com for more titles.

To Stacey—a best friend who quickly became family. You're the sister I got to choose myself.

Special thanks to my editor, Kathryn Lye, for pushing me to become a better writer. I'm grateful. To Melinda and Anna for your continuous support. To my husband and daughters for your plot-twist suggestions that always make me laugh and disrupt my stress.

CHAPTER ONE

"CAN I OFFER you a ride?" A man's deep voice broke through Brooke Ellis's stupor.

Brooke squeezed Luna's dog leash and tried to squeeze a sense of composure through herself.

Why were simple questions the hardest?

Maybe they'd always been hard and that was why Brooke had chosen to live alone in the mountains of Northern California for the past five years.

Until two days ago.

Exactly fifty-two hours earlier, a wildfire had ripped through the forest, forced Brooke and her neighbors to evacuate and destroyed lives.

Brooke turned in her gravel driveway and stared at the older gentleman watching her from inside an oversize pickup truck.

He smiled and repeated his question, "Do you need a ride someplace?"

She stepped closer, found patience in his kind gaze and her answer. "I have no place to go."

He got out of his truck and walked toward

her—he was wearing a volunteer fire-and-rescue jacket. The man may have been older, but he towered over Brooke by at least a foot and seemed to understand his height might make her guarded. He knelt and held his hand out for Luna to sniff. "There's a shelter set up in town. I could drop you off there."

Brooke indicated the two pet carriers near her feet. Archie, her one-year-old cat, slept in one. The veterinarian hospital had to evacuate its patients and he'd been sent home too soon after his abdominal surgery. Inside the other carrier, Cupid meowed. "The shelter reached capacity last night and I have pets with special needs."

"Do you have family nearby?" Luna rolled over onto her back, encouraging the man to rub her belly. He obliged the large but gentle German shepherd with a soft grin. "I could take you to a relative's place."

Another simple question. The answer wasn't so easy. Brooke managed a quick shake of her head, enough to knock the tears back down inside her.

All she had left of her life was in a large black garbage bag beside her. The family members she had were the four-legged ones surrounding her. She clutched Luna's long leash as if the leather anchored her.

The man rubbed his chin and stared at the blackened landscape behind her. Her house was nothing more than ash. Only the axle remained of her truck. The old diesel had refused to turn over and guide her to safety two nights ago. She'd had enough time to grab her animals and the one garbage bag from the truck bed, and cram into the waiting police cruiser. The roaring winds and fire-breathing sky had chased the police car down the mountain to the evacuation site.

"Do you have any plans?" the gentleman asked.

Brooke stared across the street at the decimated hillside. All her plans had been here. On the land. With her animals. Why had she hitched a ride back here when deep down she'd known? "I never imagined. I never planned for…" She lost her voice.

The same way she'd lost her voice five years ago. Only, then she'd been standing in the cemetery in San Francisco County. Beside her husband's grave. The scent of roses and gardenias had been in the air. The grass under her black heels green. The sky a brilliant blue.

Now the air was gray. Ash shifted around them like singed snowflakes.

Nothing was the same except that insistent punch to her gut.

She'd rebuilt her life on this mountain. Wept against the old oaks, screamed her frustration to the sky, cursed Fate and slowly reconstructed her world bit by bit. Day by day.

How many times could one person rebuild? Did she even have the strength? Luna sat up and nudged her head under Brooke's palm as if lending Brooke support.

"I lived almost thirty years in these mountains." Sadness shifted through the man's low voice. "This is the worst I've seen."

"What am I supposed to do now?" Brooke spoke to the sooty air. She'd discovered years ago that Fate had a bad habit of refusing to answer.

"I can't let you stay here. My wife, rest her soul, would be highly disappointed in me." The man pulled out his cell phone and tapped on the screen. "They've opened another evacuation center. Let me take you there."

"I'm just a stranger." And she felt more and more lost—like she'd misplaced a part of herself—every second she stood there.

"Strangers don't exist in moments like these." He rose and held out his hand. "I'm Rick Sawyer."

"Brooke Ellis." She shook his hand, grateful for his firm grip. It steadied her.

"Well, Brooke, how about we get you and your pets someplace safe?"

Brooke nodded. The shelter would have water and a place to sit. Maybe if she sat, she'd find a clear thought. Surely one clear thought would lead to another. Then another. Perhaps by sunrise, she'd find a plan.

Rick picked up the pet carriers and walked to the truck. Brooke lifted her garbage bag and whistled for Luna to follow.

The devastation outside the truck windows—on every street they drove on—clogged her throat and stole her words. Brooke concentrated on breathing. And repeated to herself that she had her life and her pets. That was more than enough. Fortunately, Rick looked as lost in his own thoughts as Brooke. Neither of them seemed inclined to carry on a conversation.

Too many miles of scorched land later, Rick pulled into the community-center parking lot and helped Brooke with her pets and single bag of belongings.

"Hey, Captain." An older woman with a baseball cap and orange volunteer vest sat at a folding table outside the community-center entrance.

"Evening, Darla." Rick motioned to Brooke beside him. "Have room for one more and her fur family of three?"

"I'm so sorry, dear." Darla's frown amplified the apology in her tone. "The animal rooms are full. They evacuated Cedar Ridge and Pine View Estates two hours ago. We've already overextended capacity with the last family of ten that just checked in."

"Can I camp on the lawn?" Brooke had spent two nights at the other site outside in a borrowed tent. She'd returned the tent to the family as more of their displaced relatives had arrived for shelter.

"We ran out of tents this afternoon." Darla shuffled her paperwork.

Rick rubbed his chin. "Heard of any open hotel rooms?"

Darla shook her head. "The hotels that haven't been evacuated are full with residents from the nursing homes."

Brooke swayed. Numbness, rather than panic, seized her.

"Certainly, we can find someplace." Uncertainty flickered through Darla's small attempt at a smile.

"We've got an empty in-law apartment at my son's house and a grandson who loves animals," Rick offered. "You're welcome to use the place."

They were all barely on a first-name basis. How could he open his own house to her? Just like that. Besides, Brooke helped herself. Relied on herself.

"If you aren't going to take the captain up on his offer, honey, I have quite a few families inside that will." Darla dipped her head toward the building. "They'd love a hot shower and their own bedroom tonight."

"I just…" Brooke began.

Darla adjusted the brim of her hat and squinted at Brooke. "Are you alone, honey?"

Brooke nodded.

Darla never hesitated. She rounded the table and clutched Brooke's cold hands. "I've got nine fire stations in the county and over one hundred firefighters who will vouch for Captain Sawyer and his family. The Sawyers are good people, honey. The kind you don't find much anymore. You'll be safe with them."

"Appreciate the endorsement, Darla." Rick looked at Brooke. "We're just a hardworking family that likes to help when we can."

"Your son won't mind?" Brooke asked.

Rick shook his head. "We discussed it when the fires broke out. The place is yours if you want it."

"Or I'll offer it up inside." Darla squeezed Brooke's fingers and whispered, "Take the offer."

Simple kindness was a rare gift. Hard to repay, but Brooke intended to try. "I can pay rent. I promise I won't stay long."

Darla gave Brooke's hands one more encouraging squeeze and released her.

"You're welcome to stay as long as you need." Rick hugged Darla and told her that he'd be back within the next day.

"Take this for her." Darla handed Rick a packet of paperwork and a small bag. "It's an overnight-essentials kit and a checklist for what to do after a fire."

Brooke settled the pet carriers in Rick's truck and climbed into the front passenger seat. "You're a captain?"

"Retired fire captain." Rick switched on her seat heater. "I worked at Station Twelve for most of my career."

That explained why he was in the area, volunteering and helping people like Brooke.

"Retirement took me off the mountain and in a new direction," he said.

"Do you miss living on the mountain?" she asked.

"I miss nature's quiet solitude, but I love being with my grandson and son." Rick pulled out of the parking lot. "After my wife passed, it never felt the same up here."

Brooke wondered if she'd ever feel the same again. Normal again. Nothing felt familiar, not even her worn running shoes and old sweatshirt.

Her muscles unknotted against the warm seat and forced a yawn out of her. She mumbled an apology and tried to swallow her next yawn.

"Might as well settle in." Rick turned onto the ramp for the interstate. "We've got a bit of a drive ahead of us."

Brooke rubbed her eyes. "I never did ask where your son's place is."

"San Francisco," Rick said. "Far enough so

you can breathe in some fresh air and gather your thoughts."

Brooke stiffened. Rick was wrong. So very wrong.

She couldn't think in the city. She couldn't *breathe* in the city. Not since…

"I can't."

She turned toward Rick, intending to tell him to take her back to the shelter.

"It may look impossible now." His hand, warm and gentle, settled over hers. "But everything looks better after a good night's sleep."

A good night's sleep. Brooke hardly remembered what that felt like. Most days she felt like she hadn't slept in years. She closed her eyes. Concentrated on the quiet truck cab and the comfort in Rick's simple touch. She was returning to the city. To a stranger's house. To a past she never wanted to face again.

She'd stay the night and leave first thing in the morning.

CHAPTER TWO

DAN SAWYER STOOD in line at Zig Zag Coffee House waiting to pay for his order and stared at the name flashing across his phone screen: *Valerie*.

His stomach hardened and his jaw clenched as if he was preparing to absorb the abrupt attack of an assailant. He'd accept every shot, especially from Valerie, if that protected his son.

His ex-wife had decided six years ago that traveling the world was more of a priority than her marriage and her four-year-old son. Her last video-chat attempt with Ben had been after the New Year—almost eight months ago. Even that had been cut short after a poor connection interrupted the call too many times.

Valerie's current call dropped into the missed-call list like so many things she'd missed in Ben's life: his first day of kindergarten, his first soccer goal, his first time riding a big-kid bike. Visits from the tooth fairy, the Easter Bunny and Santa Claus. Every year brought something new to celebrate and something unknown to guard against. Mismanaging Ben's juvenile diabetes wasn't an option.

Ben and Dan had worked too hard to overcome the obstacles of Ben's autoimmune disease. Ben was in a good place. A healthy place.

Nothing, and no one, would disrupt that.

"Stare at your phone any harder, you'll miss the world going on around you." The all too familiar gruff voice and laughter-wrapped scold ended Dan's stalemate with his phone, as if he'd been ordered to stand down.

"Dad." Dan glanced at the older man, who matched him inch for inch. Those knots loosened inside him. "What are you doing here?"

"Ben is fine. Numbers were perfect this morning and he even tested himself." His father put a hand on Dan's shoulder and squeezed. "Dropped Ben off at school with his book report and completed poster board just a little while ago."

That still didn't explain his father's unexpected arrival. His dad always claimed he preferred his own home-brewed coffee to the fancy, overpriced coffee houses in the city.

"It's Tuesday." His dad waved his hand around the trendy coffee house. "You always stop here before you drive Ava to her classes."

Every Tuesday for the past six months, Dan left work, picked up his best friend, Ava, and dropped her off at school. It'd started by accident.

Ava had called for a ride after her fiancé's car broke down while Kyle was on the East Coast. They'd just carried on after that. The perfect time for the two longtime friends to catch up. Most recently the drive had been paired with party planning for their friends' joint bachelor-and-bachelorette party, an event that Dan had convinced Ava they should put together as members of the wedding party.

But his father never came with Dan on Tuesday mornings. Or visited this particular coffee house. Not once in the past four years since he'd been living with Dan and Ben. Dan scanned his father, from his deep red hair to his weathered face and worn work boots. "Are you okay?"

"Never better." His dad sipped his coffee, which looked suspiciously similar to a white-chocolate mocha with extra whipped cream. "I brought home an evacuee late last night. Nice lady with a kind heart."

That news could've been delivered via text. Dan searched his dad's face, eyeing his neck as if Dan could read his father's pulse. His dad stirred the whipped cream into his coffee with a wooden stirrer as if he wanted to design a picture in the liquid. "Thought you might want to know that she has pets."

"Pets," Dan repeated. "As in plural."

His dad nodded.

That was definitely bad news. The type of news that could disrupt things at their house.

Dan had told Ben that he was allergic to animals to keep from having to get a pet. He'd started the white lie the year after Valerie had left. Dan had been afraid a pet would be too much for them; there was enough for him and Ben to get used to without adding the responsibility of a pet. After all, Ben's illness wasn't the flu or an appendix surgery that he'd recover from. Juvenile diabetes was an autoimmune disease that Ben would deal with his entire life. It required strict management every day. Thanks to help from Dan's parents and Valerie's mom, Dan had gotten Ben's juvenile diabetes under control and adjusted to his role as single parent. One year later, his mom had died suddenly, his dad had moved in and Dan's world had shifted again. Then Ben had started school and the truth about Dan not really being allergic to animals never came out.

But it wasn't a big lie. Valerie had lied in her wedding vows: promising to love Dan until death did them part. Dan's phone vibrated. Once again Valerie's name claimed the caller ID.

"Our tenant has three pets to be exact. Shelters were full. Hotels, too. Couldn't leave Brooke alone to fend for herself." Rick settled his shrewd gaze on Dan and shook his head. "That's not the Sawyer way."

No. The Sawyer way was to *always* help. Even if it meant letting go. Like Dan had done with Valerie.

Their marriage had ended over couriered paperwork, stamped with international postage, and no disputes. Dan had gained legal and physical custody of Ben. Valerie had gained her freedom.

Despite their obvious personality differences, Dan had always believed they'd both agreed on parenting styles. How wrong he'd been.

Dan had stepped in to fill both parental roles. Valerie had stepped out and never looked back. Even with Valerie's capricious nature, he hadn't expected that. His young son had lost his mother. That wasn't a wound that healed easily.

Now Valerie was blowing up his phone. And his father had invited a woman with pets into their rental apartment. The distractions were compounding. No problem. Dan just had to keep focused on their routine—the one he'd established to keep Ben healthy and safe.

Someone called Dan's name from behind the pickup counter. Dan stepped up to the cashier. Shelby, with her heavily outlined cat-green eyes and even brighter purple hair, said, "Your order is already paid for."

Dan gaped. That wasn't part of the usual routine. The entire staff knew his order by heart.

He never had to wait long—that was routine. "It can't be. I haven't paid yet."

"Another customer covered it and told me to tell you thanks for all that you do for the community." The jeweled earring in Shelby's eyebrow twitched, as if she was daring him to challenge that people in the world could be kind.

Dan glanced around the coffee shop, searching for the Good Samaritan. No one stepped forward. Dan shoved his phone into the pocket of his cargo pants and walked to the pickup counter.

If he believed in signs from the universe like Ava did, he'd look at the customer's kindness as the good to balance the bad. *Because—let's face it—everything is off this morning.*

His dad waited near the door, enthused about the evacuee from the fires. While second thoughts shifted through Dan. He hadn't rented out the in-law unit since his divorce, preferring to keep things as simple as possible, especially for Ben.

Dan silently thanked the stranger for the gesture. Stuffed the money he would've used to pay for his order along with a tip into the tip jar and grabbed his to-go order.

His dad held the door open. "Perhaps you'll discover a new appreciation for pets with our tenant."

That wasn't *ever* going to happen. Dan had

nothing against dogs. In another life, he'd pictured his home with several kids, two dogs and a wife. That wasn't his world now and that picture had been distorted years ago. Dan's world now was his work, volunteering and his son.

Besides, he wasn't about to do anything that might ruin what he already had. His life was good. He was content. Ben was happy. That was enough, wasn't it? "I don't think she'll be with us that long."

"There's a fire raging in the mountains, son." Rick settled a baseball cap on his head and studied the sky. "It was only twenty-five percent contained this morning." That could delay her return.

"Pick up groceries on your way home."

"I went to the store two days ago." Dan pulled his truck keys from his pocket.

"Not for us," his dad said. "For Brooke. Our tenant."

Dan stopped on the sidewalk and faced his dad. "You want me to buy her food?"

"I'm heading back up north." Rick twisted a plastic lid over his coffee cup. "They need help transporting supplies to the shelters."

And his father expected Dan to help their new tenant. After all, that was the Sawyer way.

He could argue that he'd forgotten to order syringes last week and had to pick those up within the hour. Mention the planning meeting he'd promised to attend for the school's Fall Festival. And detail every other ball he juggled to keep the Sawyer family moving forward. It wouldn't matter.

His dad knew Dan would buy groceries. And Dan knew it, too.

He ordered his dad to be safe, climbed into his truck and rearranged his schedule for a quick stop at the grocery store.

Ten minutes later, Ava climbed into the truck. She dumped her backpack with a thud and grasped the extra tall tea from the drink holder like it was a divine gift. "What is a sign associated with meningitis—Homans's sign, Kernig's sign or Tinel's sign?"

"Kernig's sign. If the leg can't be straightened, it's a positive sign for meningitis. Homan's is deep-vein thrombosis and Tinel's is carpal tunnel syndrome." Dan tapped his coffee cup against hers. "I'm right, aren't I?"

"You should be in physician's assistant school with me." Ava sipped her tea. "I could use your brain."

"You mean you could copy off me." Dan pulled away from the curb and merged with the traffic.

"It's wrong to copy." Ava glanced in the back seat as if making sure Ben wasn't there. "But I would use your notes. You write much neater than me."

"You say that like it's bad." Dan clicked on his blinker to change lanes. That should mute the vibration of his phone on the console and his urge to make sure it wasn't Valerie calling him again.

"Speaking of bad things, did you hear about Hank?" Ava asked.

"Kevin told me that Hank got sick last night." Dan's supervisor, Kevin McCoy, had called him on his way into work to let Dan know he was one of the senior guys on shift for the night.

"*Sick* is putting it mildly," Ava said. "Denise texted me. Hank is having triple-bypass surgery this morning. He's only forty-four."

Hank Decker was also a career paramedic and one of Dan's longtime coworkers. Dan stopped at a red light and looked at Ava. "Are you serious?"

"Wish I wasn't." Ava tapped her fingers against her cup. "What did you eat last night in the rig?"

"What does that have to do with Hank?" Dan scowled at the traffic around him.

"Come on, Dan. You and I both know the statistics of our work too well," Ava said. "You have to take better care of yourself. You don't want to become another statistic."

Dan focused on the car in front of him. Ava had to transition from her paramedic work into something less stressful. Between her military-medic background and working as a paramedic in the city, she'd pushed the limit on her stress boundaries. But Dan didn't have that kind of stress. Sure, his plate was full, but whose plate wasn't?

"If you aren't going to do something for yourself, then do it for Ben," Ava urged.

"Fine. You're right." Ben was his everything. His son was his world. And his best friend wasn't wrong. "I could stand to eat a few less french fries and add a few more days at the gym every week. That sound good?"

"It's a start," Ava said.

"Now, can we talk about coordinating the bachelor-and-bachelorette celebrations?" And move away from Dan's health and his fast track to becoming another statistic.

Dan gripped the steering wheel. Had his supervisor known about the seriousness of Hank's condition last night? Was that why Kevin had ended the call with the comment about an assistant director position opening within the next month? Adding that he considered Dan a natural fit, as if Kevin feared Dan might be next on the statistic train. Would he?

Dan took a large sip of his coffee, determined to slip in an hour at the gym later that afternoon. "I think we should stick with our original idea. Call the whole thing a coed bash and have one big party."

Surely talking about wedding plans with his best friend would get the day back on track. Back to normal. And distract him from his phone. The one that buzzed again on the console. Dan rushed on, covering the sound, "About the wedding schedule."

"You're quite popular this morning. Something I should know?" Ava grabbed his phone and held it out of his reach. Her gaze settled on Dan like the fog over the bay: heavy and dense. "You met someone."

"When?" Dan shook his head. "Last night between the heart attack and the preterm labor patient?"

"You have less than four weeks until the wedding. You need a date, or you'll be at the singles' setup table," Ava warned, as if he wasn't paying close enough attention. "Do you want that?"

He wanted his day to return to normal. He wanted Valerie to stop calling. He wanted to grab his phone from Ava. "Who's at the singles' table?"

"Women who want to date you." Ava's smile lifted her eyebrows and lightened her tone. "Especially Marlene Henderson. You remember Marlene, right? Wyatt's mom introduced you guys during her garden party in the spring. Marlene is the master gardener at the botanical garden."

And excessively gabby. Dan cringed. He'd

never met anyone capable of putting so many words into one breath so continuously without hyperventilating. Dan had taken several deep breaths for the poor woman. Fortunately, a dear friend of Wyatt's mom had a plant question and Dan had handed off Marlene, then escaped. Surely there was another guest on the wedding-invite list prepared and eager to match Marlene word for word. It just wasn't Dan.

His phone chimed. He winced and concentrated on the road. He was setting his phone on permanent silence as soon as he got it back.

"Seriously, what is with your phone? You never get so many calls." Ava crammed the party-planner binder back into her backpack. "We'll deal with party planning later. What aren't you telling me?"

Ava's insight was all too clear. One of the pitfalls of having a best friend trained to read people and their actions. Dan pulled into a parking space outside San Francisco College of Medicine and turned toward Ava.

She jumped in first. "Everything okay with Ben? Your dad?"

The concern in Ava's voice broke through Dan's jumbled thoughts. Ava cared for his family. Her interest was real and genuine. He'd always appreciated that about her. "Dad is fine. He's opened the mother-in-law apartment to a fire evacuee."

"That's wonderful and…" Ava's words drifted off as if she sensed there was more.

He supposed she could read him well enough to know there was more. They'd worked in tandem too many nights on call in the ambulance not to be able to figure out each other.

"There's more," Dan admitted. He pushed Ava's hand toward her. "Put the phone on speaker and press Play on the voice mail."

Ava glanced at the phone screen. Shock slowed her words. "Valerie called six times. Valerie, as in your ex-wife, Valerie. The ex-wife who is now with your younger brother."

Dan's heartbeat stalled as if that assailant connected with a knockout punch after all. Five years ago, Dan had been pretzeled on his son's hospital bed, Ben finally asleep on his chest. He'd been adjusting Ben's IV lines and scolding himself for his misstep in caring for his sick son. The flu had played havoc with Ben's glucose levels; the vomiting had only compounded things. Ben had been admitted to the hospital for the fourth time that year. And Dan had feared he'd never get it right.

Then the text from Valerie had arrived. Not a checking-on-her-sick-son text. But rather a picture of Valerie with her arms wrapped around Dan's younger brother, her lips pressed against Jason's cheek. The caption—Monte Carlo brought us together—in bold print underneath.

Valerie had followed that with a quick explanation: There wasn't an easy way to tell you. But we both want each other to be happy, right?

Dan had dropped the phone on the floor and curled his arms around his young son. Determined to focus on his true family and guard those he loved from harm.

Years later and he'd kept his promise. He'd gotten over his ex-wife. But he wasn't as numb to his brother's betrayal as he wanted to be.

Dan finally dipped his chin, the motion stiff, his voice flat. "That's her."

"What does she want?" Suspicion laced Ava's tone.

"Play the voice mail and we can find out." Unease twisted through his stomach again.

Valerie's lyrical voice with her upbeat excitement, like she had a really great secret to share filled the truck. *"Bon journo, Dan. Call me back, please. Maybe not now. My connection isn't the best. But call me. Ciao."*

"You can delete it."

"Why didn't you tell me this earlier?" Ava checked the time and swore under her breath. "I have to go to class."

"I don't want it to be a big deal."

He had no idea what Valerie wanted. He only knew he had to protect Ben from getting hurt by her again. This time Ben was old enough to feel his heart breaking if his mother let him down again.

"It already is." Ava tossed the phone at Dan. "You have to call Valerie back. See what she wants."

Dan gripped the phone. "You have to get to class."

"I know. I know. Text me as soon as you talk to Valerie. Otherwise, I won't be able to concentrate in neurology." Ava opened her door, climbed out of the truck and leaned back inside. "You're still good with everyone coming over Friday night, right?"

"Definitely." Several phone calls from his ex-wife and a new tenant were not going to alter his life or change his schedule. "I'm making chicken and waffles, so let everyone know to come hungry."

Ava pointed at his phone. "Call her."

The truck door slammed shut. Dan stuffed his phone in the empty drink holder and backed out of the parking space.

Call Valerie?

Not on his life.

CHAPTER THREE

I'M GOING TO SUFFOCATE.

Brooke shoved aside the thick down comforter, smacked her bare feet on the wooden floor of the bedroom and lunged for the light switch.

Light flooded across the unfamiliar four-poster bed, highlighting the rustic roses embroidered on the comforter. It wasn't enough. Not nearly enough to banish the nightmares of her past.

She stumbled into the kitchen, slapped at the light switches. The night pressed against the windows. Her fear pressed against her chest, sucking away the air and her sanity.

She should never have returned.

The clock on the microwave glowed as if mocking her lack of bravery. Rick had given her a tour of the one-bedroom cottage behind the main house less than three hours ago. Welcomed her and her pets into the unit. And she'd believed—*in that moment*—everything would be all right.

Lies. So many lies. *You're destined for great things, Brooke. Dream big. Reach for the stars, dear.*

She'd reached like her mom had encouraged her. Now she was alone, like she'd been as a child. The shy misfit scared of her own shadow.

But the shadows haunted her now with a different intensity.

You'll always be safe with me, Brooke. Even Phillip had lied. Promises couldn't be kept in a world where twists of fate took away the promisor.

She turned on the lamps in the family room. Flipped the switch for the gas fireplace. Lit up the apartment as if that would steady her world. Prove she was safe.

Brooke reached for her cell phone, her fingers slipping on the granite kitchen counter. She opened the city-map app. Typed in the address that tormented her and stole her good night's sleep.

Two-point-six miles. That was all that separated Brooke from the very corner where a drunk driver had taken everything she'd loved from her. All the promises shattered.

Inhale into your stomach. And hold it for a count of five. So many therapy sessions and still she forgot how to breathe. The urge to run seized her.

Instead her knees buckled. She had nowhere to go.

She collapsed on a kitchen stool and stared at the blue pin flashing over the corner of Bayview and State Streets. The spot she hadn't returned to in the past five years. She'd never again wanted to step foot two hundred miles from there much less twenty blocks.

Deep breaths from your stomach. Increase the oxygen. Slow yourself down. She exhaled on a five count. *Now repeat.*

Her gaze skipped around the open space, seeking something—anything—to focus on. The compact, modern kitchen encouraged even an amateur cook like herself to prepare a decadent three-course meal. The empty bar stools waited for friends to gather. The vintage couch and matching chair were worn and relaxed from years of conversations and comfortable use.

Only one word echoed through Brooke: *trapped.*

She was boxed in like the three crystal angel ornaments—*Joy, Hope, Love*—wrapped inside the wooden jewelry case handmade by her father. Her late husband had given her the angels on their third anniversary. Phillip had claimed the angels would remind her to laugh, to always find the good in everything and to never give up.

There was one other option: her former in-laws, Ann and Don Ellis. Her mother-in-law had called and offered her their spare room, but she'd had shelter then. And surely, they didn't want a constant reminder of their grief. They'd lost their only son.

She rested her forehead on the cool granite counter.

A wildfire had destroyed her house and land. She had her pets and her life—she had what mattered most. She should be grateful.

Still, she wanted to yell at the universe: *Why?*

And demand an answer for a seemingly impossible choice: face the city she feared or the in-laws she knew she could never apologize to enough.

Luna sat beside her and leaned against Brooke's leg. Brooke reached down and sank her fingers into the dog's thick fur. The counter supported her cheek, stopping her from crumpling to the floor. Her gaze locked on the paperwork from Darla.

That was a checklist for what to do after a fire. Not a checklist for what to do to rally courage.

Brooke stared at the papers until her eyes burned. Until the chaos inside her settled into something less smothering. She never moved, only inhaled. Exhaled. Then repeated. The world became less forbidding, more approachable.

A heavy knock on the front door startled Brooke. She straightened, rubbed her cheek and blinked. The first rays of the sun streamed across the kitchen counter like nature's own alarm clock, announcing the arrival of a new day.

Another knock rattled through her. Brooke signaled Luna into a stay position with the shift of her hand. Then cracked open the front door.

A younger version of Rick in a paramedic's uniform grinned at her. Except for the blond that softened his red hair, making it lighter than Rick's deep auburn. His eyes would've been green if not for the intense copper swirls. His height and build would've been well suited for a football field but filled out his uniform perfectly.

"I saw the lights on." He lifted several cloth shopping bags and his smile, then added, "Grocery delivery."

Brooke wanted to close the door. His appealing half grin could disarm her if she was someone else. Someone who believed in fairy tales, storybook romance and that once-in-a-lifetime love could happen again. But she couldn't shut the door. This was Dan, Rick's son. And her stomach growled. "How much do I owe you?"

"I'm not interested in money." He handed the bags to her.

But he wanted something. His head tipped to the side and he studied her. She set the bags near her feet and waited.

His arms remained loose at his sides, his smile easy and unforced. "My dad mentioned you have pets."

"I have two cats." *Her family.* The only support she needed. She signaled Luna to come to her. "And my dog, Luna."

He held out his hand, let Luna sniff his fingers before he scratched her head. "I'm hoping you can take your dog to one of the greenways several blocks over rather than letting her use the backyard for her business."

Brooke was confused and she was sure it showed on her face. There was a perfectly good patch of grass right on the property, why should she walk to a park? Especially when it would mean taking her farther into the city and circumstances she'd rather avoid. Dan cleared his throat. "It's nothing against your dog." Luna sagged against Dan's legs as if she forgave him. He added, "I might've told my son I was allergic to pets."

Clearly, he didn't have allergies. Or he'd have stopped rubbing Luna's back by now. There was something about Dan that soothed, even from a distance. Brooke shifted backward in the doorway. "But you're not?"

His eyebrows pulled together into a charming V. "Not exactly."

Everyone deflected to cover a truth they

didn't want to face, including handsome Dan. Even Brooke.

"It's complicated with my son," Dan admitted.

Things were often complicated. "Sure. I can walk Luna to the greenway." She forced more confidence into her voice, concealing the waver inside. "That won't be a problem."

That satisfied Dan, if not Brooke. "The grocery store is less than a mile past the greenway. A pet store not much farther away. Let me know if you need directions around the city." Luna stretched out near Dan's feet and rolled onto her back as if she couldn't get enough of his attention. As if the dog was undisturbed by his presence.

Brooke couldn't claim the same. "We'll be fine right here." *For the moment.*

"The city is great for exploring, even if you only have a few days," Dan said.

In another lifetime, she would've agreed. Brooke inhaled, using the cool morning air to shrink the curtness from her tone. "Thanks, but sightseeing is far down on my to-do list." *Somewhere below never.*

"The botanical garden and the beach can be good places to clear your mind." Dan's gaze searched her face. "Take a break. Breathe."

Or those were places that stole her breath away as she realized she couldn't hear her husband's

laugh anymore. Or how his hand had once fitted so perfectly around hers. Brooke shifted her
gaze from Dan and smoothed the tremor from
her voice. "Speaking with insurance agents will
probably be easier here. It's quieter."

"You aren't thinking about going back up
north, are you?" Dan asked, his voice quiet.

"Still working on those details."

"Do you have family in the state?" Dan kept
petting Luna as if he was more than content to
linger.

But if he lingered, Brooke would only notice
his gentleness with Luna. She would notice *him*
even more. How was she supposed to ask him
to leave his own backyard?

"I don't have any family. I'm an only child."
Brooke cleared her throat and avoided meeting
Dan's watchful gaze. "My parents came into
the parenting world rather late. But my mother
always told me that I was her greatest journey."

A simple *no* would've been more than enough.
Why did she feel the sudden need to ramble on
as if he was her kind of handsome and made her
nervous? But she hadn't considered anyone her
kind of anything in a long while.

"That's a gift, isn't it?" Dan's movements
were easy, as if he'd always taken the time to
stop by and visit with her. He added, "Having
a mom that makes her children feel like the

most special kids in the world. My mom was like that, too."

Dan blinked as if he'd surprised himself. Brooke liked not feeling so alone. "How long has your mother been gone?"

"Four years this past summer," Dan said. "We head to the lake every June to remember her."

"That's important." Brooke pressed her lips together.

The memorial of her late husband's death was in three and a half weeks. Her in-laws and their extended family would travel to the city to celebrate his memory. They'd invite Brooke to join them as they had every year since his death.

Brooke had never found the courage to face Ann and Don Ellis at her husband's grave since they buried him. "Are you sure I can't pay you for the food?"

"It's on the house." Dan stood up. "Let me know if there's anything else I can help you with."

That one-sided smile returned, capturing Brooke's focus, pulling it away from her worries. But she always relied on herself. She pushed determination into her voice. "I'll be fine. Really."

"I have errands to run." Dan's gaze searched her face as if he was searching for the right words. For something else to say. Maybe a promise that everything would be all right. Or an encouraging line his grandfather had always told him. An uplifting quote.

She'd seen that particular look too many times on her neighbors' and coworkers' faces after the accident. Dan was proof that people didn't want to know you were hurting inside. So, she did what she always did. She reassured him. She reassured him that she could go it alone.

CHAPTER FOUR

THE NEXT MORNING, Dan backed his truck out of the driveway and gaped. A familiar red-haired man and a dog walked side by side two houses down. Dan pressed on the gas. His lips pressed into a grimace.

He pulled the truck over to the edge of the sidewalk and rolled down Ben's window. "Dad? What are you doing?"

Dan knew exactly what the old man was doing. Dan always had the same routine on his day off. *Always*. Because knowing what to expect prevented unwelcome surprises and unnecessary hurt.

Today he'd drop off Ben at school, run errands and return phone calls, including Valerie's. The last was only a onetime blip in what Dan determined would be a normal day. He narrowed his eyes at his dad.

Dog walking wasn't normal for the Sawyer men. Dog walking wasn't on the schedule. After all, Dan planned to avoid his new tenant and her four-legged family.

"Brooke doesn't have a coat or hat. Refused to borrow mine so I took Luna instead." Rick pointed at the German shepherd sitting next to him. Luna's tongue rolled out the side of her mouth, giving her a lopsided, endearing grin. "Told Brooke to get some sleep. Poor girl looked wrung out."

Dan had noticed Brooke's red-rimmed eyes and pale skin yesterday. Not even that or her compact size could mask the strength Dan had sensed inside her. Something about Brooke compelled Dan to both take care of her and stand beside her. "I thought you were heading back up north again."

"Figured a walk wouldn't hurt." Rick rolled his shoulders. "My old joints could use a stretch."

"You don't walk, Dad." Now Ben would want to walk, too—perhaps even tonight. Soon Dan would be offering to pet sit or walk the dog himself. No doubt, Ava would be delighted to know he was getting more exercise. And he could use the exercise. Still, dog walking wasn't exactly what Dan had in mind.

Besides, his tenant had promised Dan wouldn't even know she or her pets were there. Now he was staring at her dog and thinking about her.

"Never too old to change things." Rick reached into his pocket and pulled out a doughnut, his eyebrows lifting up and down. "Besides, I've got treats for Luna and me."

"Dad." Dan stretched the word into a warning. Doughnuts were not in his father's restricted diet. Nor were pastries part of Dan's diet, if he intended to prove Ava wrong and show her that he did, in fact, take care of himself. And prove he wasn't going to be another statistic.

"The way I see it, the walk offsets the calories and sugar." Rick zipped the pastry inside his pocket as if afraid Dan would demand he hand it over. "I'm sharing with Luna. Ben, don't tell Brooke."

"I can't tell Brooke anything because Dad won't even let me meet her." Ben's mulish tone deepened the scowl he aimed at Dan.

"I didn't want to bother her last night. The lights weren't even on in the apartment." Although Dan had checked on Brooke. Saw the bedroom light on after he took out the trash. Saw it was still on after midnight when he'd walked out to his truck to get his phone charger.

Ben leaned out the window toward his grandfather. "Did you know Dad told Brooke that Luna can't use the grass?"

The horror in Ben's voice made it sound like Dan had ordered the dog to be chained inside its crate indefinitely.

"There's nothing saying that your father can't change his mind," Rick said.

Not happening. Dan had come up with that rule after Brooke had failed to invite him into his own apartment. After he'd brought her groceries. Every single day strangers let Dan inside their houses. Granted, those strangers were usually in medical distress. But Brooke had been distressed, too. He'd seen that much in her tight grip on the door handle and heard it in her breathless voice. The woman needed help, even if she didn't recognize it.

His response to being shut out of his own rental unit was childish, of course. But he stood by his new rule. And his plan to avoid her.

"Dad also claimed that Luna would scare me. But I've played with bigger dogs at Sophie's doggy day care." Ben rolled his eyes. "Grandpa, you have to make Dad change his mind."

Dan wanted to change Brooke's mind about him. He wanted Brooke to trust him.

"That's the thing with Sawyer men." Rick rubbed his chin. "Once we make up our minds, we get set in our ways."

"But you started walking, Grandpa," Ben argued.

"Okay. We're going to be late." Dan ended the conversation before his son and father teamed up and tried to outmaneuver him. He had to be sharp with this pair. His tenant had distracted him. That would need to stop. Brooke didn't want his help. Fine. Dan wasn't all that concerned if she trusted him or not. "Dad, keep it to one doughnut."

Rick nodded. Yet his hand landed on his other pocket, giving him away.

Dan rolled up Ben's window and glanced at his son. "If you reconsider your stance on not eating vegetables besides broccoli, then I'll reconsider my grass rule."

"Brussel sprouts aren't worth a *maybe*, Dad." Ben adjusted his seat belt. His voice lifted with curiosity. "But if you promise to let Luna in the backyard, I'll try cauliflower."

"A dog ruining the grass isn't worth you only *trying* a new vegetable." Dan slid a dose of encouragement into his tone. "If you promise to eat cauliflower every week for the rest of the school year, then we might have a deal."

"Dad, you don't even eat cauliflower every week." Ben laughed.

Dan stopped in the drop-off lane at Ben's school. "Does that mean we don't have a deal?"

Ben opened the door, grabbed his backpack and shook his head. "Guess Grandpa was right. Us Sawyer men are just stuck in our ways."

Ben hurried to catch up with his best friend, Wesley. The pair scooted to the side of the entrance and waited. A blond-haired girl with her walking stick extended joined them. Laughter ensued before the trio disappeared inside the school. Ben and Wesley met Ella every morning outside the school—the same place at the same time. One of the boys would be there to help Ella if she needed it throughout the day. That was their daily routine. Dan pulled away from the school, waving to the principal and several teachers in the car line. The same as every morning. Dan wasn't stuck in his ways.

He just *liked* his routine. Every time he'd ever detoured, bad things happened. World-tilting, life-altering things. Things that curdled his stomach, crumpled his knees and damaged brotherly bonds.

One Saturday, he'd rearranged his work shift to join Valerie and three-year-old Ben for an impromptu visit to the redwood forest. Inside the national park, Dan had walked to the bathrooms. Valerie and Ben played hide-and-seek. He'd been gone five minutes and Valerie screamed Dan's name. Ben had wandered into the forest. Valerie had lost their son. And Dan had lost years off his life. If he'd gone to work that day as scheduled, Ben and Valerie would've gone to their playdate as planned. And Dan wouldn't know how to describe mind-numbing terror or full-body panic.

Sure, they'd found Ben pretty quickly. But the outcome could have been so much more tragic. Dan had a mental list of such events. Following a schedule kept life predictable like he preferred. Like he relied on to keep Ben safe.

Why would he want to change things and risk disrupting the life he'd built? The life he liked.

One stop at the drugstore to replenish the Band-Aid stock for the school nurse, Dan ran through his schedule and pulled into his driveway. He had time to return those phone calls, take a nap, then finish his errands.

The dark-haired woman rushing toward him had him slamming the truck into Park. The blood staining her light blue sweatshirt had him jumping out of the truck. *Brooke.*

A quick assessment of Brooke from head to toe confirmed the source of the blood was the bundle she cradled. Dan moved toward her. "What happened?"

"It's Archie." She adjusted the towel around the cat and revealed a bandage saturated with blood on the animal's stomach. "Can you help us?"

Blood matted Archie's entire belly. Dan suddenly noticed the cat's eye had been stitched closed and his left ear was missing completely. How was this cat going to survive the drive to the vet's office? Dan clamped his teeth together to keep his negativity to himself.

Brooke covered the cat, the resolve in her voice strong. "Archie has survived worse than this."

Perhaps. Still, Dan wondered how many lives Archie had left. He glanced at Brooke.

Fear paled her skin, but a determination crackled in her deep brown eyes. What, beyond the wildfire, had Brooke survived? He pulled his keys from his pocket and hurried to open the passenger door. "I know where to go."

"Is it close?" Concern rattled through her words, shifting her voice into a breathless wheeze. "Is the vet's office near Bayview and State?"

"Less than six blocks away from that area." Dan set his hand on her lower back to guide her into the truck. He added, "I know how to get around the city quickly and avoid people-congested areas like that one."

Brooke dropped into the passenger seat, her gaze fixed on Archie. A tremor curled through her hands before she buried her fingers in the towel around the cat.

Dan reached for the extra towel he kept on the back seat. "It's clean. My son, however, isn't always clean and has a habit of spilling whatever he's drinking."

Brooke lifted Archie. The tremor returned. Somehow, she looked even more fragile and even more lost inside his truck.

Dan worked faster, spreading the towel across her lap. He opened his well-stocked first-aid kit and pressed a stack of extra large gauze pads onto Archie's stomach. "Don't let up on the pressure. Sophie's place isn't too far."

Dan rushed around to the driver's side and started the truck.

"Archie wouldn't get into the crate with his cone on when the evacuation order came. I took it off." Brooke adjusted Archie on her lap, drawing out a pathetic meow that matched the anguish in her voice. "We had to leave."

She wouldn't have left her pets behind—that much he knew. Only the rhythmic click of the turn signal disrupted the somber silence.

"I should've put the cone back on yesterday. I made him a recovery area. Figured he'd leave his stiches alone," she added.

The misery in her voice settled on Dan's shoulders. He accepted the weight, accelerated around a car and reminded himself Brooke needed him for transport, nothing else.

"Your dad brought Luna back after their walk." Brooke's words continued to spill out as if there was solace in the confession. "I jumped into the shower and came out to find Luna in the recovery area and blood all over. I'll clean up the apartment."

"Let's get Archie help, then worry about that," Dan said.

"I don't know what we would've done without your dad bringing us here," she said. "Or now you."

The wisp of gratitude in her voice tangled in his gut, making his own breath catch. He wanted her out of his place as soon as possible, didn't he? He reached over, touched Archie's small head rather than holding Brooke's hand to offer her reassurance.

And recalculated the fastest route to Sophie's store and his misplaced feelings for his tenant.

He never considered he'd ever transport a seriously injured animal. But he was trained to help those in need. He'd rescued animals from the wildfires with his father over the years, but he'd only ever reunited those animals with their owners and walked away to continue fighting the fire. He looked over at Brooke.

She wouldn't be easy to walk away from. That thought he trampled into a dark corner, somewhere back behind his routine, and concentrated on driving.

BROOKE CONCENTRATED ON Archie and avoided looking out the truck windows. This time she was inside the vehicle, she reminded herself, not watching a large van barrel toward her. She had to stay focused, be in the moment. Archie was her priority.

"Sophie's place is up here, just around this corner." Dan parked the truck in a loading zone and jumped out onto the street. He helped Brooke onto the sidewalk, swung open the front door to The Pampered Pooch and shouted, "Sophie, it's an emergency. We need you now."

Dan guided Brooke ahead of him, shielding her from the busy sidewalk and gaping store-front windows. And then she was inside, Dan and her fears bracketing her on either side. The city loomed outside. Archie was lying limp in her arms.

A woman, her blond hair tied back in a pony-tail, sprinted down the center aisle. "Dan, what's wrong?"

Dan pointed at the bundled cat. "Archie needs your expertise."

The woman skidded to a halt and gasped at the injured cat. "Upstairs. Follow me."

She led them outside to a wide staircase. On the second-floor landing, she pulled out a set of keys from her back pocket, pushed open the old wooden door and motioned them inside.

A deep male voice echoed down the hallway. "Sophie Callahan, that's an emergency exit, not your private entrance. There are landlord-lessee rules and a code of conduct, you know."

"Iain, we don't have time for that. You have an emergency patient," Sophie called back.

She led them into an examination room, com-plete with a stainless-steel exam table, white industrial cabinets and a carpeted cat tower in the corner. Only the cushioned seat built under the bay window revealed the room's former use as a bedroom. Not all the Victorian charm had been renovated out of the old building, softening the commercial space.

"I have no more kennel space, Sophie. We went through this last night." The man's deep voice continued to blast from somewhere inside the flat. "I won't be able to get into my supply room if we add another kennel in this place."

Bare feet slapped on the wooden floor. A tall man moved into the room, slipped on his Crocs and stepped into the adjoining bathroom to wash his hands. "My landlord is very bossy. Hello, everyone. I'm Dr. Porter and who do we have here?"

"This is Archie." Brooke stepped to the table and unwrapped the towel. "He had abdominal surgery after being dropped out of a moving car on the interstate. I think he and my dog, Luna, took out all his stitches."

Iain zeroed in on the cat and took over for Brooke, his touch gentle, his voice mild. "When was the surgery?"

"Four days ago." Her fingers dug into the clean section of the towel, but the tremor inside Brooke refused to surrender. She couldn't lose Archie. She'd lost most of her family already. Brooke pushed her words past her panic and filled in Iain on the rest of the details.

"The shelters were full. My dad brought Brooke and her pets to the city the night before last." Dan's hand landed on Brooke's shoulder.

His simple touch—steady and composed—held her together. But he was a stranger. And she couldn't rely on his touch.

Iain looked at Sophie, his gaze intent and his voice urgent. "Can you find Gwen? Tell her to prep for surgery now."

Sophie sprinted out of the exam room.

"This will take some time." Iain lifted Archie into his arms and moved to the doorway. "You're welcome to wait. There's fresh coffee in the kitchen."

Iain offered nothing more. No false platitudes or false hope. She stood in a strange veterinarian's office, relying on an unknown veterinarian to save a part of her family. Leaned into a stranger's touch on her shoulder for comfort. She was surrounded by strangers. Yet the loneliness forgot to claim her. Rather, these strangers offered reassurance. But surely that was only their jobs. Only their training. After all, she was every bit a stranger to them.

Voices bounced against the hallway walls outside the exam room. A door opened and shut.

Sophie stepped into the room. "Iain Porter is the best veterinarian I've worked with. He'll do everything he can for Archie."

Dan's hand dropped away from Brooke's shoulder. She missed his touch before she could caution herself not to. "What now?"

"We wait." Compassion radiated from Sophie.

In her positive voice. In her soft grip. "I don't know about you, but if I can stay busy in moments like these, it stops the worry from consuming me."

"Sophie owns the pet store downstairs." Dan's small smile offered silent encouragement. "If you want to stay busy, I'm sure she can help."

"I accept only willing helpers," Sophie corrected. "As it happens, I have new guests downstairs. They're also fire evacuees. Several foster families couldn't take the animals into the shelters with them, so I brought the animals here."

"How many animals did you take in?" Dan asked.

"Eight last night." Sophie rubbed her cheek. The visor of her Pampered Pooch baseball cap failed to hide the dark circles under her puffy eyes. "We had to move the cats up here with Iain to make room for the dogs. Then three more dogs arrived before sunrise."

The pet shop owner looked exhausted, yet she hadn't stumbled once with Archie and Brooke. She'd jumped in and helped. The same way Brooke had never ignored a call for help from one of the overcrowded animal shelters up north. She tossed the towel in the trash can and faced Sophie. "What can I do?"

"I plan to work on rearranging the storage room in case I need to add more kennels." Sophie paused in the doorway. "I could use someone to feed and walk the dogs, if you're up for it."

Walking meant sidewalks. Shop windows. Six blocks away, the site of the accident loomed. But in what direction? Panic pinched the back of her neck. There had to be something else. Something inside. Brooke pointed at her blood-stained sweatshirt. "I'm not sure this is appropriate dog-walking attire."

"I've got you covered." Sophie motioned into the hallway as if she was a tour guide. "We have extra Pampered Pooch clothing in the stockroom. Someone usually needs to change during the day."

"I'm not very good with city streets and directions." She wasn't very good with *the city*. Dread streamed through Brooke, alarm rushed her words. "Are there small dogs that need a bath or exercise in the play yard?"

She bit into her lip. She'd seen a play yard in the back, hadn't she? Everything had blurred after she'd discovered Archie bloody and limp on the apartment floor. Everything except Dan's presence.

"Good point." Sophie poured herself a cup of coffee in Iain's kitchen. "Laura can walk outside. Yes, there are several small dogs requiring baths and even more who need playtime."

Brooke exhaled. She could handle this. She'd

avoid the shop windows, keep to the back rooms and concentrate on the animals, not her worries.

"I'm going to take Sophie up on her offer." Brooke held her hand out toward Dan and struggled not to feel awkward. There was nothing to be awkward about. "Thanks for the ride. I'm sure you'd like to get on with your day. Sleep or something."

"Dan is a machine." Sophie laughed. "The only person I know who can function on less sleep is Ava, his best friend and former partner."

Brooke studied Dan. "What happened to Ava?"

Dan took Brooke's hand and looked into her eyes. "She fell in love."

"You make it sound like a disease." Sophie elbowed Dan in the side and glanced at Brooke. "Don't listen to him."

Brooke tried not to listen to that hum of awareness inside her. Tried to ignore the feel of his hand wrapped around hers. When had she last held a man's hand? When had she last wanted to? "You don't need to wait for me and disrupt your schedule."

"You'll need a ride back to my place." Dan tilted his head and eyed her. A challenge in his green gaze, as if daring her to refuse his help.

She should. She managed just fine on her own. Always had. But Brooke said, "That would be nice." She turned and followed Sophie onto the fire-escape landing.

Behind her, Dan asked, "How much rearranging in the storage room are you doing, Sophie?"

"I've got it handled." Sophie skipped down several steps, her pace quickening along with her voice.

"Where's Brad?" Dan persisted.

"Working a case." Sophie opened the back door into the kennel area and eyed him. "Before you ask, Erin and Troy have the morning off after staying late last night. I've got this figured out."

"Show me what we're moving, Sophie." Dan motioned the women inside.

"Rearranging my storage room is not on your list today, Dan." Inside the back room, Sophie spun around and set her hands on her hips. "I know you have a list of your own things to do like you always do."

"I could be wide-open, all day," Dan countered.

His gaze bounced away from Sophie and Brooke. He had a list and driving Archie here hadn't been on it.

"Not a chance." Sophie narrowed her eyes. "You can't fool me. We're both overcommitters who really need to work on saying no."

"Okay. I have a full schedule," Dan admitted. "But I can give you a hand rearranging the storage area, too. Besides it'll go faster with two of us."

"I'm not asking." Sophie sorted through

a drawer of purple shirts and handed one to Brooke. "You already help me out so much that you should be put on payroll."

"I don't want your money, Sophie." Dan held out his arms. "Now, are we going to stand here and waste more time arguing or just get to work?"

"We're getting to work." Sophie shut the drawer with more force than required. "And I'm going to figure out how to pay you back."

"It's really not necessary," Dan said.

That had been the same answer he'd given to Brooke after she'd wanted to pay for the groceries. Brooke looked at Sophie. "Does he always help out without being asked?"

"Always," Sophie said. "He's the most reliable person I've ever known. Once he's given his word, he doesn't break it."

He kept his commitments. That was something to admire. But he had limits. He'd told Brooke that Luna couldn't use his perfectly good backyard. He'd doubted Archie would survive the drive to the pet store. That she'd seen in his shadowed gaze. And he hadn't introduced Brooke to his son yesterday. She'd watched the pair return from school, stroll through the backyard and disappear inside their house. Their laughter had lingered in the afternoon breeze long after the back door had closed.

His heart might have limits. Brooke's did, too.

She stepped into the bathroom to change into the Pampered Pooch shirt and retrace those boundaries around herself. Reminding herself that she preferred to be fine over heartbroken.

CHAPTER FIVE

Dan joined Sophie and Brooke on their tour of the pet store and mentally rearranged his schedule, building an hour at the pet store into his timeline. Iain would care for the cat. Archie was one of the lucky ones. As for Brooke, who would care for her?

The wildfires had displaced so many families, changed lives and taken lives. He wanted to be with his dad, helping as much as he could. But he had Ben, and his son came first. For now, he'd assist the rescues inside Sophie's store and figure out later how to do more for the victims of the fires.

"This is the new calm, quiet area. Several of the rescues needed to be away from the day care." Sophie opened a door with *Cats Only* swirled across the glass insert. "Obviously it's a work in progress."

Brooke stepped over to a floor-level kennel, knelt down and peered inside. Her voice dropped to a whisper. "Are they sick?"

"Traumatized." Sophie lowered her voice. "Rex is the worst case I've seen in a long time."

Brooke set her palm flat on the kennel door. "I used classical music for Luna. Fleece blankets and mood lighting, as well. She was an abused and terrified one-year-old puppy when I took her in."

"That'll be perfect for in here." Sophie lowered to one knee on the other side of Brooke. "Comfortable and soothing is very much needed right now."

Did his in-law unit have the same soothing effect for Brooke? He should pick up softer towels and thicker blankets for the unit. Dan straightened. The unit was perfectly fine as it was. Still, purchasing a few new items was nothing more than he'd do for any evacuee from the fires, not just Brooke.

Dan peered inside the kennel at the dog burrowed in the far corner, curled in on himself in a tangle of skin and bones. A pair of deep soulful eyes watched them without blinking. Brooke had given him a similar wide-eyed look in his driveway earlier. Both proved hard to disregard. "Rex doesn't look like he's eaten in the last month."

"He was rescued from a hoarding situation up north. The homeowners had left before the fire and abandoned every animal on the property." Sophie stood up, bitterness and fury ricocheting through her voice.

Horror and anger shifted over Brooke's face.

"We don't know much more, but it wasn't good or safe for Rex and the others." Sophie wiped a hand over her eyes as if that would re-arrange the reality of the dogs' lives.

Dan knew firsthand it wasn't so easy. He'd witnessed neglect and abuse, both human and animal, over the years as a firefighter and para-medic that left him speechless. No matter how many times he'd blinked, the reality never changed. Now those images were a part of him.

"But, hey, we can change that." Brooke looked into Rex's kennel. "I'm going to feed your friends, then I'll be back. I promise I'll be back."

Dan believed her. But would Brooke be back if it was him and Ben? He shook himself, hop-ing to knock that thought out of his head. He wasn't asking.

Dan followed Sophie and Brooke into the storeroom. Sophie directed Brooke to the dog kennels and new arrivals before introducing her to Laura, one of Sophie's part-time employees. Laura and Brooke disappeared outside with two rescues.

Sophie turned toward Dan. "Ready for the heavy lifting?"

"Let's do this," Dan said.

The one hour extended into two. Dan finished off a bottle of water and pushed his phone calls to his supervisor and Valerie to the following day. He allowed himself a minute to admire the reorganized storage unit. He had to get back on schedule.

"Dan." Sophie motioned for Dan to join her at the cats-only entrance. She pointed inside the room. Relief shifted through her voice. "Look at that."

Brooke sat on a pile of blankets in front of an open kennel. Rex's head rested on her thigh. Beside her, an empty food bowl sat. Two misplaced souls found comfort in each other. Dan struggled to look away from the sweet pair. Worse, he wanted to wrap Brooke and Rex in his embrace and make promises he couldn't keep. He squeezed the water bottle until the plastic crackled and crumpled, trying to break up his stray impulses, too.

"Am I interrupting?" Iain asked behind them.

No, the vet was saving Dan from himself. Dan turned around, concentrated on Iain Porter and on the fact that his life was perfectly fine. Perfectly full with his son, his dad and his friends. Dan was happy and content and definitely not interested in messing that up. Besides, Brooke was a temporary tenant in his in-law unit and little more than a stranger. He only hoped his reckless thoughts to comfort Brooke were temporary, too.

"Brooke coaxed Rex out of his kennel and got him to eat." Sophie wiped at her eyes.

"Impressive." Iain shifted to look inside the

room and waved to Brooke. "I still need to examine Rex when he's ready."

"You might need Brooke with you," Dan suggested. Dan, on the other hand, did not need Brooke with him. He'd prove that as soon as he left and got on with his day.

"Not a bad idea," Iain said. Brooke stepped out of the room. Iain didn't waste time. "Archie made it through, but I'd like to keep him overnight for observation."

Brooke nodded. Dan tensed, waited for the impact, ready to offer his support.

Yet Brooke stood stoic, clearly able to support herself. Dan retreated a small step, reminding himself he was content supporting himself and his son.

"Can I see him?" Brooke asked.

"In about an hour," Iain said. "We'll have him moved into a more comfortable kennel."

"Did Archie cause more damage to himself?" Brooke squeezed her hands together. Worry flattened her mouth, and she lowered her voice. "Did Luna cause damage?"

"There was an infection at the surgery site. Several clots beneath the incision." Iain touched Brooke's shoulder, his voice reassuring. "They were trying to heal him."

"He was lethargic. I thought it was the stress of the shelter and then the car ride," Brooke said. "Luna, my dog, wouldn't leave him alone."

"Smart dog," he said. "They often sense things before we do."

"You'll tell me what I owe you," Brooke said.

"We'll deal with that later," he said. "I have some patients to see. And it looks like you have a friend waiting."

Brooke looked behind her into the calm room. Rex had retreated into his kennel, but his head stuck out, his gaze locked on the door. "That's Rex."

"Archie is going to be fine," Iain said. "It'll just take time."

Brooke shook Iain's hand and slipped back into the calm room.

Sophie leaned toward Dan. "Brooke is going to be fine. She just needs time, too."

Dan rubbed his hand over his chin. He didn't have time to give Brooke. He looked at Brooke and his insides shifted like the pins on a safe lock dropping into place. But surely that was only Dan's natural response and his first-responder training to assist people in need. He wasn't built to walk away without helping.

Well, he'd helped Brooke and Archie. That was certainly more than enough of his time for one day. Besides, after Valerie had left and the divorce had been finalized, Dan had locked up a part of himself, deleted the combination and moved on.

Dan checked his watch, calculated he could

still get to the pharmacy for his dad and run into the grocery store for dinner before he picked up Ella and Ben. He glanced into the cat room. Brooke was already settled in with Rex.

She hadn't invited Dan to join them. He hadn't asked. She was a stranger. A stranger with a soft heart and compassion for wounded animals. She'd help heal Rex and any other rescue inside Sophie's pet store.

But Dan wasn't wounded. He didn't need to be rescued. Not now. Not ever.

Dan stepped outside The Pampered Pooch and inhaled. The city rushed by: the bus brakes squealing a block away. Drivers honking. Pedestrians skipping the crosswalks for faster routes. Dan blended into the crowd and found his balance again.

CHAPTER SIX

BROOKE ESCORTED THE sibling pair of Yorkshire terriers into their kennel, then checked on Bennie, the corgi, and Astrid, the beagle, in the neighboring kennels. The dogs slept curled up in the fluffy blankets Sophie had given Brooke earlier. If only Brooke could find the same easy contentment as the rescue dogs.

She glanced into several other kennels, searching for a restless soul like hers. Surely one of the rescues wanted another quick run in the small play yard. A treat. A distraction.

Yet the only one desperate for a distraction was Brooke.

She was less than half a mile from the accident site. She'd lied about not knowing her way around and avoided leaving the pet store. After all, she was needed inside these walls. Outside, she would need to run.

Was it wrong that she just wanted to keep pressing Pause inside the safety of the pet store?

Brooke left the dog room—she didn't want her discontent to disturb the calm animals.

"You, my dear, need this and this." An older woman with chin-length white-gold hair peered at Brooke. Her expressive eyes were magnified by a pair of sleek trendy eyeglasses. She pressed a hot cup into one of Brooke's hands and a muffin into the other. "I'm Evelyn Davenport, but you can call me Evie."

"Thanks." Brooke inhaled the steam from the cup, drawing in the warmth.

"We usually keep the Irish coffee for after hours." Evie tilted her chin at Brooke's cup. "But there are times when only Irish coffee will do."

"Thank you." Brooke sipped the coffee, certain the hot liquid would finally soothe the chill inside her.

Evie wrapped her arm around Brooke's waist and guided her into the storefront. "You couldn't have taken the time to eat what with worrying about Archie."

Brooke's mother used to embrace Brooke the very same way—one steady arm around her that Brooke had believed would always anchor her. Always support her. Brooke was grateful for Evie's kind gesture. She hadn't realized how much she'd missed the simple support. First with Dan. And now with Evie. Still, she let it last for only a minute. She'd stood on her own for too long to stop now.

"Sophie filled me in about Archie's condition this morning," Evie continued, her voice infused with the warmth Brooke sought. "Dr. Iain Porter is an excellent vet and somewhat of an animal whisperer, even though he'll deny it. You came to the best place."

"Thanks to Dan." Brooke had been panicked and lost. Fortunately, Dan had pulled into the driveway. Once again, a Sawyer had come to her rescue—she owed them.

"Dan and Rick are like family. We take care of each other." Evie picked up another muffin from the tin on the counter.

"But I'm not..." *Family*. Her family was four-legged and carried deep scars like Brooke. They were all she needed. Her fingers curved around the coffee cup as if searching for Dan's touch. His hand had been even warmer wrapped around hers. But she'd given up wanting to hold hands with a man. And she was more than fine with her decision. She was *fine*.

"You're here with us now." Evie peeled the wrapper off the muffin. "And already caring for our rescues like they're your own."

Sophie arrived and took the cinnamon-streusel muffin from Evie's hand. "Evie's day isn't complete or successful if she hasn't fed everyone."

"I wouldn't have to hover and chase you down if you'd only stop and eat like a person should." There was scolding in Evie's voice, but the affection lit up her eyes.

How long had it been since someone looked

at Brooke like that? Since someone hovered over her just to make sure she was all right.

"Why would I do that?" Sophie hugged Evie. "Then I'd miss out on these bites of deliciousness, which are some of your best by the way."

When was the last time someone had hugged Brooke? Not as part of the protocol for a grieving widow. But a good-natured, I-just-want-to-share-my-affection-with-you, feel-good embrace that gave as much as it received? The urge to retreat to the calm area seized her. Surely, if she took a moment to herself, all her wishful thinking would cease. Surely, she'd believe she was fine by herself. Surely, she'd remember the danger in opening her heart.

Besides, there was safety in that comfy corner in the quiet room she'd put together for Rex and the other dogs. Rex had already crawled across the floor earlier, edging close enough to touch Brooke with his nose, craving the affection but too fearful to reach for it. She could relate. He'd given Brooke the smallest tail wag for her efforts. That was enough for Brooke. Animals had been enough for Brooke these past five years. They were all she wanted now.

"This batch really is quite tasty." Evie grinned and replaced the lid on the muffin tin. "What do you need me to do today?"

"Thanks to Brooke, we've worked with all the canine rescues." Sophie toasted Brooke with her muffin. "Dan came back with the kids and he's going to help me upstairs with the cat kennels. If you could run things in here that would be terrific."

"The best part of my day is meeting new people." Joy spread across Evie's face. "I like to help them discover the things they didn't know their four-legged loved ones absolutely needed. Want to join me, Brooke?"

Brooke wanted to forget the support of Evie's arm, the talk about family, the almost too easy camaraderie with Sophie. She wasn't there to build something in the city. She wanted to escape.

A year's worth of therapy sessions after the accident, and Brooke was declared ready for the next step of her life. Brooke had stepped into a cabin on a remote mountain, surrounded herself with rescues and healed.

Sharing Irish coffee and fresh muffins, while tempting, wouldn't help her heal now. There were too many reminders of her past. Too many reasons to leave.

Brooke wasn't there to make friends. Even if Sophie understood Brooke's natural reserve and shared passion for animals. Even if Brooke was drawn to Sophie's no-questions-asked, simple acceptance. Brooke was there long enough for Archie to recover and for her to find a new home. "I think I'll check on Rex."

A girl with curly blond hair, holding a folded cane in one hand and resting her other hand on Ben's elbow, stepped through the doorway. The cute pair stalled Brooke's retreat.

"Evie." The boy waved Evie closer to them. His whisper wouldn't meet the criteria of even the most lenient of librarians. "Someone left Rex's kennel door open."

Blond curls sagged against the girl's cheeks as if weighed down by her worry. "Ben says Rex is shaking bad. Really bad."

"Like his-skin-is-going-to-slide-off-his-bones bad," Ben added.

"Evie, we didn't mean to scare him." The girl explained, "Ben was describing Mom's changes to me room by room."

Evie hugged both children and offered encouragement.

Ben's gaze collided with Brooke's over Evie's shoulder. Brooke wanted to reassure the little girl. She stepped forward and cleared her throat. "It isn't you guys. Rex is really stressed."

"Mom told me that Rex is scared and doesn't know that he can trust us." The girl pushed a pair of lavender glasses up her nose.

"She's right. I left his kennel door open, so he'd know this place is different than his old home." Brooke set her coffee and muffin on the checkout counter and reached her hand out to the boy. "I'm Brooke."

He shook her hand with a firm grip and introduced himself as Ben Sawyer. Brooke could've guessed he belonged to Dan, given his copper hair and height. Ben guided his friend's hand to Brooke's.

The girl grinned, introduced herself as Ella Callahan and added, "Your hand is so warm, like my mom's. I bet Rex wouldn't shake so much with something warmer to wear."

"That's a brilliant idea, Ella." Brooke grinned at Evie. "We need to get Rex one of those stress vests. Where can we find one in the store?"

"Aisle four in the dog section." Ella smiled as if she heard Brooke's surprise. "I helped stock the entire store with Mom and Evie. I know where everything is."

"When I forget, I always yell for Ella." Evie cupped Ella's cheek, drawing the little girl's smile wider.

Ben dipped his head, hiding his laughter in the collar of his hooded sweatshirt.

"I'll remember to holler for Ella, too." Brooke was quite certain she wouldn't forget this pair.

"Are you working here now?" Ben pointed at the logo on Brooke's purple shirt. "You have a Pampered Pooch shirt on."

"It's on loan." Brooke smoothed the wrinkles out of the shirt. "Your grandpa Rick invited me and my pets to stay in the rental apartment at your house for a little while."

Ben stared at Brooke. Confusion made his mouth drop open. "But you're not old."

Brooke picked up her coffee cup and caught her laughter behind the rim. Evie rushed to greet a customer at the front entrance, her own laughter trailing behind her like a silk scarf in the breeze.

"Brooke's voice is crisp and brisk like Mom's, Ben." Ella socked Ben in the shoulder and scolded him. "Not wobbly like Evie's gets when her throat can't find its voice. Brooke can't be *old* old."

"Grandpa Rick told me about the nice lady staying with us." Ben stressed the words *nice lady* as if that explained everything. And in case he wasn't clear, he said, "And Grandpa Rick always calls Wyatt's mom and Mia's mom and even Evie real nice ladies."

Ella's eyebrows drew together, and her mouth pulled in. "He also calls Ava's mom a nice lady all the time."

"See." Ben slapped his palm on his forehead. "That meant Brooke was supposed to be old."

"You're not secretly old, are you, Brooke?" Ella tilted her head toward Brooke. "Evie and Ben's grandpa talk about their friends who've declared war on aging."

"Grandpa says several of their friends are losing the war even with their doctors' help." Ben shook his head, his chin dropped toward his chest as if he was miserable. "It's a shame, really. At least that's what Grandpa always says."

What wasn't a shame was meeting this adorable pair. Brooke said, "I don't think I'm *old* old, unless you consider Ella's mom *old* old and Ben's dad."

"I knew I wasn't wrong about your voice." Ella cheered back up.

Brooke saw Sophie in Ella's full smile. And Ben's green eyes matched his dad's. For the first time in a long while, that hole in her heart throbbed against her chest and made Brooke wonder again. Wonder if her children would've had her eyes and her husband's laugh. Wonder what if…

Brooke firmed her knees and stepped away. She couldn't go there. Not now. Not here.

Reminded herself to focus on the sweet, not the bitter, like she'd once learned to do. Ben and Ella were the sweet and she was grateful she had this pair to assist her with Rex. Finally, that throb faded into its ever-present ache that scuffed her voice. "Why don't we get that vest for Rex?"

"What color vest do you think Rex would like?" Ben asked. "Brown would match his fur."

"What color do you like?" Brooke asked.

"Blue would match my soccer team," Ben said. "But gray matches most of my clothes."

"I like purple. It smells sweet and magical."

Ella unfolded her cane. "Wyatt's mom has lilacs in her garden and my favorite place to sit is by those flowers and the fountain."

"Sounds like a perfect secret garden." Perhaps Brooke could find a place with a lush garden that would embrace and soothe her.

"I think there are fairies in the garden, but we haven't found them yet." Ella's frown fluttered across her face, disappearing before it took hold. "Wyatt's mom is helping me search. She has a special house to grow her plants in. We think the fairies like to spend time in there, where it's warm and safe."

"Sounds like Rex and his kennel." Brooke followed the pair down the center aisle and smiled at Evie. The older woman held up several different feather cat toys for the customer's inspection.

"If you left Rex's kennel open, did he come out?" Ben asked.

"Yes, earlier this morning." Brooke picked up a tennis ball from under the shelf and set it back in the bin on the endcap with the others.

"How'd you get Rex out of his kennel?" Ella turned down aisle four. "Mom couldn't get him out."

Brooke paused in front of the colorful array of soothing vests. The tags recommended the snug-fitting jackets to calm a dog's anxiety and offer constant comfort like an enduring hug. The kind Brooke might miss, if she let herself linger with this welcoming group too long. "Can you keep a secret?"

Ben guided Ella closer to Brooke. The trio huddled together in the middle of the aisle, their heads bent toward each other as if blocking out anyone trying to eavesdrop.

Brooke lowered her voice. "Rex couldn't resist the peanut butter or the string cheese."

"That's a high-value treat." Authority spread through Ella's voice and pushed her shoulders back.

Ben gave a firm nod to back up his friend's claim. "We know that because Ella and I help with the animals."

"We only get to use peanut butter for something really special." Ella grimaced. "Usually we give out tiny crunchy biscuits or kibble."

"I thought Rex could use something special," Brooke said.

Ella smiled. "Everyone needs special things."

"Grandpa Rick told me that your house burned down." Ben brushed his copper bangs out of his eyes and studied Brooke. His green gaze was somber, but his voice was hopeful. "Did you get something special, too?"

"A nice place to stay with my pets until I find a new home." That was so much more than other families waiting at the shelters. Brooke wasn't sure how she'd repay the Sawyers for their kindness, but she would.

Ben's mouth dipped into a frown and he scratched his head.

"But you need something for yourself, Brooke." Ella hopped up and down and clutched Ben's arm. "We should tell your dad, Ben."

Definitely not that. She was indebted to Dan already. She didn't need anything else, especially from Dan. "Your dad already helped me with my cat Archie this morning."

Dan had been capable and gentle. Had given her an extra towel, bandages from his personal supply and a steadiness that had allowed Brooke to regain her composure and rein in her panic. He'd stood right beside her when Dr. Porter relayed the news that Archie had survived. She'd considered staying right there, relying on Dan for support. Until she'd locked her knees and remembered that she'd never allow her knees to buckle.

"What happened to Archie?" Ben chewed on his bottom lip.

Brooke explained about Archie's stitches and his surgery.

"Archie is gonna need something special, too." Ben pointed over Brooke's head. "The cat section is over there. Does he like toys that squeak or ones with bells?"

"Or ones with feathers?" Ella tucked her curls behind her ears. "He probably can't play right now. He needs something to cuddle with. Mom got me a fluffy unicorn after my last eye surgery. I still sleep with it every night."

"I got a bear wearing a Bay Water Medical shirt the last time I went to the hospital." Ben pulled a blue vest from the rack and handed it to Brooke. "My pancreas doesn't work like it's supposed to. But Dad says I'm getting really good at checking my blood like the nurses showed me how to do. The hospital isn't bad, but I'd rather not go."

"Have you been to the hospital?" Ella asked.

"I have, and like Ben, I'd rather not go back." Brooke picked up a fleece dog blanket, forced herself to stay in the moment. In the sleepless hours of the night, she could sometimes still hear the machines beeping and humming from her time spent in the intensive-care unit. But she'd healed, just like Archie and Rex would. That ache in her chest pulsed as if reminding her that she still had to rebuild somewhere. "Should we head to the cat section?"

"Do you have other pets besides Archie?" Ben asked.

"Cupid is my silver cat with only three legs.

Luna is my dog." Brooke lifted up the fleece blanket covered in cat and dog paw prints. "Luna likes to sleep on couches when I'm not there. I think this might protect your dad's couch."

Ben touched the blanket as if testing its softness. "Can we meet them? My dad won't let me have a pet. He *says* he's allergic."

Brooke set the vest and cat supplies on the checkout counter to cover her frown. Why would Dan lie to his own son?

Evie shook her head. "Your dad is no more allergic to animals than I am to chocolate."

"That's what we decided." Ella grimaced.

"Lincoln's mom is allergic to cats and her nose gets really red and her eyes really puffy if she touches a cat." Ben drummed his fingers on the counter. "Dad's eyes don't even get red or puffy even when he cries."

"You saw your dad cry?" Ella asked.

"His eyes got all watery, like one time when I woke up in the hospital and he was sitting next to me." Ben shrugged. "I gave him my teddy bear."

"Then what happened?" Ella asked. "Did tears run down his cheeks? Tears ran down my dad's face when he married my mom. I felt them on my cheek when he hugged me real tight."

"My dad hugged me and the bear at the same

time." Ben scratched his chin. "Then I went back to sleep."

Evie wiped at her own eyes and busied herself rearranging the muffin container. "Well, I have reasons not to overindulge in chocolate and your dad has reasons not to have a pet even if he isn't allergic to them."

"Not a very good reason," Ben muttered.

"I bet there is one very good reason." Evie cut the tags off the dog vest, her gaze soft as she eyed Ben.

Evie's love for the children was more than obvious. Dan's love for his son would be just as strong. Just as protective. Ben was no doubt the reason for Dan's white lie. Was Dan's love only reserved for his son? *Love.* Where had that come from? She'd fallen in love before. The head-over-heels kind. The once-in-a-lifetime kind. She'd be too greedy to consider a second chance. Brooke reached for that invisible pause button to stop her tumbling thoughts.

A strong hand landed on Brooke's lower back and settled as if to catch her when she fell. Brooke glanced over her shoulder. Dan stood just behind her, his smile gentle.

"Can I please meet Brooke's pets?" Ben asked.

Dan shifted his attention to his son. "Before we disrupt Brooke's evening, we need to make dinner and concentrate on your homework."

"What about Archie?" Concern widened Ben's eyes. "We can't leave without Brooke and Archie."

"Archie is going to spend the night here with Dr. Iain." Brooke was going to spend the night in Dan's rental apartment. He'd be a shout away. Only a short run would take her to his back porch.

A small shift and she'd be under his arm, within his protective embrace. A small shift and she'd be a welcome part of the pet store.

Perhaps in another lifetime she'd risk again.

"Well, Brooke needs a ride home," Ben argued.

"I can take a cab," Brooke said. She worked better alone. She was safe alone. "I want to see Archie before I leave."

"Ben can start his homework with me upstairs," Ella suggested.

"Then Brooke can sit with Rex until Dr. Iain lets her see Archie." Ben touched his dad's arm to keep his focus on him. "Rex is really scared, Dad."

"Fine. We'll stay until Brooke has visited Archie." Dan ruffled Ben's hair. "But then we're going home."

Ben nodded and guided Ella out of the storefront, as if the pair wanted to avoid his dad offering another suggestion.

Dan shook his head. "They are quick when they want to be."

Brooke had to be quick, too. Otherwise she might find herself discovering even more to like about Dan.

CHAPTER SEVEN

SOMETHING CHIMED THROUGH the house and interrupted Dan's carb-guesstimate tally for Ben's day. The sound chimed again. Not shrill enough for a fire alarm. Not piercing like a siren.

"That's the doorbell," Ben yelled. His feet smacked against the hardwood floor. "I'll see who's here."

Dan sliced Ben's sandwich in two, dropped the knife in the sink and rushed to intercept Ben. Dan hadn't recognized the doorbell—no surprise. No one ever used it. Their visitors consisted of Ava, who already had a key, and the postman, who left any packages hidden behind the chairs on the front porch. Their neighbors were friendly but distant. With a big extended family spread over several blocks, folks never walked over to borrow an egg or cup of sugar.

And no one came over at 7:30 a.m. Ten minutes before Dan had to leave to drop Ben off at school.

Ben peered through the window beside

the front door and jumped up and down. "It's Brooke and Luna."

Brooke. Dan yanked open the door. His gaze tracked from her head—her hair neatly in place, her cheeks flushed pink, her eyes lively and bright—to her purple Pampered Pooch shirt, which was wrinkle- and stain-free. Same for her black yoga pants and worn tennis shoes. A quick scan of Luna—the dog's tongue lolled from the side of her mouth as usual—signaled all was well.

If his breath came easier, it had nothing to do with Brooke's well-being. He searched deep inside himself, trying to force his frustration to the front. He should be irritated at her unexpected arrival. He should tell Brooke that they were leaving. And then he should leave. Without her.

Instead, something almost cheerful filled his greeting, as if her visit was the highlight of his day.

Brooke skipped over her reply. "Sorry to bother you guys so early."

This wasn't a morning conversation or invitation to coffee. Not that he wanted to have coffee and conversations with Brooke. He wanted to get on with his day, as he'd planned it. Without Brooke. "We're about to leave for school."

Brooke twisted Luna's dog leash. "I'll be quick."

Dan narrowed his eyes. Nothing, in his experience, was ever quick. Not doctor's appointments. Or short lines at the grocery store. Or school projects.

The school-committee chairs liked to call and ask for Dan's assistance on quick projects. Those projects turned into an entire day building the backdrop for the school play or a dunking booth for a school fund-raiser. Still, he had to admit the dunking booth had been fun to construct and raised quite a bit of money at the Spring Festival, and the students already begged to use it again at the Fall Festival at the end of the month.

Ben looked up from where he was kneeling beside Luna. "We have time. Dad drops me off really, *really* early."

"Punctuality is a life skill." Dan lifted his eyebrows and he stared at his son. "You don't want to make a habit of being late. You'll miss too much of your life."

Ben buried his head in Luna's neck, but not before Dan caught his drawn-out eye roll. Dan smoothed out his smile and concentrated on Brooke. Her purple headband held the dark strands away from her face and emphasized her round deep brown eyes. Eyes he could fall into if he wasn't careful and alert.

Brooke spoke, her voice hesitant. "Sophie called this morning."

Dan pulled back. "Is Archie okay?"

Brooke blinked and focused on him. "He's stable but Dr. Porter needs to keep Archie at least another night. Sophie called about Rex."

Dan stumbled over his relief for a cat. Who was Rex? He had an image of a dog curled in the back of the kennel, more eyes than body.

Ben jumped up, worry flashing across his face. "What happened to Rex?"

"He isn't doing well." Brooke touched Ben's shoulder. "Sophie had several more arrivals last night. Dr. Porter and Sophie think Rex needs to be someplace quieter, where he'll feel safe."

"He'll feel safe here." Confidence puffed Ben's chest out.

Ben's absolute certainty softened Dan. That was all he'd ever wanted to give Ben: a safe home. One without chaos. One with stability and love.

Brooke shifted to look at Dan.

Again, her dark brown gaze pulled him in. Her wide soulful eyes called to him. Made him want to learn everything about her. Made him want...

But he already knew her flaw: she was a rescuer. She'd take in more and more pets. Turn his rental unit into its own boardinghouse. And Dan would let her. It was her eyes that would convince him.

Yet Brooke was not a complication he wanted

in their lives. She'd distract him. And that could put Ben in danger. Like now, he should be guesstimating Ben's carb intake for the day, not falling under her spell.

"Sophie wanted to know if Rex could stay with me."

"Rex isn't afraid with you." Ben poked Dan's side. "Rex only came out of his kennel for Brooke. She had to feed him with her hand."

Dan wasn't surprised. Brooke had a quietness about her that soothed everyone around. He'd seen that yesterday at the pet store and only after a few hours with her. Still he said, "Won't Luna scare him?"

"We're hoping just the opposite will happen." Brooke unwound the leash from her palm and set her hand on Luna's head. "But we won't know until we introduce the two dogs. We won't do that unless you give the okay for one more evacuee to stay here."

"You have to say yes, Dad." Ben latched onto Dan's arm, his fingers digging in. "You always tell me that we have to help whenever we can."

Dan had meant people. Brooke was qualified. But was Dan prepared to handle the disruption?

"We have to help Rex, Dad," Ben insisted.

"I'll keep Rex in the apartment with me." Brooke's words bounced over each other as if she sensed Dan might say no. "There's nothing you'll need to do. I promise."

How he hated that word. Empty and meaningless unless backed up with actions. That's where most people failed. No one wanted to put in the work to keep their promises.

"But we can help, if you need us," Ben offered.

"I appreciate that." Brooke shifted her full smile on Dan. "You won't even know Rex is here."

But he knew Brooke was there. That was the most unsettling part. That smile and her expressive gaze had lingered in his mind last night for far too long. No, the dogs didn't concern him. But Brooke—she did. "Let's drop off Ben and introduce the dogs."

Ben jumped up and pumped his arms over his head. "We're getting another dog."

And Dan was getting a headache. He grabbed his keys from the hook on the wall. If he kept his eyes open and his focus on the truth—Brooke was as temporary in his life as an ice cube in the sun—then nothing would go wrong.

One minute out of the driveway, Ben cuddled with Luna in the back seat of the truck. And Dan wanted to wrap his arm around Brooke.

Dan really had to figure out a way to help Brooke get back to her old life quickly. His was already being turned upside down. And that said nothing about his misplaced thoughts. His current one included: *believing that Brooke sitting next to him felt right.* He shoved on his sunglasses. Clearly, the bright morning sun obscured his vision.

The next hour passed in a blur. Dan watched Luna and Rex bond—even he hadn't doubted the dogs would get along. The universe seemed to be conspiring against him. Maybe it was that white lie about pet allergies that had done him in.

Dan loaded Rex and his few belongings into the back seat of the truck, promised Sophie he'd return for more dog food and waited for Brooke to come out of the pet store.

"Sorry." Brooke buckled her seat belt and shook her head, her tone bemused. "I really need to get another shirt before I go back inside The Pampered Pooch. A customer thought I worked there and flagged me down on my way out."

"Sophie will appreciate that," Dan said as they drove away. "You seem to know your way around a pet store."

"I've spent a lot of time inside them," Brooke said. "I've been a dog trainer and foster mom for hard-to-place pets for the past five years."

"That explains your comfort with the rescues." And why Rex was comfortable with her. The dog recognized Brooke was safe. "I never did ask if there was anything you needed."

"Besides a new car, furniture and a home?" The weariness in Brooke's voice settled into the truck cab like the fog in the summer: dense and cloying. Brooke reached behind her for Luna as if she needed the contact.

"I can help with the car. I don't recommend my shopping skills unless you like boy jeans and superhero T-shirts and bunk beds."

"Don't you ever get tired?" Brooke touched his arm.

Her hand was light and small, but the warmth speared deep inside him like the sunlight burning away the fog. He wanted to cover her hand with his and make promises he never intended to keep. "What?"

"Don't you ever get tired of helping everyone around you?" she asked. "I overheard you offer to help rearrange the dog kennels at the pet store. Construct backdrops for the play at the school. Then Ben reminded you about restocking the nurse's office before he climbed out of the truck. Now you've offered to car shop with me. You never even flinched."

"I get it from my dad," Dan said. *It's the Sawyer way.* Those were his father's words every time Dan and his brother joined their parents to serve meals on holidays. Deliver food and clothing to shelters. Or simply bring cookies to a sick neighbor. "Dad has always been the first to help. The first to jump in whenever he sees a need."

"But who helps you?" Brooke asked.

Dan pulled into his driveway, searching for

the last time he'd asked for help. His father supported him, but Dan tried not to lean on him too much. His dad still hadn't managed to learn to say no to other people and Dan refused to overextend the older Sawyer. "What about you? Don't you get tired of taking in rescues and animals in need?"

"I'm a widow," Brooke said, her voice matter-of-fact as if her status explained her compulsion to rescue animals.

Dan set the truck in Park and shifted toward her, wanting her to see and hear the sincerity in his apology.

But Brooke continued, "After my husband passed, I heard the same advice often—get a pet and you won't be alone. Think about the bears and snakes in the mountains if you don't want to think about yourself. I found Luna by accident in a shopping mall parking lot. Her owners were about to chain her to a dumpster."

Maybe it wasn't such an accident after all. Dan got out of the truck and joined Brooke by the passenger door.

"Luna blossomed with every foster cat or dog I invited into the house." Brooke opened the passenger door, took the dogs' leashes and guided them out. "And I wasn't alone."

But was she ever lonely? Dan pulled the kennel from the truck bed and followed Brooke to the side gate and into the backyard.

"Cupid arrived and stuck." Brooke took the kennel from Dan and set it beside the front door. "Then Archie stuck, too."

What was it that let them stick beside Brooke? What if he wanted to stick? Dan took a step away from the front door of the apartment. "And Rex?"

Brooke reached down to pet Rex's head. "He'll blossom with kindness and then he'll be ready for his forever home."

"That's one of Sophie's favorite phrases, too." Dan crossed his arms over his chest. "But how do you know you found the right family? How does the family know they picked the right dog? Forever is a long time."

Brooke pulled the apartment keys from her pocket and stared at him. "You have to try."

That was a huge ask and an even greater risk. "What if you're wrong?"

"It's easier for the family." Brooke frowned. "They return the pet to the shelter and leave to return to their lives."

Or not so simple. Not so easy. Someone had to pick up the pieces and try to rebuild.

Brooke had to rebuild her life. He'd done that, too, after Valerie had left. Still, he hadn't been alone. He had his father, Valerie's mother and his friends. Brooke was alone. His stomach clenched.

"The pets are left bewildered and even more

scared. Unsure of what they did wrong." Brooke hugged Rex. "Why they were abandoned again."

That feeling that opened a pit inside him— he didn't ever want to experience it again. "But you keep trying."

"Absolutely." Brooke tipped Rex's face up to hers. "I trust the right family will be found for each animal. Until then, I shower as much love and affection on each one as I can."

That was her way: kindness. But what about Brooke's forever family? Did she want one? Were her pets enough? Ben and his father were enough for Dan. He might've envisioned things differently at one time. But he'd been wrong, and he'd adjusted. "What now?"

"I set up Rex's kennel, then give him space and time," Brooke said.

Was that what Brooke needed, too? Space and time? Sophie had said that much in the pet store. "I'm sorry about your husband." *About the loss of your forever family.*

"I appreciate that." Brooke straightened and cleared her throat. "I should get Rex sorted."

"I should get going, too. I have…"

Brooke's smile chased the joy up into her eyes, lighting her face and interrupting Dan. She added, "You have a yellow brick road to build."

"Yes, that, too." Dan laughed. "Believe it or

not, building props and sets for the play isn't all that bad."

"Neither is cleaning out a litter box," Brooke teased.

"I'll take your word for it." Dan stepped off the porch and headed to his house. He kept himself from looking back at Brooke. Yet he listened for the soft click of her door.

In his bedroom, he rummaged around the back of his closet, digging through piles of sweaters and sweatshirts. On the top shelf he found what he was looking for. On his way back through the kitchen, he grabbed a pen and wrote on a piece of scrap paper. "In case you get cold."

He left the EMT sweatshirt and the note on Brooke's doorstep. Because everyone deserved simple kindness. And he was determined to offer her that much for as long as she was there.

CHAPTER EIGHT

"WE WERE DESPERATE last night," Brooke huffed at both Rex and Luna and tugged them away from Dan's backyard. Guilt and dread wove through her. Ahead of her the wrought-iron gate loomed. The city sidewalks beyond.

She glanced at the far corner of the lawn. The spot in the backyard where she'd snuck the dogs to last night to let them take care of their business. Everything in her begged her to creep back over there.

Walking in the city was *not* fine, like she'd told Dan. Her feet slowed on the path as if she was slogging through quick-setting cement.

Surely, she could manage one block. *One step at a time, Brooke.*

One step at a time had been her mantra after she'd been discharged from the hospital and had to face organizing her husband's funeral and the end of what was supposed to have been a fairy-tale, decades-long marriage, just like her parents' and in-laws'.

Grief had overwhelmed Brooke's in-laws and

they hadn't been able to help Brooke with the memorial decisions. Brooke's own parents had been gone for quite a few years. Brooke had faced her new reality alone. She'd managed, if only one small step forward each day.

Brooke rubbed her neck, forced herself to inhale around her coiled airways. Surely, she could walk one block alone now.

The rumble of a truck pulling into the driveway drifted down the path. Dan was home.

After her accident, coworkers had sent cards and well-wishes to the hospital. Her boss had driven her home, yet it'd been awkward and strained, with the right words too hard to find. Neighbors had visited, but never stepped beyond her porch, as if Brooke's grief was contagious. She'd stopped inviting people inside, concealing her pain behind a small smile and distant wave.

She wasn't convinced a forced smile and absent wave would be enough to fool Dan.

"Okay, Rex," Brooke said. "We'll sit here until you're ready." *Or I am.*

"Everyone okay?" Dan stepped through the gate.

Brooke squatted beside the boxer and fiddled with his collar, hiding her face from Dan. The shudder in her tone wasn't as easy to remove. Her words skipped and tangled. "Rex isn't... He isn't sure he wants to venture into the city."

Neither was Brooke. Brooke touched the

boxer's head, willing her inner fighter to step forward.

Dan leaned down to pet an excited Luna. He held his other hand out for Rex to sniff. "Hey, buddy. I bet you'll get really high-reward treats if you walk today."

The cheerful coaxing in Dan's voice captured Brooke's focus. "You know about high-reward treats?"

"Ben gave me a tutorial on the way to school this morning about the difference between rewards and treats for the dogs." Laughter trickled through his tone, too little to catch.

"He's a smart kid." Brooke inhaled, concentrated on Dan. "He dropped off a list of Sophie's approved dog treats for me this morning."

Surprise shifted through his low voice. "I wondered where Ben had run off to between breakfast and packing his backpack. He never likes to get up early and always presses Snooze on his alarm more than once. Today he was dressed before his first alarm went off."

Rex inched closer to Dan's side and gently tapped his nose against Dan's palm. The churning in her stomach relented. "I think he likes you."

She could like Dan, too. There was something about him. With everything on her plate, though, now wasn't the time for her to be aware of Dan. Now wasn't the time to be aware of any *man*. As if she hadn't lost those feelings for companionship and a relationship with her former husband.

"Have any of those high-reward treats stashed in your pocket?" he asked.

"I do." Brooke lifted her chin, more for herself than him. "I wanted to use those on our walk." Because she was going to walk.

Dan's eyebrows pulled together as if he hesitated to state the obvious. "But Rex isn't walking."

Neither was Brooke. Rex leaned his full body weight against Dan's leg as if encouraging him to stay there. Where both the dog and Brooke wanted him. "He'll walk soon." So would she.

"Let me try to walk him." He held his hand out for the leash.

Would he take her hand if she set it in his? "Are you sure?"

"Let's go for a walk." His reassuring smile made her want to believe she'd conquer her fear once and for all with him beside her.

Brooke hadn't depended on anyone else in quite a while. Still, something deep inside her wanted to reconsider. Something inside her wanted to depend on him to get her past the driveway. But Dan wasn't hers. Not to confide in. Not to lean on. Brooke handed him Rex's leash and pushed herself up. "We only need to go to the end of the block." That was all she'd promised herself.

"One block it is." He adjusted Rex's leash in his grip. "Then I have to get to the grocery store or Ben won't have anything for his school lunch except high-reward dog biscuits."

"We can't let that happen." She tugged on her sweatshirt, putting her spine into place. "Although Ben also gave me a recipe for homemade dog treats that people can eat, too."

"Did he?" Dan asked. "That explains the additional items on the shopping list."

"Put these in your pocket." Brooke pressed a plastic bag of hot-dog pieces into his palm.

Her fingers brushed against his skin. Only the slightest connection, yet her nerves responded. She wanted to hold his hand.

Dan held open the gate, Rex beside him, and motioned to her. "Let's see if we can get out of the driveway."

Brooke rubbed her chest, willed her heart to slow down. Her distress clung like a sticky shadow. The houses around her were eclectic and varied in their building styles, spanning many decades. One common thread tied the neighborhood together: they were all homes. Less than four blocks away, the business and residential sections collided and meshed. But not here. There were no wide storefront windows for her to repeatedly check for the reflection of a reckless driver racing toward her. There was comfort in that, wasn't there?

In the driveway, Dan mimicked Brooke's hold on Luna's leash and shortened Rex's to anchor him at his side. "When does Rex get a reward?"

"When he does something special." Brooke's fear refused to step aside.

"Like getting to the sidewalk," Dan suggested.

"Today that is definitely enough."

Dan studied the dog. "Do you think he was abused?"

"Or neglected. Either way, walking or being on a leash wasn't a happy experience for him." Sadness and regret leaked into her voice before she could contain it. There'd been a time she'd loved nothing more than wandering the city streets, window-shopping and taking in the eclectic architecture. Now she was breathless and hadn't left the driveway.

"We should change that."

"I'm going to try," Brooke vowed.

She glanced down the street, counted the houses that stood between her and the stop sign. The street was empty, both of pedestrians and traffic. Only the rapid beat of her heart buzzed in her ears.

"He wants to like this." Dan slipped Rex a treat. The white tip of Rex's tail wagged erratically against his legs as if the dog wasn't certain how his own tail worked.

Brooke wasn't sure how she'd managed to reach the corner without giving herself away. Brooke praised the boxer. "A successful beginning." For them both.

Dan bent down on one knee in front of the dogs. "Want to try another block?"

"I promised you only a block." Brooke touched Dan's arm to steady herself. "We can go back."

Dan looked at Rex's face and grinned. "I think he wants to go one more block."

She wanted to not like Dan. Not appreciate his patience with Rex. *With her.* How could she refuse without explaining it wasn't the dog, it was her? Brooke forced a strained smile. "Then we should take him."

Brooke scanned the street in front of her, skipping from a closed garage to an empty bus stop to a motorcycle wedged between two parked cars. Her gaze never settled. She had to be prepared.

A dump truck shuddered to a stop. Brooke jumped and bumped into Dan. She mumbled an apology yet remained close to his side. Close enough that he could wrap his arm around her waist and tuck her against him, if he chose to. If she wanted him to.

One block turned into two, then three. Every

block, Rex transformed. First his tail curled up over his back, then wagged freely. Soon his floppy ears lifted as he began to take in the world around him. He kept close to Dan, never venturing too far ahead on the leash.

Brooke never ventured farther than a finger's reach of Dan. Sweat trailed down her back, despite the cool morning air. Dan never commented when she lingered at each corner, checking and rechecking for oncoming cars before crossing.

Dan paused and let Rex sniff a garbage can. "He's like a different dog."

"You've been patient with him. He knows you're in control and will protect him, not harm him." Brooke glanced at Dan. She wanted to believe, too, but pulled herself back. "I imagine you're the same with your patients."

"I wasn't calm or patient when Ben was first diagnosed with diabetes." He smoothed his hand over Rex's leash as if the reflective threading revealed the past. "I was at work. My nanny, a second-year college student, had called my mother-in-law. Luann called my dad. No one wanted to disturb me for what they'd suspected was most likely the flu. Ben had been feeling off for several days."

The pain in his voice caught inside her, blocking her own worries. Brooke matched her pace to Dan's, wanting to stay beside him like he had for her.

"Every day was like an endless marathon. But we learned and slowly got his diabetes under control, then Ben thrived." Dan looked over at her. "Rex is starting to do the same and it's only his first walk."

"Thanks to you," Brooke said. Brooke wasn't exactly thriving. But she was walking. On a sidewalk. In the city. She'd always been alone with her fears. But not now, with Dan. For that, she was grateful.

"I doubt that," Dan said. "More likely it's you."

Brooke smiled. "We'll call it a team effort."

"I've been a single dad since Ben was four," he said. The firm resolve in his tone pulled her focus back to him. He added, "Since the divorce, it's always been only Ben and me."

Brooke understood. He had boundaries. He had a team: him and his son. That was enough for him. He wasn't looking to expand. Neither was Brooke, no matter how much she liked referring to herself and him as a team. "Did you know there are dogs trained to assist patients with diabetes?"

Dan frowned at her. "Did Ben tell you that?"

Brooke nodded. "Although, I'm already familiar with therapy dogs. I've trained several over the years."

"I probably could have used the assistance when Ben was first diagnosed." He touched his throat and shook his head as if uncertain where that truth had come from.

But Brooke sensed he wanted her to understand. And she did. His team would only ever be two people.

He continued, his voice cautious, as if he hesitated to reveal so much to a stranger. "Ben was four and my wife called to tell me that she was extending her trip in Monaco for another two weeks. She'd already been gone for three weeks on one of her quick, revitalizing getaways."

"What did you do?" Brooke asked. Dan's willingness to talk about himself humbled her. Two houses away, a garage door raised.

"I told her if she didn't come home, then the marriage was over," Dan said. "I waited two months. Waited for Valerie to call my bluff. Waited to call hers. She never returned. I didn't know about Ben's condition at that point."

A car peeled out of the garage and slammed on its brakes. Brooke yanked on Luna's leash and lunged backward. She motioned for both dogs to sit, trying to cover her erratic response. She latched onto Dan's story, willing her pulse to slow. "When you found out about Ben, did you tell Valerie?"

His gaze trailed over Brooke's face and narrowed.

Brooke touched her cheek. Certain her reaction had leached the color from her face. What would she say? How would she explain? He'd opened up to her. But some secrets were better left unshared. She wouldn't burden anyone else with her own struggles.

He pointed a finger at her. "You're thinking that surely finding out that your only son has juvenile diabetes would be enough to board the first plane home to be with him."

Brooke exhaled. He'd mistaken her alarm as dismay about Valerie. Brooke never hesitated. "Absolutely." Then again, Brooke doubted she'd have left her child in the first place. Her inner mediator tapped on her shoulder, reminding her about the importance of remaining impartial. Every story had two sides.

"That's what you would've done." Dan checked the traffic on the street and motioned for the car to continue backing out.

It granted Brooke a moment to gather herself and, in the process, gather her own indignation. "That's what any mother would do."

"Valerie isn't any mother. My mother always told me that Valerie danced to her own tune— one that she was compelled to share with the world." He tugged on Rex's leash, encouraging him to walk. "Valerie told me I was better suited for the medical issues, given my paramedic background. She really does faint at the sight of someone's blood."

Brooke stopped at the intersection, drawing his gaze to her. The dogs sat and watched him, too. "Still, she never came home?"

"Four months after that phone call, I filed for divorce." He shook his head.

But his solemn, cold gaze and reserve in his tone, as if refused to be affected by the past, alerted her. Like her former clients who never answered a question directly during one of her mediation sessions. "There's more."

He shifted his gaze over her head. "The divorce took over a year to finalize because of Valerie's extensive travels."

"She never came home to see her own son that whole year?" Her bewildered tone bounced between them.

"She sent birthday cards that arrived late and Christmas presents in October. She was even late to our wedding so it's not surprising." He allowed Rex's leash to extend fully, giving the boxer more sidewalk to explore. "Valerie also found someone to travel with her. Someone not tied down with the responsibility of a child and full-time job."

Tied down wasn't as distasteful as he made it sound. Brooke was quickly becoming less and less neutral. "Is Valerie still with this other man?"

"As far as I know." He started walking faster, as if he could walk away from his past.

"Do you know anything about him?" Brooke increased her pace to stay beside him. "Surely if he was decent, he'd tell Valerie to come home and see her son." Brooke wanted to demand that Valerie return home to see her son.

"I know all about him. I grew up with him." The indifference in his voice only emphasized the significance. "The other man is my younger brother."

Brooke's mouth dropped open. She kicked her inner demons aside and focused on Dan. "Your ex-wife hooked up with your brother?"

"Jason was always the fun one. The charming adventurer who never liked to be in one place for very long. The same as Valerie. He's a professional gambler now." His tone was detached, as if he hadn't known his brother his entire life. As if his brother was no more relevant than last year's celebrity gossip. "Jason is the one who dared."

"But you dared more." Brooke grabbed his arm, swinging him toward her. "You dared to stay with your son and tackle being a single father. You took the biggest risk."

"And in my opinion, the most rewarding one."

He encouraged the dogs' quick pace again and offered no more glimpses into his past.

Only the sound of a passing car and the bass of a stereo in a nearby apartment disrupted the silence between Brooke and Dan. Brooke counted the blocks left to reach Dan's house. Only three.

She'd managed four square blocks without jumping out of her skin. She had Dan to thank for that. His bold trip down memory lane and his hurt, restrained and powerful, had nudged aside her own fears.

Back at the apartment, with Dan's past behind them, where she suspected he preferred it, Brooke accepted Rex's leash from him.

He rubbed Luna's head, then Rex's. "I'm off to the store."

"Do you mind if I join you? I need a few things." Very few. But she didn't want to go alone. She didn't want to be alone. Not yet. At Dan's hesitation, she added, "I promise, no more talk about your past."

She kept her promise, and exactly one hour later, Dan parked the truck in the driveway and gaped at Brooke. "I cannot believe you've never had chicken and waffles."

The surprise on Dan's face tugged a small laugh free. The sound was muted and off-key to her own ears, as if her laughter had rusted over the years.

"You're going to like my chicken and waffles," Dan vowed.

She'd liked grocery shopping and the sense of normalcy even while nothing about her situation was normal. Picking out the perfect unbruised apples and debating over spinach or lettuce reminded her that some things remained the same no matter where she was. That settled her. Even if being out in the city did not.

She wanted that to be all that steadied her. But Dan calmed her. He hadn't offered pity after she'd mentioned her husband's death. The sincerity in his simple apology had wrapped around her like an embrace.

Today, he'd bought every ingredient for the homemade dog treats. His thoughtfulness for Luna and Rex softened her. His love for his son tapped on a heart she refused to open. "I'll try your chicken and waffles. Though there's something about mixing breakfast and dinner that doesn't feel right. Syrup on fried chicken sounds like two food groups that don't go well together."

Not like she and Dan went together. Not that she'd considered her and Dan *together*. Or anything close to that. Dan had his whole life in the city. Brooke was only passing through. And so much was still up in the air for her, while so much was settled for Dan. How would she find a home, a job, her life again?

Not to mention figuring out how to avoid the site of her accident.

Still, she'd discovered two of her favorite places: Beaux Arts Bakery and Mission Sushi were still open in the Golden Heights District. Thanks to Dan. That wasn't enough to erase the bad memories, was it?

Brooke opened the back-passenger door and slid the cloth grocery bags up her arm. For now, it'd be enough to appreciate this one sweet, simple moment.

"Taking everything in one load?" Dan asked from the other side of the bench back seat.

"Always." Brooke grinned. Sweet and simple was all she wanted right now. Nothing more. Nothing that required her heart or a courage she'd lost in the accident. "It's the only way to carry groceries. I've been doing this since I was a kid. Saves time."

Dan stacked grocery bags into his hands, his smile crooked and appealing.

Something inside Brooke shifted—something inside her chest like those pesky butterflies that romance movies liked to reference. How many years had it been since she'd experienced a fluttering? Was it wrong that she indulged, for only a breath? Before she adjusted the groceries in her grip and adjusted her thoughts.

She'd made a deal years ago: if she never opened her heart, she'd never hurt. Even more, she'd never hurt others. The thought of causing Dan pain clipped those butterflies' wings.

Besides, they'd taken one trip to the grocery store, not been on a first date. Butterflies and racing hearts were for the poets and screenwriters, not widows like her. Brooke walked around the truck and stepped beside Dan. "See, perfectly balanced. You're the one who's a little off-kilter."

Dan didn't straighten. Only gaped at the front porch. Nothing about him moved, from his stiff shoulders to the grocery bags that had stopped swaying, as if Dan's tension stalled the air.

Brooke looked up at the striking woman propped against the porch railing. Her blond hair was cropped at the perfect angle to swing elegantly against her defined jawline. Her white pants blended with the white railing, while the sleek trench coat and bold blue sweater came together in an effortless, classic style.

"We brought food, too. But you can never have too much food, can you?" The woman's open smile shifted into high wattage with her bright laughter. "Can you believe it took more than thirty-six hours to get here from Dubai?"

"Valerie." Dan's voice sounded strained and detached, at odds with the woman's vibrance.

That was Dan's ex-wife. The dismay inside Brooke flatlined those butterflies. Valerie was poised like a princess, ready to lean over the railing and wave to her admiring throng of fans. Except Valerie wasn't a princess and Brooke was no adoring fan.

"I've been texting and calling." The sunflower-yellow scarf around Valerie's neck seemed to infuse her voice with extra warmth and cheer. "This shouldn't come as a surprise."

Muscles flexed in Dan's cheek and tracked along his jaw.

Brooke noticed the subdued man standing in the shadows behind Valerie, decided he was most likely Dan's brother. Dan's past had just walked right into the present. And Brooke thought dealing with the ghosts in her past was difficult. Brooke whispered, "How long has Valerie been trying to reach you?"

"Since Tuesday." Dan's voice was bewildered, as if he was still processing that his ex-wife and estranged brother stood so close. "I called her back. Left her a message. She never called again."

Brooke stepped closer to Dan until her shoulder connected with his arm. He'd supported her during their walk, even though she hadn't confessed her real fears. She'd do the same for him now.

Dan shrugged. "I thought she'd given up and moved on to something else."

Brooke failed to stop her scowl from drifting into her voice. "Looks like she showed up instead."

"I should've known." A low curse drifted into the afternoon breeze, as if Dan had accepted the reality but disliked it all the same. "Valerie called and texted more in the past week than she has in the past year."

"She could've put her travel plans in one of those texts," Brooke suggested.

Dan nodded.

Brooke waited beside Dan. He never moved. Not even a twitch, as if he stood sentry in the driveway and intended to remain there indefinitely.

Valerie's smile never faltered as her gaze moved to Brooke, then over the neighborhood like she was lost in pleasant memories. "Is Valerie always so gracefully poised and composed?"

Dan shifted and focused on Brooke. One corner of his mouth relaxed and tipped upward. "Always. It's her gift."

Dan had a gift, too. A gift for making Brooke believe she was valued thanks to one of his all-encompassing looks. He gazed at Brooke, made her imagine she was the only one who mattered to him in that moment. Brooke blinked. This wasn't about Dan's effect on her. His ex-wife and brother stood twenty feet away. "Where are your house keys?"

Dan kept his gaze locked on Brooke as if she anchored him. "In my left hand."

Brooke took the keys and squeezed his hand holding the grocery bags.

"I'm not inviting them inside." Dan's voice came out as both a warning and simple fact.

"Okay." The dormant mediator inside Brooke leaped to attention, reciting strategy. *All parties should feel heard. Active feedback is your strength.* "But we have gelato melting and chicken that needs to get in the refrigerator or I'm definitely not sampling your chicken and waffles later."

Dan closed his eyes. Less than a five count, as if pulling himself together.

Brooke squeezed his hand once more and walked up the stairs onto the porch.

CHAPTER NINE

DAN SQUEEZED HIS eyes closed once more. The hair on the back of his neck prickled as if he'd conjured the past. He followed Brooke. Tunneled his vision until he saw only Brooke's dark hair and blue sweatshirt.

Never had he been so reluctant to be home.

Besides, Dan had places to be. Several, in fact, like Hank Decker's house to drop off the dinner he'd agreed to deliver that afternoon. The entire EMS team had put a calendar together to bring meals to Hank, his wife and five kids while Hank continued his recovery. He had to return calls from his supervisor and the drama teacher at Ben's school.

None of those places included a reunion with Valerie and Jason at his own house.

Dan didn't know what to say to the pair on the porch. "Welcome home" seemed absurd. "What took you so long?" sounded too passive-aggressive, as if he still harbored unresolved anger. "Get out" would be rude.

Dan settled for no greeting.

Brooke unlocked his front door. He flattened his palm on the door above Brooke's head, holding it open and himself together. Brooke slipped under Dan's arm and stepped inside. Valerie never waited for a formal invitation and swirled into the house as if her welcome had never been in question.

Valerie sank down in the center of the couch in the living room and ran her hands over the chenille cushions on either side of her. "I always loved this sofa set at your parents' house. I'm glad Rick brought it with him. Sitting here always felt like a warm hug from your mom."

Dan curled his fingers around the bag handles. What would his mother say now? Would she offer warm hugs all around? The only person Dan wanted to pull closer was Brooke. He never talked about the past. He'd never wanted to feel the sting that always accompanied the truth or the memories.

Somehow walking with Brooke, the blade sliced a little less deeply. If he tugged Brooke into his side, would the knife cleaving through him now hurt less? He cleared his throat and adjusted his focus.

Jason stopped beside the curio cabinet and set his hand on the intricate antique handle. "You kept it?"

Dan didn't need to look at the shelf to know

what piece his brother referenced. He said, "Mom did."

They both knew that was a lie. Jason had given Dan the phoenix poker chip on Dan's nineteenth birthday. After Dan responded to a house fire and lost his first patient. Jason had told him it was a reminder to always keep rising from the ashes—his work mattered. He mattered. Would Jason be surprised to learn that Dan also kept several decks of playing cards and their collection of various sports caps, along with a box of photographs in the attic?

Valerie took the grocery bags from Jason and peered into the curio cabinet. She frowned at the shelf, her tone dismissive. "Jason has thousands of poker chips littered all over his apartment. He can send you a full set and an extra."

There wasn't a set of that particular poker chip. It was the only one in existence. Designed by Jason himself. More regret and grief shifted across Jason's face. Only a flash before he retreated behind his impassive mask.

His brother stood close enough to clip with a right hook, yet the distance was more like a bottomless chasm. Was that all that stood between Dan and his brother now? Insurmountable distance. And resignation. The loss of his brother gutted Dan. He rubbed his chin as if he'd been punched.

"I got Kahlúa coffee cake from Whisk and Whip Pastry. I know it's your favorite, Dan." Valerie's lyrical voice commanded attention. She set her bags on the kitchen counter, then pulled out two boxes. "And Rick's favorite, pumpkin-cheesecake-stuffed monkey bread. Don't you love fall flavors? I wasn't sure about Ben, so I picked up chocolate espresso beans. All kids like chocolate, right?"

Dan shifted his attention to Brooke, unsure if her frown was for the espresso beans or that Valerie didn't know Ben's favorite dessert. Brooke would put her child first. She'd know her child's favorites. If Dan was a different person and this was a different time, he'd have looked for someone like Brooke.

Dan ignored Valerie's bakery offerings and piled his groceries and Brooke's on the counter. "Why are you here, Valerie?"

"We wanted to see our family." Valerie set down the boxes and gripped the bar stool.

"Why now?" Suspicion deepened Dan's voice.

"Do I need a reason to want to see my own son?" Valerie's tone was baffled, as if she was surprised Dan would ask.

"You haven't attempted to see him in years." Dan turned away, yanked open the pantry door and dropped several cans of soup on the shelves with a dull thud.

"I'm Brooke Ellis." Brooke reached out to shake Valerie's hand. But her gentle voice reached out to Dan as if encouraging him to contain that twitchy irritation inside him.

Brooke added, "I'm staying in Dan's rental apartment. Rick and Dan offered the apartment after I had to evacuate from the wildfires up north."

Brooke would be a mother who fought for her kids. Fought to be with those she loved. She'd lost her husband. Yet Dan sensed she hadn't lost her ability to love. He'd seen her with the rescues, then later with Ben and Ella. But he wasn't interested in Brooke or her heart. He was already committed to Ben. Dan dug through another grocery bag.

"I cried looking at pictures of the devastation." Valerie took Brooke's hands, her voice warm. "I'm sorry, but you couldn't have asked for a better place to recover. The Sawyer men were built to assist those in need."

Who helped the Sawyer men when they were in need? Dan glanced at his brother. The rim of Jason's black baseball cap shadowed his gaze, blocking Dan from really seeing him. Once upon a time, Jason and Dan had only depended on each other. And they'd always had each other's backs. Now the Sawyer men helped themselves.

Brooke stepped toward Valerie, her voice

pleasant, her smile welcoming. "How long do you plan to be in town?"

Valerie pulled out plates and napkins from the bakery bag, then opened the coffee-cake box. "That depends."

Dan paused on the other side of the kitchen counter and eyed Valerie. She'd never liked schedules and committing. Not like Dan. Even Jason had used to keep an up-to-date calendar on his phone that included everything from birthdays to his part-time work schedule. Had Jason taken on Valerie's carefree nature? Had his brother changed that much?

"I have business to take care of, then travel plans will be made." Jason eased away from Dan and Valerie, as if he intended to observe from the sidelines. The same way Jason had done after he'd learned about his adoption status four years ago.

"He has business at the golf course," Valerie quipped.

Dan studied his brother, searched for his childhood friend. Only he found a man, serious and standoffish. "You play golf now? What happened to poker?"

"Only miniature golf," Jason replied.

Dan blinked and recovered as if he'd absorbed another punch, not a glib line from their childhood. Still, Jason's response had knocked Dan for a loop. "And only on—"

"Wednesdays," Jason said, finishing for him. The edge of his mouth creased—that was the only break in his brother's withdrawn expression.

One high school summer, Dan and Jason had played miniature golf every Wednesday. Not for the sport. Rather for Jason to see Ashley-Lynne, the blond-haired Southern transplant with the wide smile and bright eyes. Through eighteen holes of pirate traps and windmills, Dan had coached Jason on what creative things to say to Ashley-Lynne. One month and too many rounds into the summer, Jason discovered his courage and finally asked out Ashley-Lynne. Only to learn one of their friends had already asked her out the day before. Dan had teased Jason the rest of the summer for being a day late and a date short. Jason had laughed and vowed he'd be the first for everything. He'd lived up to that promise. Did he still?

Valerie sliced a section off the coffee cake, set it on a plate. She moved into Dan's view and thrust the plate at him. "I hope we haven't ruined your afternoon plans."

Valerie's eyebrow quirked as if questioning whether Dan and Brooke were more than landlord and tenant.

"Actually, our afternoon is quite full." Dan avoided the coffee cake and put away more groceries with speed and efficiency, as if he was a clerk restocking the store for a bonus. "As well as Ben's."

"You can't keep me from seeing him." Valerie's voice was matter-of-fact.

"I'm not." Dan unloaded another grocery bag and scrambled to fabricate an excuse. "Ben is at school until three fifteen. Then he has soccer practice and a birthday party at his best friend's house tonight."

"I'll go with you to pick him up from school." Valerie handed Jason a plate of coffee cake.

"I'm not picking him up. Wesley's mom has car pool duty today." Dan closed the refrigerator and reached for the last grocery bag. "It's Wesley's birthday tonight. Ben and Wesley have been talking about this night for the past few weeks."

"I don't want to disrupt Ben's plans." Worry shifted over Valerie's face. "I remember how important my friends were at his age."

Dan offered nothing to soothe her concerns. How could she recall her middle school classmates and fail to remember important things about her own son?

Dan looked at Brooke and wondered if he would ever know all the important things about her. Definitely the wrong time, wrong place. He finished putting away the last of the groceries, as if that would unhitch the snag in his chest. He couldn't *like* Brooke.

Valerie sliced another piece of coffee cake and handed the plate to Brooke, as if they'd met for their weekly coffee and dessert. She said, "I'd like to see Ben this weekend."

Valerie eyed Brooke as if she expected Brooke to convince Dan to agree. Dan couldn't promise he wouldn't confide more of himself to Brooke. Or that he wouldn't let her sway him. That wasn't good.

"I'll be in touch about this weekend." Dan folded the last cloth grocery bag and stacked it on top of the others. "Now, Brooke and I need to leave."

Dan's hand fell against Brooke's lower back. A bold move that truly put in question their strictly tenant-landlord relationship. Yet she didn't move away.

"You just came home." Valerie studied Brooke as if searching for a weakness.

"To drop off groceries. We weren't expecting company and we have things to do." Dan's fingers flexed against Brooke's back, encouraging her to play along.

That heavy silence returned. Only now speculation and interest hovered in both Valerie and Jason's gazes.

"This is delicious, Valerie." Brooke pointed her fork at her plate. "Where will you be staying while you're in town?"

Valerie beamed at her.

"Valerie's mom lives in the Heights," Dan offered. "I'm sure they're staying at her house."

"Mom isn't home." The light in Valerie's voice and face dimmed like a cloud passing over the sun. "You know Mother doesn't like people in her house when she's out of town."

No. Dan didn't know that. He'd dropped Luann off at the airport to fly to Port Canaveral, Florida, to catch her cruise. Luann had refused to get out of the truck until Dan had shown her the floral-printed house key on his key chain—the one to her house in the Heights. Dan took care of Luann's home whenever she traveled. And Valerie's mom enjoyed several vacations a year, declaring she'd earned the reprieve.

Suspicion curled through Dan. What had happened between Luann and Valerie? And how would that affect Ben?

Valerie busied herself with the pastry box lids.

Jason tossed his paper plate and piece of intact coffee cake in the trash can. "I have a suite at the Fog City Hotel."

"I've always wanted to stay there." Valerie wiped her hands on a napkin. "We should check in and get settled."

Dan picked up a pen and piece of paper. He wrote across the paper and handed it to Jason. "Call Dad. I know he'll want to hear from you."

"Thanks." Jason stuffed the paper in his back pocket and walked toward the front door.

Valerie walked off, calling out, "I expect you'll be in touch about this weekend."

Dan expected he wouldn't.

CHAPTER TEN

BROOKE LINGERED IN the living room behind the others. Valerie simply drifted onto the porch like sunflower petals floating on the wind. Dan remained in the doorway, as if the wooden door propped him up. So many unspoken and unresolved emotions strained the silence. Brooke wanted to prop herself up, too.

Jason stepped beside Dan. The brothers matched each other in height. Yet Jason's brown hair lacked any hint of red and his build was leaner, like a marathon runner's.

Jason paused as if he wanted to say something to Dan but held back. His clear blue gaze collided with Brooke's. She saw the regret before Jason shuttered his features. She understood then the true meaning of a poker face and how Jason succeeded at the gaming table.

In her past life as a mediator, Brooke had worked numerous cases that had all started with the same stilted awareness. The reward in her work had always been returning harmony between feuding people. Easing the discord among families and strangers. The Sawyers were a family of strangers. The underlying pain in the division was easy to sense.

Her interference might not be welcomed. But how could she walk away? Rick and Dan hadn't turned away from her. Perhaps she could give something back to Dan and Rick before she left. First, she needed a strategy.

Dan shut the front door and turned toward her.

"Do you want to go and get coffee?" she asked. For a first step, it wasn't the best.

Dan scrubbed his hands over his face. "I'm afraid I won't be good company right now."

"I get it." Brooke had used the very same excuse with her in-laws on more than one occasion. She held on to her smile, walked into the kitchen and filled the coffeepot with water.

"I can make that." Dan dropped onto a kitchen stool.

"It's not a problem." Brooke pulled a bag of bagels and a container of cream cheese from the refrigerator. Fresh coffee and tea along with snacks had been a customary part of any room where she'd met clients. Even more, preparing something made her feel useful now.

Dan picked up the container of blueberry cream cheese and frowned.

"Blueberry adds the perfect amount of flavor. Not too sweet, not too plain." Brooke tapped the counter, drawing Dan's gaze to her. She repeated one of her mother's favorite lines. "Sometimes it's the little things that completely change the mood of the day."

His flat tone weighed down the edges of his mouth. "The little things dismantled my marriage."

Brooke tipped her head and studied him, her gaze searching his somber face. Dan didn't appear to want a mood change.

"Valerie always thrived on the big moments," Dan continued. "Chairing a fund-raising gala, hosting a Christmas soiree or acting as a tour guide through the Swiss Alps for two dozen family and friends."

Brooke sliced a bagel in half. "What about you?"

"Don't get me wrong. I enjoyed myself most of the time." Dan straightened and pushed the container away from him. "Until Ben was born."

Ben. He changed Dan's mood. And only from a mention. His face relaxed, his eyes lit up. Brooke's stomach clenched—she would've known a love like that. For her child. If only...

"Then I discovered the quieter, simpler moments were the lasting ones. Rocking my infant son to sleep. Hearing Ben's first squeaky laugh as if he'd swallowed his own giggle. Watching his first wobbly steps." Dan's hands flexed on the counter as if he prepared to catch his wobbly toddler all over again.

She'd missed all those simple moments, too. She cleared her throat. Her words were raspy, like an unfinished gasp. "But you have those special memories. That matters." She had only what-ifs.

Dan nodded. "I realized all the rest was simply noise and chatter. I stepped back, and Valerie kept moving."

Brooke had to keep moving, too. She'd been wrong about the mediation. Somehow, she'd skipped right past mediator and treaded into friendship territory.

"Sorry. I shouldn't have dumped that on you." Dan rose and poured a cup of coffee, held it out to Brooke.

She shook her head. She was sorry, too. Sorry she'd misplaced her mediator—the one that was supposed to help Dan and his family find harmony. "Do you miss Valerie?"

Brooke slammed her lips together. Was that even appropriate? Brooke wasn't sure anymore.

"A therapist on staff at the hospital helped me come to terms with the divorce." He stared into the coffee mug he cradled in his hands. "Sometimes I miss the idea…"

He trailed off, his words lost in the dark liquid. That was for the best. "Does Ben miss her?"

"Around his fifth birthday, he stopped asking

when his mom would come home. By the time he turned six, Ben had stopped asking about her, period." Dan sipped the coffee. "Valerie will charm him now. That's her way. She'll win him over."

"Is that such a bad thing?" she asked. Was it a bad thing that Brooke wanted to know if Dan would miss her once she moved out of the cottage?

"Absolutely." The tension in his voice collided with his scowl. "Valerie forgets to take her own vitamins. She's squeamish with needles. How can she care for a boy with diabetes?"

"She could learn," Brooke suggested. Brooke would learn, too. To be a mediator again and leave the friendship to those more qualified.

"This is the woman who believes chocolate makes people happy." He pointed at the bag of chocolate-covered espresso beans on the counter. "As a toddler, Valerie indulged Ben with chocolate milk, chocolate doughnuts and chocolate-chip pancakes for *breakfast*. Her reasoning—to make sure Ben's entire day could be a happy one."

"That's…" Brooke touched her mouth as if that would help her find the right words.

"Unhealthy. Unsafe," Dan filled in for her. "And yet, all Valerie wanted was for her son to be happy."

"Good intentions. Wrong approach," Brooke

offered. Brooke had searched Valerie's face for a sign of insincerity. A hint of disingenuousness in her voice. She'd discovered only heartfelt emotion in Valerie's quiet blue eyes. She should dislike Valerie, shouldn't she?

"I want Ben to be happy, too." Dan set his coffee on the counter next to the beans. "But even more, I want him to be safe."

Brooke wanted that, too, for Ben. And herself. "What about your brother?"

"Jason," he said. He straightened and shook his head. "That's complicated."

And still raw. Still painfully raw. She heard the anguish in his voice. That memory lane was gutted, yet perhaps not completely washed out. "It's only as complicated as you make it. My mom always told me 'sometimes you need to let things be what they are, not what you want them to be.'"

"We don't know each other anymore. I'm not even sure what I want our relationship to be. Or even what it is." Dan pulled out his phone and turned away from her. "I really need to make some calls."

And Brooke really needed to leave. He hadn't asked for her advice. Her counsel. Or her friendship. She walked to the back door. "I should check on the dogs and call Iain about Archie."

"Brooke," Dan said.

She turned around. Dan stood in the middle

of the kitchen, looking lost, as if he'd misplaced his home and wasn't sure where to find it.

Their gazes connected and held. The vulnerable shadows underneath his deep-set eyes asked her to stay. His words told her to leave. Brooke wanted to help him find whatever he'd lost. Help him regain his balance again. Yet she needed to give him space. And herself. Needed to break the connection.

"Thanks," he said. His voice was rough, drawn-out, as if from deep inside him.

One word that encompassed so much.

"Anytime." Brooke let herself out and rushed across the small yard. Running from her own tumbling emotions—the very ones Dan stirred up inside her.

THIRTY MINUTES AND one hot shower later, Dan walked barefoot into the kitchen. Fresh coffee still scented the air and the bagels waited on a paper plate. And Brooke's advice swirled through him.

He hadn't been wrong. He really didn't know what things were between him and his brother. He might've wanted to find out, if not for Ben. He had to protect his son.

He was concerned about Valerie letting down Ben. How many times had he come home to find Ben crying in his crib as an infant? Valerie's explanation: *a baby should learn to cry it out.* As for supervision, Valerie had spent more time organizing her next social engagement than watching her three-year-old son in the playroom. *Kids need to learn independence, Dan.*

Parents were also supposed to teach their children boundaries and healthy eating habits and provide unconditional love. What happened if Valerie's chocolate decadence didn't fix Ben's unhappiness? What if she allowed him to over-indulge and sent Ben's glucose levels too high? Would she leave Ben alone to deal with it himself?

Dan massaged his chest, forcing the panic to retreat. Ben was safe. Healthy.

But Valerie was back. And he couldn't trust she'd changed.

Even worse, he couldn't trust Ben to keep his expectations low and his hopes in check. After all, Ben was a ten-year-old kid whose mother had returned. Ben would believe those secret wishes for a regular mom and reunited family would come true now. How could Ben not believe that?

Valerie would most likely disappoint Ben. Dan accepted that. But what if Valerie caused more damage than Dan could repair?

Worry reclaimed him. Looking away, he spotted the decadent coffee cake Valerie had brought over. Kahlúa coffee cake had been his

favorite. Before he'd vowed not to become a statistic and started to clean up his diet. Before he'd
learned to appreciate the simple things.

He reached for one of Brooke's bagels and
walked over to the toaster.

The front door opened and closed. Booted
footsteps echoed across the wooden floor. Dan
stared at the toaster and skipped over any greeting to get to the important part. "Did you know,
Dad?"

"Not until your brother called me today."
Rick draped his jacket over the empty bar stool.
"Got here as fast as I could."

Dan retrieved his bagel from the toaster,
tossed the too-hot sections on the plate and
picked up the cream cheese. Jason had called
their dad, like Dan had suggested. Would Jason
listen when Dan told him that he'd always considered Jason his brother and still did, blood ties
or not? That Jason being adopted never changed
how Dan felt. Would Jason believe him if Dan
told his brother that he'd missed him?

That was a surprise. How much he'd really
missed his brother—feelings Dan had never admitted or faced. Until today.

Rick pulled a bag of spicy pumpkin seeds
and a bag of dried mangoes out of the pantry.
"When did we start eating organic?"

"I put Brooke's groceries away with ours."
Dan spread cream cheese across the bagel. The

groceries had kept him from stumbling over his chaotic emotions and blurting out whatever came into his head. That and Brooke. "Set them over there. She's coming for dinner later."

"Is that so?" Rick examined the bag of mangoes as if tropical dried fruit was one of his all-time favorite snacks.

"It's not like that, Dad. Between Rex, Archie and now Valerie and Jason, the plate is overfull." Dan bit into the bagel before his dad accused him of arguing too much. Blueberry spilled across his mouth, sweet and flavorful like Brooke had claimed. Maybe he could expand his plate. He took another bite to disrupt that misguided thought.

"Who's Rex?" Rick poured coffee into a mug.

"Another rescue from the fires. Sophie took him in but her crowded kennels only made the dog more scared. Brooke is helping." The same as she'd helped Dan today.

Valerie and Jason had surprised him. Dan searched for the anger he was certain boiled inside him but discovered only a low simmer of suspicion about Valerie's intentions.

"We have more animals?" Rick added sugar and a heavy pour of creamer to his coffee. Humor coated his voice. "Does Ben know?"

Dan found his first real smile since his grocery store trip with Brooke. He usually sprinted through the grocery store, intent on getting to his next destination. Brooke had made the store a destination in itself, instructing him on proper apple selection and the best season for different fruits. "Ben was already over at Brooke's first thing this morning to check on everyone and explain the benefits of diabetes therapy dogs to Brooke."

"That boy won't give up." Rick chuckled and glanced at the clock on the stove. "Where is he? He should be home from school by now."

"Nichole picked him up from school for a sleepover tonight with Wesley." Dan was even more grateful for Ben's best friend and his mom.

Dan had called Wesley's mom before he'd gotten in the shower. The boys had met in kindergarten and been inseparable ever since. Both single parents, Nichole and Dan had swapped stories about their exes during their first stint in the ticket booth at the school Halloween Trick-or-Treat Bash. Over the years, Nichole and Dan had relied on each other for car pools, classroom and soccer snack rescues and volunteer assistance.

Nichole hadn't flinched at Dan's news about Valerie's unexpected return. At the end of the call, Nichole had explained that Wesley's half birthday was in exactly eight days, therefore Dan hadn't outright lied to Valerie. Besides, she'd declared, the boys were always happy to celebrate anything. Dan was grateful for Nichole's long-time friendship and support.

"Where are Valerie and Jason?" Rick asked.

"They went to check into their hotel."

Rick picked up a butter knife and sliced off a piece of Dan's bagel. At Dan's frown, his dad shrugged and said, "It looks good. Never tried blueberry cream cheese before."

Neither had Dan, but he liked it. And he liked Brooke. Interesting that his dad chose Brooke's bagel over the coffee cake, too. Or maybe it wasn't. His dad always preferred the down-to-earth, like Dan's mom. His dad always insisted the key to his long-lasting marriage was his wife's even temper, even in the face of his recklessness.

"Do you think Luann knew that Valerie was coming home?" His dad swiped the other half of the bagel off Dan's plate. "This is quite good."

"I don't think Luann would've booked a transcontinental cruise if she'd known," Dan said. "Valerie told us that her mom doesn't like people in her house while she travels."

Rick lowered the bagel and frowned at Dan. "But Luann invites us to stay at her house every time she travels."

Luann had offered the same invitation last week at the airport like usual. Luann always invited Ben to enjoy the theater room and indoor Jacuzzi, often telling Dan it was her right as Ben's grandma Lulu to allow Ben to have all-night movie marathons at her house.

If anything, Dan believed Luann wanted people in her home more often as if that might chase away the loneliness he'd always sensed just beneath her wrinkled smile. "Doesn't make sense unless Valerie is hiding from her mom."

Rick picked up the other bagel and sliced it in half. "Valerie probably got the dates wrong for her mom's cruise. Simple misunderstanding."

Not the first time and easy to believe. Valerie lived according to her own calendar. Her son's own birthday wasn't a fixed date on her schedule. Dan doubted the exact dates of her mother's transcontinental cruise would've been penciled in, as well.

Still, Dan had sent an email to Luann about Valerie's return home.

After Valerie had decided not to come home years ago, her mother had offered to pay for Ben's hospital bills and other expenses. Dan had explained that he wasn't interested in Luann's money. He wanted her to be involved in her grandson's life. Luann had been delighted. There was only one task Dan had eagerly handed over: shopping for Ben's clothes. Luann still outfitted Ben. Only now the pair turned back-to-school shopping into an all-day adventure that included a trip to the movie theater and other treats.

Luann liked to declare retirement hollowed out her mind and left behind cobwebs, but Dan knew the seventy-four-year-old remained as perceptive and sharp as ever. Luann wouldn't have scheduled a cruise on the same day her only daughter was coming home.

"What now?" Rick smeared extra cream cheese on the bagel and handed half to Dan.

"That's what I'm trying to figure out." Dan chewed on a bite of bagel and considered Valerie's agenda.

"Valerie has to be allowed to see Ben." Rick set the butter knife in the sink.

"I know," Dan said. "I'd like to talk to Ben first. I just don't know what to say."

Like he hadn't really known what to say to his brother moments ago. Dan had wanted to ask, "Figure out you're a Sawyer yet?" Jason's last words to Dan had been that he needed to figure out who he was. But Dan had held back, Jason had seemed too reserved, too closed off. Jason used to get like that when they were kids. Dan always gave his brother space. He'd given Jason five years. Surely that was long enough, wasn't it?

"How about something simple like 'Ben, your mom is back in town'?" Rick loaded his coffee cup into the dishwasher.

"Then what do I say when Ben asks for how long?" Dan asked.

"Let Valerie answer that herself."

"She'll break his heart this time." And that would break Dan's heart. Ben had been four the first time Valerie had abandoned him. Too young to criticize her. Too innocent to resent her.

Rick stepped around the counter, set his hand on Dan's shoulder and squeezed. "And we'll be here to help him put it back together."

"Doesn't sound great," Dan said.

"No," Rick said. "But Valerie is here, and you have to do what's right."

Dan shoved off the stool and paced into the kitchen. Dan's parents had raised him to know right from wrong. Taught him to do right by people. He lived those lessons every day.

Still, shouldn't Valerie have been expected to do what was right six years ago and not abandon her own son? Shouldn't Valerie have known what was *right*? Dan crushed the paper plate in the garbage can and tossed away his irritation. The past had been lived. He had to focus on the present. His parents had also taught him the power in second chances. But that meant trusting that Valerie was home for the right reason: her son.

Dan checked his emails on his cell phone, hoping Luann might have already responded. Surely Valerie's mother would know what her own daughter was up to, wouldn't she?

"I'm having dinner with Jason and Valerie tonight," Rick said. "Do you and Brooke want to join us?"

Dan stuffed his phone back into his pocket. "I think Brooke has had enough Sawyer family drama for one day."

"Well, did she stay with you after Valerie and Jason arrived?" Rick asked.

Dan nodded. Brooke had not only stayed, she'd intervened as if she'd known Dan had struggled to match his words and his thoughts.

"Then a little drama isn't going to scare her away that easily." His dad grinned and whistled as he walked toward his bedroom.

Dan stepped to the window and stared across the backyard at the apartment. Something must've compelled Brooke to stay. Surely, she hadn't stayed only for Dan. But he didn't know much about Brooke other than she loved animals and was a widow.

He should probably get to know Brooke better. After all, he should know the person living on his property. And it wasn't as if learning more about Brooke would lead to anything. Dan was way too careful to allow that to happen.

CHAPTER ELEVEN

DAN'S KITCHEN LOOKED like a restaurant right before the buffet opened. He'd prepped all the chicken for the frying pan. A large bowl of batter rested on the counter beside the warm waffle maker. The mayonnaise and maple-syrup spread waited, already prepared.

He checked the clock on the oven. Thirty minutes until his friends arrived. Plenty of time to bring a plate to Brooke. Dan left the kitchen, convinced he was only returning her groceries and keeping his word. After all, he'd promised Brooke chicken and waffles, not a long-term relationship.

Brooke opened the door. Surprise lifted her eyebrows and her voice. "Dan."

"You said you'd try my chicken and waffles." *You never said you didn't want to get to know each other. Or to date.* Dan lifted the plate higher, blocked that incessant voice and his heart. "Don't tell me that you're backing out now."

"I didn't think…" She glanced at herself, her voice trailing off.

She wore her usual workout pants and Dan's sweatshirt. The one he'd given her to keep warm. She looked comfortable. And comforting.

She might be different from Valerie: grounded and practical. Traits he'd come to appreciate after his divorce. But that didn't make Brooke or any woman good for him. He was committed to Ben and the life he'd built. Love and relationships weren't on the menu. Not tonight or any night in the future. He said, "I also brought your groceries."

She slipped her hands free from the arms of the sweatshirt and grabbed the bags.

Tucking her hands up inside her sleeves was her habit. Would she be less cold if he held her hand? *No*. Tenants didn't hold their landlord's hand. Neither did friends. And they were somewhere in between, somewhere in the no-complication zone. "If you promise not to feed the dogs your chicken and waffles, we can sit on the back patio and let the dogs wander around the yard."

"Are you sure?" Her gaze searched Dan's face.

The concern in her brown eyes made it impossible for him to look away. That scale slipped to the more personal. And the truth slipped from Dan. "My divorce shook my world six years ago. The end of my marriage hurt pretty bad.

But I recovered and moved on for my son. This afternoon, I needed a moment to process Valerie and my brother's return. I had that."

She read him almost as easily as Ava. How was that possible? Maybe it was that Brooke was the first person Dan let close enough to really look at him in a long while. He had to stop letting her do that. He had to stop himself from spilling his secrets. Now.

He adjusted the two plates, reached down to pet Luna's head and slid that scale back to the impersonal. This was only supposed to be a kindness to his tenant. "If we don't eat soon, Luna is going to eat for us."

Brooke lifted the grocery bags. "Let me put these in the kitchen."

She returned and stepped onto the porch, Luna beside her. Dan said, "Sorry about your groceries. I was a little distracted."

"You had every right to be distracted." Her smile was sincere, her voice kind.

She never pressed him to dig deeper or share more. Even though he could have. Might have, but he reined himself in and remembered what this was.

Today, he'd revealed things to her he'd never told anyone. He'd been caught up in helping Rex, he assured himself. He'd always walked with a purpose. Toward a destination. Except Brooke had felt like the reason he was there.

And the longer he stayed beside her, the more he'd opened up. Clearly, he had to stop walking with her and head back to the gym.

Dan tipped his head, keeping his voice light. "You really aren't planning on feeding your chicken and waffles to the dogs, right?"

"No." She laughed. "Though I'm still counting on Ben's help to make those dog treats." Brooke left the apartment door open and followed Dan to the paved patio area.

"Speaking of Ben, he wanted me to invite you to his soccer game tomorrow." Dan handed her the plates and concentrated on brushing the leaves off the cushions on the chairs around the small gas fire pit.

Brooke sat, clutched the metal chair arms and stared at the food as if Dan had given her plates of worm-infested rotten apples.

"No pressure." Worry shifted through him. What had he said? He sat beside her and smoothed out his voice as if she was a patient he had to calm before an IV stick. "You don't have to go."

She lifted her head, blinked at him like she'd only just realized he was still there. "I think it would be nice."

Dan searched her face. Her gaze was clear, her mouth soft. No tension. No paleness. He hadn't imagined her reaction, had he? "Really?"

She nodded.

Lightness spread through him like the sunrise after a difficult night at work, promising a new day and another chance. He frowned. She'd agreed to a soccer game, not a first date. Still, the pleasure wouldn't dim. Why wasn't that making him uneasy? A light-brown-and-black head peeked out of Brooke's front door. Dan latched onto the distraction and whispered, "Look who's coming to join us."

"Maybe Rex will make it past the front door with you here." Brooke handed Dan one of the plates, her movements slow.

Dan kept his voice low to avoid startling Rex. "Should I call him over here?"

"Let's go with no pressure."

That approach worked well for Dan, too. Easy. Casual. Everything the night was supposed to be. Although something like anticipation swept through him. "Sounds good to me."

"I can eat this in any order I want, right?" Brooke unwrapped her plate. "And take my time trying a bite of chicken and waffle and syrup together?"

She could take all night. Dan uncovered his plate. "But it's delicious as one bite."

Brooke eyed him, then her food.

"Seriously, eat it any way you want." Dan toasted her with his fork. "No one is here to judge you."

"Then I'll go for it." Brooke cut off a piece

of chicken, added a corner of the waffle and dipped her fork in the syrup. She took a moment to chew and taste the bite like a judge on a TV food show. "There's something strangely satisfying and pleasing about this dish."

He could tell her the same about being with her. But the night was about chicken and waffles, not relationship building. "Then you like it?"

"I do." Brooke put together another bite on her fork.

"I told you so," Dan teased.

"You were right." Brooke concentrated on her plate.

The sun dropped away, granting the evening its turn, and time slowed. Enough for Dan to appreciate the moment.

When Brooke had finished half of her chicken and waffles, and his plate was almost cleared, Dan propped his feet on the edge of the round brick-and-stone fire pit. Cupid jumped onto one of the empty chairs and cleaned his paws as if he'd sampled the chicken and waffles, too. Luna stretched out in the grass. Rex lingered in the doorway, more out than in.

Brooke leaned back in her chair and glanced at him. "Are you really okay?"

Dan wiped a napkin over his mouth. Not to hide his frown. He was more confused that her question hadn't irritated him. The night was supposed to be casual. His mind had other ideas and once again forgot Brooke wasn't his confidante. "In some ways, I guess I knew this day would come. That didn't make it any easier, but I'm all right. Ben was too young for a broken heart the first time Valerie left us. It won't be the same this time."

Brooke leaned toward him and reached out.

Her hand almost connected with his arm, his heart almost skipped inside his chest.

But then Ava's sudden voice warned from the other side of the fence, "You better have enough chicken and waffles for everyone, Dan."

Dan set his plate on the side table and stood up. His friends, led by Ava, strolled into his backyard. Ava clutched her wedding party planner. Sophie brought in two tall thermoses and cups. Brad carried a cooler. Kyle walked in last, grocery bags in both of his hands.

Ava gave Dan a one-armed hug and leaned back to study him. "You forgot, didn't you?"

No, he hadn't forgotten. He'd lost track of time. When was the last time that had happened?

At his continued silence, one red eyebrow arched, and Ava added, "It's Friday night. We're meeting here for the coed bash planning."

This was the part where Dan told Brooke he had to follow his schedule. This was the part where Dan let Brooke escape back inside her apartment. This was the part where their time together ended, as he preferred.

"It's okay." Kyle punched Dan's shoulder. "We've got you covered with appetizers, drinks and dessert. But first I need to know if there really is more chicken and waffles."

"Upstairs." Dan dropped into his chair as Kyle and Brad fist-bumped their delight. His friends introduced themselves to Brooke quickly and simply: Brad was Sophie's other half. Kyle was engaged to Ava. Which gave Dan no chance to prove he could be a polite host.

Brooke started to stand. She reminded him of Rex: wide-eyed and ready to lunge back inside his kennel. Dan opened his mouth to tell Brooke she didn't have to stay. His friends could be overwhelming, but they meant well.

Sophie chimed in first. "Brooke, you can't leave us. We might need your vote against the guys."

"That's true." Ava waved Brooke back into the chair. "Please stay."

Brooke sat down slowly as if still unsure. Dan wanted to take her hand and protect her from whatever spooked her.

"Can you fix me a plate, please?" Sophie cradled Cupid and grinned at Brad. "I have a new friend."

"Me, too, please." Ava added several air-blown kisses in Kyle's direction.

"Who's getting married?" Brooke pulled her legs up onto the chair and wrapped her arms around her knees.

"Mia and Wyatt." Ava stole the last bite of waffle from Dan's plate. "Mia is a photographer and Wyatt is an ER doctor at Bay Water Medical, where Dan works, and I used to."

"Mia took the adorable photographs of the rescues at The Pampered Pooch." Brooke tucked her hands up inside the sleeves of the sweatshirt. "Evie told me about her."

Now Dan could stop focusing on holding her hand.

"We're finalizing the details for their joint bachelor-bachelorette party tonight." Sophie raised her arms to give Cupid the space to make himself more comfortable on her lap. "Wait until you see Kyle's place."

Dan looked at Brooke. "His place is a man cave on steroids with all your favorite childhood games thrown in."

The group spent several nights a month at Kyle's place, challenging each other for bragging rights. All generations included, from Ava's mom to Evie and Dan's dad, to Ella and Ben. Currently the Prime Timers, as the parents referred to themselves, held the top score on Ping-Pong and air hockey. Claimed it was all about finesse. Dan and Kyle claimed it was all about their craftiness.

"You're invited, of course," Sophie said. "It's next Friday."

The sincerity in Sophie's voice indicated her offer wasn't offhand or given out of politeness. Sophie was genuine and earnest, as if she and Brooke were already good friends.

Dan stared at Brooke's empty doorway. Rex had disappeared inside. Dan should've let Brooke leave, too.

"I'm not sure I'll be here," Brooke said.

Nothing Brooke said wasn't true or fact. Dan was merely disappointed he'd finished his chicken and waffles. Disappointed Bay Area Pioneers—his football team—had lost last weekend. However, he was not disappointed Brooke would be leaving. After all, friends encouraged each other to do what was best for them. Leaving was best for Brooke. He'd support her like a friend should.

"You have an open invite, anyway," Ava said.

Dan added, "You should come if you're here."

Brad and Kyle returned with twin plates, both piled high with waffles and chicken. Kyle frowned at his plate. "We had to fry more chicken. I'm not sure we did it exactly right."

Brad shook his head. "You can't fry anything wrong. Just add more syrup."

Silence—the good kind, not the Valerie-just-returned-unannounced kind—surrounded the backyard. Twenty minutes later, stomachs full,

Kyle collected the empty plates and tossed them in the trash. Brad refilled everyone's drink cups.

Ava picked up her party-planning binder and set it on the small table beside her. "This evening was scheduled to be about final party plans. But we already know we aren't going to be productive with the elephant in the room."

Tension sharpened the silence.

Dan kept his focus on Ava. He'd only just admitted he liked Brooke. That wasn't the elephant Ava referred to. And that wasn't elephant-sized news. Valerie and Jason's return certainly qualified. But how had she found out? He said, "You talked to my dad."

Ava winced. "Your dad told my mom that Valerie and Jason were back."

Sophie opened a container and took out a brownie. "Then Evie dropped off brownies at Ava's house this afternoon and Ava's mom told Evie."

"Both Wyatt's mom and Mia's mom got the full story from Ava's mom during their weekly afternoon tea-and-coffee meet-up," Kyle explained.

Dan left the brownies untouched and handed the tin to Brooke. A sugar rush would only confuse his already twisted emotions. His father was excited his son was back home. His dad no doubt wanted to share the news. Dan wanted to analyze the situation and figure out Valerie's agenda. He wanted to figure out if he still had a brother. Then he'd decide if he wanted to celebrate.

Ava glanced over at Brooke, her tone ominous, as if their parents predicted the future correctly, too. "Our parents have the market cornered on grapevine gossip."

Kyle shuddered. "It's disturbing really and I'm marrying into this."

Brad cradled the brownie tin and leaned away from Kyle. "It's not too late to get out."

Ava slapped Brad's leg, grabbed the brownies and handed the container to Kyle. "It's way too late. Our wedding date has been decided."

"No one is getting out of anything." Sophie brushed brownie crumbs off her hands. "The problem with the parents is that none of them thought to tell *any* of us."

"How did you find out?" Brooke set her elbows on her legs and leaned forward as if intrigued.

Dan was more interested in Brooke's reaction to his friends than the gossip train. Had he helped her relax?

"By accident. Like we always do." Ava grimaced.

"I called Rick earlier tonight to ask if he'd consult on an arson case." Brad looked at Dan. "Your dad answered the phone, called me Jason and told me he couldn't find the restaurant. I told Rick it was me. We talked about the case and let the name mix-up slide."

Dan shook his head. "I keep telling my dad to check the caller ID before he answers the phone. But he claims he *always* knows who's calling so he doesn't need that new technology."

As if his father really could see into the future. Dan wished his dad possessed that skill, then Dan would know what to expect and how to shield Ben from any potential harm.

"Sounds just like Rick." Ava's gaze zeroed in on Dan. "So, it's true? Valerie and Jason are back in town?"

Dan exhaled into the evening air. Maybe he shouldn't have eaten the second chicken-and-waffle sandwich. "They were waiting on the front porch when Brooke and I returned from the grocery store today."

"No announcement? No forewarning?" Sophie raised her hands like a magician about to pull a rabbit from a hat. "Just poof. Here we are."

"Pretty much," Dan said. Although in hindsight, he had a premonition. All those phone calls and texts he hadn't replied to surely contributed to this mess.

He should've prepped Ben better. Yet each year that Valerie failed to surprise them with her return, complacency set in and Dan built a life where he was everything Ben would need.

More questions from the gang ensued. Most answered by Dan. Some fielded by Brooke, to Dan's appreciation. Nichole had stepped in to take Ben for the night. Now Brooke stepped in to support Dan. But he wasn't reading more into Brooke's support than the friendly gesture it was.

The inquiries rolled to a stop with Dan's statement: he didn't know Valerie's plans or her intentions.

That led to several minutes of speculation.

Sophie suggested that Valerie was tired of traveling and missed her home. Except that was Sophie's inner family side speaking about her own need for roots.

Kyle wondered if Jason had encouraged Valerie to come back. That was Kyle speaking as an older brother who adored his sisters and wanted his whole family within walking distance. Kyle kept encouraging his own sister to move back from England.

Ava added that Valerie's mom might be ill. That was Ava's loyalty to her own mom coming out—she was battling MS.

Ava's suggestion might've had merit if Dan hadn't dropped Luann Bennett—a healthy and happy seventy-four-year-old—at the airport for her cruise. And received the subsequent photographs she'd forwarded to her grandson of herself on the ship—ballroom dancing and winning bingo. They weren't pictures of an ill passenger.

But Dan's friends circled back to the very heart of the matter quickly.

Brad asked, "What about Ben?"

"What can we do?" Sophie touched Dan's arm. "How can we help?"

Dan valued his friends. Their constant support, given freely and without expecting any sort of payment, filled his life. Dan looked at Brooke. He didn't need more friends, did he? He said, "I'm not sure what to do."

"Well, we're here." Kyle claimed another brownie and stood up. "For whatever you need."

"Even if you just want to lose at Ping-Pong," Brad offered.

Laughter eased through Dan and his argument. "I wouldn't have lost if you hadn't convinced Ava to tilt the table at the last round."

"Winners don't get distracted." Brad stood up, too. "We have singular focus."

"Until your wife walks by and smiles at you." Kyle earned a high five from Dan.

Brad leaned down and kissed Sophie, openly and honestly. A man not afraid of his feelings. Dan almost envied him. *Almost.*

Sophie asked Brooke if she could visit Rex. The women disappeared inside the apartment. Brad and Kyle walked over to the basketball hoop in the corner of the yard. Ava followed

Dan inside to clean up. And like that, the evening returned to normal as if his friends understood Dan needed that the most, even without asking.

Dan walked into the kitchen and shook his head. He hadn't considered it possible for Kyle and Brad to make more of a mess than he already had.

"This is not helping you to not become a statistic." Ava picked up the monkey bread and coffee cake on the kitchen table, then dipped her chin at the fried chicken. "Did you know Hank is retiring?"

"Hank never mentioned it when I saw him." Hank had five children to support. The stress of the job almost killed him. A career overhaul made sense for Hank.

"Have you considered a change?" Ava turned on the faucet, drizzled soap over the stack of prep dishes and started washing.

Dan had not. He was fine, handling the stress and balancing his life. Maybe he slept even less than usual most days. And some calls—even the minor ones—stuck to him a little longer, leaving deeper imprints that were proving harder to shake. But a decade in the rig was bound to do that to a person. The exhaustion and cynicism were typical.

"I have enough change going on around me

with a new tenant and now my brother and Valerie back home." Dan set more pans beside the sink, grabbed the disinfectant wipes and scrubbed the counter.

He had to concentrate on Ben. His son was going to have a big change now that his mother was home. Dan didn't need to be altering his career, too. One that would put him behind a desk and into a classroom. How much help would he really be? If he was behind a desk, he wouldn't be available for Ben throughout the day. Like now. He'd have to say no to the last-minute school projects, the volunteering and being present for school events. He hadn't said no since Ben had entered school. And he'd never used work as an excuse to get out of helping. A daytime shift would change everything.

Still, he'd have his weekends. Wouldn't be on call for twenty-four hours. And he'd have a regular work schedule. Did he even know how to sleep at night anymore? He'd been working nights since his first year on the job. Dan scrubbed the counter as if it would suddenly reveal an answer like a crystal ball.

"Not all change is bad." Ava handed him a stainless-steel bowl to dry instead. "You don't have to fight it so much."

"I can change," Dan argued. Choosing *not to*

wasn't a sign of his resistance. "I walked this week with a dog."

Ava turned off the water and leaned against the counter. "How was that?"

Refreshing. Freeing. He'd opened up to Brooke more than he had to anyone in a long time. And yet he hadn't resented it. He said, "It was fine."

"It was more than fine." Ava shoved him in the chest with her wet hands. "I saw how you looked at Brooke out there just now."

"It's too dark outside to see much." He picked up the clean frying pan and avoided looking at his best friend.

"It was light enough to notice your gaze lingering on Brooke," Ava challenged. "You even smiled whenever Brooke smiled."

Dan concentrated on putting away the dishes. "I was engaged in the conversation that included Brooke's participation."

"You watched her even when she wasn't talking," Ava countered. "She's gotten under your skin."

Like a splinter. As soon as the fragment was removed, the irritation stopped. The inflammation healed. Brooke was the furthest thing from an irritation. That was the problem. She would leave. Dan worried he wasn't as immune as he wanted to be. Brooke's absence would linger inside him. And he didn't know how to fix that. "It's nothing."

"I told myself that, too, with Kyle." Ava lifted her left hand, revealing her diamond engagement ring. "Look how it turned out."

Ava had fallen head over heels in love. Dan wasn't that foolish. He'd never rush into love. He only ever rushed out in the field, where he was trained and prepared. "I'm not interested in Brooke like that. I'm just grateful she was there today with Valerie and Jason."

"Me, too." Ava opened the coffee-cake box. "I would've told Valerie to leave. That she wasn't welcome here."

Dan handed a butter knife to Ava. "I considered it."

"But it isn't the right thing for Ben." Ava cut a small piece off the coffee cake and popped it into her mouth. A muffled hum flowed from her. She swallowed and cut another piece. "This is divine."

"Valerie brought that over and the monkey bread for my dad." Dan grinned. "The coffee cake is a favorite of mine."

"Now I touched this, so I have to eat it." Ava chewed the second piece and glared at the coffee cake. "I suppose it was considerate of Valerie to remember your favorite things."

He only really wanted Valerie to remember her son and his favorite things. "That's Valerie."

"What happens next?" Ava shut the coffee-cake box and set the monkey bread on top of it.

"I'm going to shoot a few baskets with Brad and Kyle." Dan mimicked the perfect basketball shooting form.

"Not what I meant." Ava walked to the back door.

"I know." Dan followed her outside. "But I don't have any answers."

"Well, maybe Brooke will." Ava nudged her elbow into Dan's side. "Because I also noticed how she looked at you."

"Aaaa-va." Dan scrubbed his hands over his face and stretched out her name.

"I'm in love." Ava poked him again. "Don't blame me for wanting everyone to be as happy as I am."

"We have other single friends, like Kyle's sister. Spread your joy on Iris," Dan said.

"Fine." Ava laughed and headed toward the rental apartment. "But don't think I'm giving up on you."

Dan was happy. Maybe not the blissful, cloud-nine kind that Ava floated around on. But clouds dispersed and dissolved. Then he'd face-plant right back into reality. He was satisfied with his feet on the ground and his kind of happy.

Dan intercepted a pass between Brad and Kyle, shot and scored a basket. He high-fived Brad, then joined their debate about what to wager. This was the only kind of happy he wanted.

CHAPTER TWELVE

LAUGHTER FROM THE basketball half-court drifted through the open apartment door. Sophie concentrated on Rex, coaxing him out of the bedroom into the family room. Luna switched from one side to the other, sniffing Rex as if to encourage him, then returning to sit beside Sophie as if showing Rex what she wanted him to do.

Finally, the sweet boxer scooted out of the bedroom and curled beside the arm of the couch.

"Ella is going to be so relieved. She's been worried about you." Sophie knelt in front of Rex, rubbed behind his ears and glanced over at Brooke. "Ella gets that from me. It's an occupational hazard. I worry about every animal as if they are my very own."

"That's what makes you great at your work." Brooke's former boss had often told her the very same thing throughout her five years at Nash Legal and Mediation Services. Brooke had cared about every client and had always pushed until both parties were satisfied. When had she stopped believing that her role no longer mattered? That she wasn't needed?

Sophie sat on the floor beside Rex, resting her back against the couch. "I'm not always so great at my job."

Sophie's frown matched the misery in her tone. Worry pushed Brooke closer to Sophie, yet Brooke stumbled for the words. How long had it been since she'd comforted someone else? Sure, she'd asked Dan if he was okay. Wanted to reassure him, but she'd caught herself and retreated thanks to Ava's arrival.

Something echoed inside her. Her therapist's instructions: *nurture your support system, Brooke. Always.*

But she was only a guest here. Passing through. These weren't *her* friends.

Still, she set a new resolution for herself. Once she'd moved into her new home, she'd work on making a new friend or two. For now, she'd try to bring back Sophie's joy.

Ava burst into the apartment. "Did you ask Brooke yet?"

Brooke held up her hands. "Ask me what?"

"How much do you like Dan?" Ava swept Cupid up into her arms and sat on the recliner.

Brooke's gaze fell on the jewelry box sitting on the fireplace mantel, with the three angel ornaments tucked inside. *Always find the good,*

Brooke. The joy. Brooke stepped closer to the women. "Dan is great."

Sophie sweet-talked Rex until the boxer rolled onto his back. He was quickly rewarded with a belly rub. "For the record, this isn't about setting you up with Dan."

"Unless you want us to. We can make that happen." Ava grinned from the recliner. Ava's straightforward manner made her impossible not to like.

Cupid curled up on Ava's lap, happy and content, as if Ava was also a trained cat whisperer. Luna set her head on the armrest of Ava's chair. Ava reached over, giving equal affection to both the cat and the dog. Cupid and Luna soaked up the attention. Ava added, "Although, you're already wearing his sweatshirt so maybe you don't need our help."

Flames pulsed underneath Brooke's skin, warming her entire face from the neck up.

"Don't listen to Ava. She's in love and wants everyone to be happily paired off," Sophie said.

Ava pointed at Sophie. "You're in love, too, don't deny it. And you want the same for our friends."

Sophie grinned and nodded. "However, we aren't talking to Brooke about love right now. This is about hiring her."

The heat in Brooke's cheeks faded. Love wasn't a topic she wanted to discuss now or later. Love was past tense. She'd already loved. But work could be a part of her present. She'd found joy in her work. "You want to hire me."

"Nothing permanent," Sophie said, assurance in her voice. "I know you have plans to leave. But I'm in a bit of a bind."

"A dog bind to be specific," Ava added.

"I don't think Dan will let me take in another dog," Brooke said. Dan had been great with Rex and Luna. Brooke suspected that was only because they weren't permanent residents. Still, he'd eased up on his rule and allowed the dogs into the backyard tonight.

"Dan would say yes if you asked." Ava nodded at Brooke, confidence bracing her words.

But one evening hardly transformed Dan. He'd most likely want to avoid taking another walk with Brooke and the dogs. Allowing the dogs into the backyard was the perfect compromise. Although he'd been the one to extend their walk that morning. Brooke rubbed her hands over her face to stop her circular thoughts. She needed to identify what deserved her focus. That tactic had always gotten her clients' attention in the meeting room.

"I'm serious." Ava's smile stretched wide. "He'd agree for you."

Brooke seriously needed to redirect her mind. Before she forgot herself and started to believe Ava.

"It doesn't matter. The dog's owner, Earl Powell, would never agree." Frustration sank into Sophie's tone like an anchor. "Earl has already turned down my qualified foster families. Every single one of them."

Brooke sat on the opposite end of the couch, facing Sophie and Ava. "Maybe you should start at the beginning."

Ava and Sophie shared a look. Laughter filled the air then, pure joy radiating from the duo. Brooke smiled. It had been ages since her heart had felt so light.

"Sorry," Ava said. "It's like you've been part of our group forever."

She was a part of something. Happiness bolstered Brooke's confidence. She wanted to settle in for the night with these women. But that wasn't part of her new plan. Friends were for later—after she'd moved to her new home. Good plans had specific, definable steps for a reason. Ones she needed to follow to ensure success.

"Here's my problem. Earl Powell is an eighty-six-year-old gentleman whose family needs to put him into assisted living." Sophie paused and inhaled as if gathering herself. "His daughter Cara came to see me because Earl has a senior dog, Sherlock, who needs to be rehomed, too."

"Dan and I have transported Earl before. He's set in his ways, cantankerous, generous and an excellent storyteller who loves his dog more than anyone." Affection warmed Ava's voice.

"Earl loves his dog so much that he's refusing to move into assisted living until Sherlock is settled with a family that he approves of." Sophie dropped her head on the sofa cushion and stared at the ceiling.

"But both Earl's and Sherlock's safety is at risk every day he remains alone in his house," Ava said.

"What about his daughter Cara?" Brooke suspected the family had valid reasons for not taking the dog. But she always preferred to gather all the information she could.

"Cara travels for work and cares for her grandkids," Sophie said. "One of her granddaughters has asthma and severe allergies."

"And Cara doesn't want Sherlock to spend his senior years alone and always outside at her house," Ava said.

That proved his daughter liked animals. Cara would be patient with her father's concerns for his dog. But for how long? At some point, her father's safety would have to come first, even before his beloved Sherlock. Brooke asked, "What can I do?"

Sophie lifted her head and locked her gaze on Brooke. "Pet mediation."

"Is that what it's called?" Ava asked.

Sophie rushed on, ignoring Ava, "Brooke,

I've watched you at the pet store with the animals and the customers. You have a special way with both.

"I need help getting Earl to release Sherlock to another family. A good one, of course." Urgency was there in Sophie's tone and a quiet understanding lingered in her gaze. "His bond with his dog is just so very strong."

Brooke wished she had her cabin. She'd take Sherlock home to live with her, too. Yet Earl might not approve of her, either. "What makes you think I can convince Earl to let Sherlock go to a new home?"

Sophie scooted closer to Brooke. "Like I said, you're really good with pets and people. Everyone trusts you."

One more statement her former boss had made often: *people trust you, Brooke. It's a gift.* But Brooke struggled to trust the world. Still this wasn't about her. This was about a man and his beloved dog.

"And there's Valerie," Ava said. "Dan told me he appreciated Brooke being with him today."

Brooke wasn't looking for a relationship. That wasn't part of her new support system she intended to build. But Dan's words flipped her insides and almost made her reconsider. *Almost.*

Meanwhile, she could help Earl and Sherlock. Her work had always fulfilled her and eased the loneliness. "When can I meet Earl and Sherlock?"

"Really?" Sophie asked. "You'll do this?"

At Brooke's nod, Sophie jumped up and hugged her.

Brooke returned the enthusiastic embrace. And if she hung on a little longer and a little tighter than normal, that was only because Sophie held on to her.

CHAPTER THIRTEEN

DAN'S GAZE CONNECTED with a familiar couple walking behind the visiting team's soccer goal. *No.* Anger spiked his blood pressure. Frustration slammed his teeth together. He dropped his chin, glared at the grass and worked to unclench his jaw.

Dan glanced at the bleachers behind him. Irritation turned his voice brittle. "Dad, did you invite them?"

"Valerie mentioned the soccer game last night at dinner. I assumed you'd already spoken to her about it." Rick shifted on the bench and stood up. "I'll go talk to them."

Well played, Val. Dan set his hand on his father's arm. "It's okay, Dad."

"This isn't what you planned." Rick shook his head.

Nothing ever went as planned with Valerie involved. Dan forced a few deep breaths and walked with his dad toward Valerie and Jason. "She wasn't going to wait."

Unfortunately, Dan hadn't prepared Ben for

the news of his mother's return. Ben had spent the morning with Wesley and Nichole, while Dan had refereed two early soccer games. Dan only saw Ben long enough to unknot the shoelaces on his soccer cleats and tell him to play hard.

Dan stuck the flag he used as linesman into his back pocket and swallowed his urge to yell "Out of bounds."

Or perhaps the foul should be called on Dan. Had he made a mistake not telling Ben last night? He'd wanted his own time to process. To plan. Valerie had taken that from him. Now he'd let down Ben. His son liked to plan ahead, too.

Ben would be mad. How could he not be? Dan crossed his arms over his chest. Upsetting Ben always chewed up his insides.

He checked his watch. Less than a minute until the game started again. Could he usher Valerie and Jason off the field and back into their rental car in thirty seconds?

"Sorry we're late." Valerie hugged Rick. "Jason had a business call."

The referee blew the whistle signaling the start of the second half and the end of Dan's stalling. Time was up. In twenty-five minutes, Ben would meet his mom.

Both teams sprinted onto the field. Dan moved into position on the sideline. It was for the better. Nothing about Valerie's arrival made Dan want to sit and get comfortable.

Valerie chatted with Rick about hiking and exploring the peninsula across the Golden Gate Bridge. She paused and asked, "Which one is Ben?"

Dan choked as if a soccer ball slammed against his windpipe. How could she not recognize her own son? Never mind Ben was the only redhead on the field. Dan had sent pictures to Valerie often.

His father pointed to Ben. Valerie launched back into her hike, describing the sea cliffs and the green and crimson pebbles across the beach. Dan moved farther down the field.

Jason stepped beside Dan. "Ben is Number Fourteen."

Dan nodded. Should he be pleased his brother hadn't required help finding his own family?

"Ben has skills." Jason shaded his eyes with his hand and tracked the play toward the visitor's goal. "Serious ones."

What was the catch? Pretend the silence of the past few years never existed? Act like they always watched soccer games together? Make his brother the villain? But in what story line? Dan rubbed his forehead. He'd worked twenty-four-hour shifts early in his career and hadn't ever been so tired. So weary.

Jason walked beside Dan along the sideline,

toward the opponent's goal. Maybe it was the exhaustion of the constant second-guessing, the constant endless questions. Whatever it was, Dan opted for a fact, something real, and said, "I tell Ben all the time that he takes after his uncle."

Jason paused and glanced at Dan. "Ben doesn't play football like you?"

"Basketball and soccer." Dan wasn't as proficient in either sport. Not like his younger brother had been. Dan studied Jason, saw the disbelief and grief. Or perhaps that was Dan seeing his own feelings. "Ben is lean like you, with the same quickness, speed and lightness on his feet. Ben could've used your advice and assistance."

Jason rubbed his hand over his face. Dan was certain he saw regret in his brother's shadowed gaze. Was it regret that he hadn't been there? Or something else? All Dan knew was that standing beside his brother at his son's soccer game, he wished they hadn't lost so many years. But wishing got him nowhere.

Jason shifted and tracked the play on the field. "If Ben planted his foot and angled ten degrees to the left, he would've made that goal."

Dan accepted Brooke's advice. *Accept things as they are.* He said, "You should tell him that."

Jason shrugged. "It'd be easier to show him."

"Then do that." The offer slipped out, yet only

surprise shifted through Dan. Surprise that he didn't want to take back his words.

"Really?" Jason asked.

Dan nodded, opening the door very slightly for his brother. He wanted Ben to know his uncle. Buried deep inside were the good memories when Dan and Jason had been best friends without secrets between them. Everything had shattered once Jason had learned he'd been adopted. But to Dan, Jason was only ever his younger brother. Then there was the fallout with Valerie. And then so much water on the bridge it had collapsed.

But Dan missed his brother and that loss ached inside him like a damaged nerve.

"Ben usually goes to the park with Wesley on Sunday afternoons." Dan pointed to Number Eight on the field. "They could both use some pointers if you can make it tomorrow."

"Yeah, I'd like that." His smile waned. But the pleasure was there in his low voice. "I'd like that a lot."

"I've been wanting to visit the park and the botanical garden there." Valerie lifted her hand and waved. "Look, there's Brooke."

Nichole and Brooke returned from the restrooms. Dan had introduced the two women before the game. Brooke had wished Wesley a happy birthday. Nichole had grinned and confessed that it was Wesley's half birthday, but

Brooke's birthday wish wasn't entirely inappropriate. That launched their conversation, which had continued through the first half without a hiccup.

Dan's gaze connected with Brooke. Her smile wobbled as her hand landed on Nichole's arm. Nichole pushed her glasses up and her shoulders back. Brooke slid between Jason and Dan.

Nichole faced Valerie eye to eye. Both women surpassed the height requirement for a supermodel. The similarities ended there. Valerie filled every inch of her stature. Nichole hadn't quite adjusted to her height and was often more clumsy than poised. Yet Nichole was brilliant, witty and observant—traits she used to her advantage. She might drop the soccer snacks on the grass. But she could clean up and design a computer program in her head at the same time.

Nichole reached out to shake Valerie's hand. Valerie waved away the gesture and wrapped Nichole in a full embrace. The kind family shared after an extended absence. The kind that wouldn't allow Nichole to remain detached.

"Oh. Okay. We're hugging." Nichole adjusted her glasses and patted Valerie's back with three quick precise taps.

Brooke frowned. "I didn't realize Valerie was such a hugger."

"Valerie embraces everyone." Dan hadn't held anyone like that in a long while. He wanted to wrap his arm around Brooke, tug her into his side and hold on. As if that was his right. What was wrong with him? His son was about to meet his mom, he wasn't sure how to reach his brother and all he wanted to do was get closer to Brooke.

Brooke bumped into his side, jarring Dan's debate. She whispered, "Nichole looks uncomfortable."

Dan laughed. "Nichole has a wider-than-normal personal-space boundary."

"That Valerie just crossed in a big way." Brooke bit into her lower lip. "Should we help?"

"Valerie is releasing her now." Dan stepped away from Brooke. He didn't embrace his acquaintances or friends. He couldn't start with Brooke. Or he'd become like Valerie, hugging everyone all the time. Was it a problem that the only person he was interested in hugging was Brooke? He added, "Watch out. You might be next on Valerie's list."

Brooke retreated, closing the distance between Dan and her. Putting herself within hand-holding reach. But if he held her hand, he'd want more.

"We're having a picnic at the park tomorrow." Valerie beamed at the group and linked her arm with Nichole's. "I'll pick up the food while Jason works with the boys on their soccer skills. Then we can hang out for the afternoon."

Or not. This wasn't a quaint family reunion. This was awkward and complicated. Picnics were for families who wanted to share memories and reconnect. That wasn't them.

Dan glanced at Brooke. What would she tell him? Small steps forward mattered. That had been her praise to Rex on their walk. It was a simple picnic. One afternoon.

Nichole looked at Dan and worry pinched her eyebrows together. "I have a Fall Festival committee meeting for tomorrow afternoon. I can't stay at the park the whole time."

"I can be there." Brooke stepped beside Dan and glanced at him. "If you want."

A PAUSE BUTTON would be useful right now. Dan needed a few minutes to collect his scattered thoughts. Work out his explanation to Ben. And reveal Valerie's arrival.

But he had no pause button. The referee blew the whistle and ended the game. Parents cheered for Ben's team. Dan struggled to find his applause. Seconds passed. The players shook hands. The coach called the team together. But for less than a minute.

That wasn't nearly long enough. He willed the coach to talk more. But the team dispersed.

Nichole slipped away to intercept Wesley, giving Ben more privacy.

Ben crossed the soccer field. The rush of

victory hurried his steps. Dan high-fived Ben, then wrapped his son in a tight hug. Time wasn't stopping. And Dan had passed the stalling limit. He released Ben, set his hand on his thin shoulder and nudged his son around.

"Ben, this is your mom and your uncle Jason." Dan's voice was flat, even to his own ears.

"Surprise." Valerie opened her arms as if certain Ben would welcome her open embrace.

Ben had always been tuned to Dan and Rick's emotions, even as a small child. A deep thinker, Ben often relied on caution and his observations. He didn't step into Valerie's arms. He simply clutched his soccer ball and planted his cleats in the grass.

Jason dipped his chin at Ben and remained in place as if he understood Ben's reserve.

Ben's voice quieted, signaling the first hint of anger, as if Valerie was ruining everything. "Why are you here?"

Dan wanted to know exactly how long Valerie planned to stay this time. Surely, she wasn't intending to become a permanent fixture in Ben's life. Valerie never did anything permanently. How long before she wanted to experience more than what her son and the city could offer? Or worse, how long before she took Ben for ice cream and forgot to check his numbers?

Valerie lowered her arms and stepped forward. Her smile swirled through her lilting voice—the combination always aided her in winning over people from every generation. "I wanted us to get to know each other."

"Right now?" Ben's face pinched along with his voice.

Brooke bent down beside Ben, her movements slow as if she feared overstepping Ben's personal space. Yet she remained close enough to offer Ben her support. "Your mom's probably hoping you guys can spend time together in person."

Ben faced Brooke. "Why?"

Dan wanted that answer, too. He'd only received a cryptic reply from Luann. A one-line response. We all need to talk in person.

Brooke gave Ben her full attention, as if to let Ben know that she'd heard his concern. Her voice was gentle. "Maybe because she's missed a lot of your life and wants to make it up to you."

Dan wished he believed that. He wanted to believe that for his son.

Ben tipped his head toward Valerie, but kept his eyes on Brooke. "Did she tell you that?"

Ben's skepticism soured Dan's anger. Ben was too young to be a cynic like Dan. He stepped beside his son. "Your mother hasn't told us anything."

"When did she get here?" Ben asked.

"Yesterday," Dan confessed. Ben needed as much of the truth as Dan could provide. Ben relied on Dan for that. He'd already let down his son. "Brooke and I came back from the store and your mom and uncle were on the front porch."

Ben narrowed his gaze on his dad. "When were you going to tell me?"

"Tonight." After Dan figured out how best to protect Ben. Valerie wouldn't hurt him intentionally—being malicious and having a mean spirit weren't part of her makeup. Still, she would hurt Ben at some point. Because Valerie's nature rejected responsibility and the instinct to grow roots.

"Everyone is waiting for me. We're supposed to go to Roadside Burgers." Ben glanced at Valerie and Jason. "We won our game."

"We watched the second half," Jason said. "You have excellent ball control. I might have a tip or two to help you with scoring from the left side of the field."

Ben relaxed his hold on his soccer ball. "Dad says you were one of the best soccer players on the field in high school and college."

"I know my way around a midfielder and center back," Jason said.

"Cool." Ben shifted his weight from one foot to the other. A challenge shifted through his voice. "What did you guys do after you won a game?"

"The team went to Olive Brand Pizzeria and

ate more slices of pizza than we should have." Jason held Ben's gaze.

"Every time?" Ben asked, his voice serious, as if Jason's answer mattered.

For the first time since Jason's return, Dan saw a glimpse of his younger brother in the twitch of his mouth.

"Every time." Jason nodded, his voice as serious as Ben's, as if he'd just made a pact with his nephew.

Dan exhaled. His brother understood Ben, the child, perfectly. He hoped Ben might reach the old Jason and convince him to stay around. Dan knew he couldn't. There was too much murky water between them.

Valerie set her hands on her hip and scowled at Jason. "We're celebrating at the Glass Violet Restaurant. I already made reservations."

She completely ignored the tradition of the soccer team. No surprise there. She'd ignored the pediatrician's advice on the best baby foods, been determined that an infant Ben would eat the same foods as the adults. And now eating cheeseburgers and sweet-potato french fries wasn't part of her plans, either.

Horror widened Ben's eyes and he grabbed Dan's hand and tugged.

Dan squeezed Ben's fingers. "Wagyu beef isn't really his sort of thing, Val."

"Why not? Glass Violet is one of the top-ranked restaurants on the West Coast." Confusion pulled Valerie's perfectly arched eyebrows together. She studied Ben as if she couldn't understand him. "It's a culinary experience."

"So is dunking your french fries into your double-fudge chocolate milkshake," Jason said.

Ben held his fist out for his uncle to tap. Jason paused. Dan willed him not to let his nephew down. Finally, Jason bumped his fist with Ben's.

Something rapped inside Dan. It was the start of a connection between Ben and Jason.

"That's rather disgusting." Valerie grimaced. At the fist-bumping or french-fry dunking, Dan wasn't sure.

Dan clarified, "Not to ten-year-old boys."

Valerie understood national traditions like New Year's celebrations and Fourth of July parties. Simple traditions escaped her. But Jason understood Ben and what kids liked. Dan and Jason had teamed up to sway their parents to agree to Sunday-morning treats and Friday-night outings. They'd been so successful that root beer floats and doughnuts should've been a staple food group in their childhood diet.

"Fine." Valerie rubbed her hands together as if preparing to toss glitter to celebrate her even-better idea. "We'll order french fries with dessert after the fourth course. It'll be different and fun."

Ten-year-old boys ate one continuous course, preferably with their hands and using their sleeves as napkins. Not that Ben couldn't behave at a nice dinner. He just shouldn't have to tonight.

Okay, Dan thought. This was small. Inconsequential. But it was the first ripple of change Valerie caused. What more waited?

Ben stepped back, clearly hoping to escape the glitter.

"Why don't you try something different tomorrow night?" Brooke suggested. Her voice was grounded and reasonable, not dazzling and enchanting.

Or never. Dan stomped on his worry.

"Tonight, Ben should celebrate with his team." Brooke touched Ben's shoulder. "Ben told me it's a tradition to go to Roadside Burgers whenever his team wins. He wouldn't want to be the one to break any traditions this close to the playoffs."

Brooke recognized the significance to Ben. Dan couldn't let that matter. Couldn't let that slide her out of the friend zone. Nor would he appreciate Brooke's assistance as anything more than friendly support. He could fight his own battles. That he liked Brooke standing beside him wasn't a critical misstep in his feelings.

The smile Ben aimed at Brooke covered his entire face and steadied Dan.

Ben grabbed his grandfather's hand. "Come on, Grandpa. Everyone is waiting for us."

"I'm part of the tradition that pays for dinner and this is my cue to leave." Rick hugged each of the women.

Dan called Ben back, stopping him midzip on his soccer bag and before his cleats sprinted across the field. "You need to say goodbye to your uncle, Brooke and your mom."

Ben fist-bumped his uncle again and mentioned the park. Then he fist-bumped Brooke and promised to help walk the dogs. Finally, he offered a wave and polite goodbye to Valerie, then hustled toward his team.

Rick glanced between Dan and Valerie. "Can I suggest that the adults head to Valerie's restaurant and work things out like grown-ups for Ben's sake?"

"That sounds splendid." Valerie transferred her delight from Rick to Dan. "We'll meet you at seven for dinner."

Valerie hugged Brooke and added the dress attire for the evening. Then she joined Jason and left as if everything was decided. No more discussion required. Dan agreed with his dad. They needed to talk. Yet a four-course meal in an upscale restaurant gave Dan indigestion. There'd be no easy out. Too much holding back. Too much forced reserve in a public setting.

Dan glanced at Brooke. "I understand if you'd

rather not go to dinner. But I'd really like you to be there."

"Why?" Brooke asked.

I like knowing I can take your hand, if I'm so inclined. Not that he ever would. He said, "You can talk to Valerie better than I can."

At her hesitation, he added, "There's Wagyu beef on the menu."

"But there's french fries and homemade milk-shakes at Roadside Burger." Brooke tapped her chin. "Ben invited me to join them."

"Did he?" Dan asked. Ben often reserved postgame dining for his teammates, his grandpa and Dan. Ava had only gone once, and she held honorary auntie status. Often Rick and Ben celebrated while Dan prepared for work.

"You can order french fries with dessert." Dan clenched his teeth together, biting into the desperation he heard in his own voice. He accepted that Valerie and he had to talk. Accepted that he didn't want to have that conversation with her alone. But that Brooke was the only one he wanted with him. Well, that made him slightly anxious on a whole different level.

"That might be one adventure too many for the same night." Brooke touched his arm. "I'll stick to the Wagyu beef."

"Then you'll come with me." Relief flowed through Dan. Along with the reminder that he was leaning on her like he would Ava or Nichole. Nothing more.

Brooke nodded. Hesitation, not confidence, leaked into her tone. "If you'll walk the dogs with me in morning."

As if he'd refuse. "I'll walk them tonight after dinner."

CHAPTER FOURTEEN

DAN STARED AT his menu and tried to ignore the small talk at the table. Red wine was preferred over white. Valerie would pick the bottle. Brooke and Jason chose lobster-stuffed mushrooms over calamari. Dan wanted water, three less courses and to get to the important stuff: Valerie's plans.

The waiter memorized their orders, collected the menus and slipped away as discreetly as he'd arrived.

Valerie beamed at Brooke as if more than content to continue the get-to-know-you portion of the evening. "Do you ever travel?"

"I used to." Brooke arranged her silverware on the table as if organizing her thoughts.

The wistful catch in Brooke's voice pulled Dan into the conversation. Brooke must've traveled with her late husband. How much had her life changed after his death? How much did she regret?

Dan missed those brief pauses in the routine. Would a night away be enough for Brooke or would she want something more extravagant?

Brooke continued, "It's more complicated to travel now with my pets."

What if Brooke could bring her pets? Dan stilled. Traveling with Brooke and her dogs wasn't the focus tonight. *Or ever.* "Traveling is Valerie's life."

"There's nothing wrong with following your passion." Valerie passed the water glasses from the waiter around the table. "People would be happier if they did what they loved."

Brooke squeezed a lemon into her water. Nothing sour squeezed into her tone. "Sometimes people have to do things they don't like, to get to do what they love."

What did Brooke love to do? Dan picked up a lemon from the small plate, considered sticking it in his mouth. Maybe the bitter taste would force him to focus. This dinner wasn't about Brooke and learning more about her.

Jason picked up his water and tipped the glass at Brooke and Dan. "Sometimes doing things with the people you love is more than enough."

"It's more magical when you're all in an exotic location." Valerie dropped dinner rolls on everyone's plates.

"Only to you," Jason countered. He pushed away the roll and the beer Valerie had ordered for him.

If Jason had meant to dent her resolve, he'd failed. Valerie's optimism required no time to recover. "Well, Jason is a professional poker player. He also gets to do what he loves and travel."

"I've never been good at cards," Brooke said. "Sounds like you must have better skills."

"Or better luck," Jason said.

"Don't let him fool you," Dan said. "He's been patiently and diligently studying poker and the players since high school. It's more than luck."

Jason grinned and relaxed into his chair as if relaxing into a good memory. "You never had good luck."

"You'd think my little brother would've helped me out with some advice." Dan speared a stuffed mushroom on his fork, comfortable in the memory and the common ground with his brother. "Instead, Jason invited me and my friends over for poker tournaments and took all our pizza-delivery money."

"I did give you a cut of the winnings for filling up the tables." Jason aimed his knife at Dan.

"Quite enterprising," Brooke said.

"And fun," Dan said. "We even invited our dad and his friends to join in."

"I'm not sure Dad has played since that night," Jason said. Laughter lingered in Jason's tone, as if hesitant to come out. As if his brother hadn't laughed in far too long.

Dan let his own laughter roll across the table. "Dad has worse luck than me."

"Jason is quite talented. Recently, though, luck hasn't been a very kind companion." The softness in Valerie's voice only added a sharper point to her words. "Wonder what side of the family that comes from."

Valerie had always preferred to veil her criticism inside a compliment. His brother's laughter quieted.

"Poker is a long-term game." Both Jason's face and demeanor stiffened. "And you have to know when to leave the table."

"You also have to play again to win," Valerie quipped.

Dan eyed his brother. He used to be able to read him. Yet Jason mastered the art of masking his emotions. Now his face was much leaner, giving him a harder edge. Even the laugh lines around his eyes looked shallow. Dan asked, "You haven't been playing?"

Jason shook his head but offered nothing more.

Dan wanted to press. But this wasn't the time. His brother had always lived for the next game. The next shuffle. The next deal. What had changed?

Valerie sampled the wine and gave her approval to the waiter. That was where her approval ended. Disapproval twisted her mouth into a grimace. "Jason calls it bankroll management."

Not a surprise. Jason had always excelled with finances, budgets and numbers. Math had never been Valerie's forte. Then again, her father had funded Valerie's every whim until his death. Dan had taken over their household finances, assuming that responsibility in their marriage, as well. Dan had expected she'd have learned on her own. The money in her trust fund wasn't endless. "Budgeting isn't bad, Valerie."

"You sound just like your brother." Valerie pierced her mushroom cap with her fork.

"Thanks for the compliment." Dan toasted Jason and earned something from his brother he hadn't seen in a long time: a genuine smile.

"Enough money talk. Ben needs a passport." Valerie grinned around her bite of mushroom as if she'd suggested Ben should get a new haircut.

Dan blinked. The connection between him and his brother disconnected like a dropped call. While Valerie's comment splattered on the table as if the waiter dropped Valerie's fish, whole and still breathing, in front of them all. Dan opened and closed his mouth. "Why would Ben need a passport?"

"So he can travel with me." Valerie straightened and waved her fork absently between herself and Jason. "Or us."

"You want to take Ben with you?" Dan asked. Clearly, he was like that fish, gasping for air and clarification.

"Absolutely." Valerie pointed her fork at Dan. "He's old enough to start experiencing more of the world, Dan."

"Ben is ten." A child. A kid who loved soccer, basketball and game night with his family and friends. How much more of the world did a ten-year-old need to see? Dan pushed away his plate. The lobster and mushroom were at war in his stomach.

"I've met ten-year-olds who speak multiple languages and have been flying international flights alone since they were six." Valerie served the remaining appetizers to everyone as if being the proper hostess was her only concern.

But those weren't Dan's kids. Or his responsibility. Or his concern.

"You want Ben to have a passport," he repeated, desperate to believe he'd heard her wrong.

"Ben should travel," Valerie said.

"Why?" Dan asked.

"I always wanted to travel as a child, but Father's work kept us home," Valerie said.

Her father's work had provided a large estate in the city and comforts few knew growing up. Dan also knew from Luann that Valerie's father had promised Valerie the world, but he'd passed away before he'd given it to her. Apparently, Valerie still expected to have it.

"I want to give Ben the chance that I didn't

have." Both of Valerie's palms flattened on the table as if she needed help supporting her claim. "As his mom, I have that right."

Dan had rights, too. Like to refuse. "I have full custody—legal and physical. You signed the divorce papers."

Valerie stacked the appetizer plates, set them aside along with his argument. "I'm still his mother. The courts want children to spend time with both parents."

"But not out of the country." *Without his father.* Exasperated, Dan wasn't sure if his statement was true or not. But the panic surged like multiple defibrillator charges on his chest. She wanted him to put Ben on a plane to fly overseas. *Alone.*

"Why not?" Valerie challenged. "I'm talking ten days to two weeks. Nothing permanent."

The only permanent thing in Valerie's life was her continuous travel.

Dan looked across the table at his brother. Jason had retreated again, his face impassive as if he'd checked his hand and simply waited for the table to place their bets. Had Jason known this was what Valerie wanted? Ironic that Dan would insist Jason be there from the minute Ben stepped off the plane to the second Ben boarded for his return flight home. As if Dan was going to agree to this. As if Dan trusted Jason more than Valerie. How could that be?

Jason hadn't been a part of Dan's inner circle for more than six years. And yet, clearly, the bond was difficult to sever. The trust difficult to break. Or was that only more useless wishing on Dan's part? It'd been a long while after all.

He tried to focus instead on Brooke. She sat beside him: steady, calm, unfazed. He shouldn't have asked her to come tonight. He should tell her to leave and enjoy her evening.

Brooke reached over, slipped her hand into his.

The chaos inside him receded. The gentle strength in her touch grounded him. Her grin was small, but endearing. Quick, but encouraging. Dan swallowed his offer to walk her out.

Brooke aimed her smile at Valerie, compassion in her voice. "I'm not sure Dan is comfortable with Ben traveling outside the country without him."

Brooke understood Dan. Why couldn't Valerie? Dan held on to Brooke's hand as if she anchored him. Selfish, he knew. This wasn't Brooke's fight. His fingers remained locked around Brooke's as if they belonged together. As if they were meant to conquer the world side by side.

Valerie picked up the wine cork and lifted her arms up as if she'd won the jackpot and the round. "Then Dan can join us, too."

"I can't just fly to Europe or wherever you

are, Valerie." Dan struggled to silence the impatience in his voice. Valerie had never wanted to understand. That clearly hadn't changed. "I have a job. Responsibilities here."

"You always did have too many responsibilities." Valerie tapped the cork on the table and eyed him. "But our son should come first."

How many sleepless nights had he spent at the hospital with Ben? Even more at home. Then there were the frantic phone calls for advice to the doctors and nurses he knew from work. The uncertainty. The constant worry. The fear of being unable to fix his own son. The helplessness. Ben had never come second. Not then. Not now.

Brooke's grip tightened around his hand, reminding Dan that he wasn't alone. That he had support. Then and now.

"Everything Dan does is for Ben. Always," Brooke said. Her voice was kind but firm. "But I'm certain you already know that, Valerie."

"I know that Ben deserves the opportunity to see the world." Valerie twirled her wineglass between her fingers. The resolve in Valerie's tone matched Brooke's. "I believe Ben should be given the choice."

"He's ten years old," Dan repeated. Brooke's touch was like a mute button on his frustration. His voice never slipped past mild. Perfectly suited for the hushed atmosphere in the upscale restaurant.

"That's certainly old enough to have an opinion," Valerie countered.

Also, old enough to get hurt if Valerie changed her mind at the last minute. That said nothing about caring for him, making sure he had the right medicine and proper supplies. "Ben doesn't need to travel for you to spend time with him. You only need to come here."

"He has you *here* in the city, Dan." Valerie raised her hands as if spreading out a map of the world in front of them. "I can show him so much more."

"Where would you take Ben?" Brooke asked, her voice interested, her manner calm.

Everything Dan was pretending to be. He kept Brooke's hand tucked inside his. He liked the idea of Brooke being with him and his family too much. He'd come to his senses at some point. Then he'd let go. But that was later.

Even Jason leaned forward as if interested, too.

Valerie tapped her chin. "Monaco. The coast of Italy."

Those were the same places Valerie had wanted Dan to visit, despite his full-time job and obligations. Places, if Dan was honest, he'd like to visit. If not for his job and those obligations that came first. If not for wanting to give Ben the best home he could afford.

Jason frowned. "The Amalfi Coast is too hard to get around. And Monaco is better suited to adults."

His brother sounded as perplexed by Valerie's suggestions as Dan felt.

"Fine." Valerie pressed a napkin into the corner of her mouth and recovered her smile. "There's always Venice and Scandinavia."

Jason rubbed his hand over his chin, his gaze narrowed, a look of uncertainty overtaking his expression. "Dan and I would've only wanted to swim in the canals in Venice when we were Ben's age."

"Or at least get into daily splash wars," Dan suggested. That earned a grin from Jason and a scowl from Valerie.

"We'd have gotten into a sleep-off in Scandinavia, daring each other not to fall asleep since it would've been daylight all day," Jason said.

"They have sleep masks," Valerie said.

Jason shook his head, his voice skeptical. "Not any that a ten-year-old will keep on."

"Fine." Valerie retied her silk scarf as if rearranging her proposal. "Where do you suggest we take Ben?"

"Simple." Jason shrugged. "Liverpool, England, to see a soccer game."

Dan toasted his brother, warming to that suggestion. "I could be tempted to travel for that."

Brooke leaned forward, excitement in her tone. "Could you really get tickets?"

Jason tipped his head, curiosity in his dark gaze. "Would you be interested in joining us?"

"I was just curious." Brooke sat back and pulled her hand away from Dan's as if she'd overstepped herself.

Dan wanted to take her hand back.

"I'm sure Jason knows someone who can get us tickets to a soccer game," Valerie interrupted. "However, I don't think that's the best idea for Ben."

"Why not?" Brooke asked the question on Dan's mind. And from the rise of Jason's eyebrows, on his mind, too.

"Surely Ben has enough exposure to soccer here at home." Valerie's voice was earnest and sincere. "Shouldn't his vacation be about learning and seeing new things?"

Brooke's chin dipped up and down. "That is part of traveling."

"Ben would be visiting soccer stadiums larger than anything he's ever seen," Jason argued.

Dan waved his hand toward his brother. "That would be new."

"It can't be about soccer, soccer and more soccer." Valerie's fingers tensed on the stem of the wineglass, yet her face remained composed.

"Why not?" Dan asked. If it was about Ben, then it should be about what Ben liked.

"There are over thirty soccer leagues in Europe." Jason grinned and thanked the waiter for his entrée. "It could really be *all* about soccer."

"What else, though? It needs to be about more than that." Valerie held up her hands. "Let's do this. Everyone tell me your favorite childhood vacation."

Everyone quieted. Only long enough for the rest of the entrées to be placed on the table.

Brooke's soft laughter broke the silence. "We were supposed to spend Christmas in the Florida Keys one year. But bad weather and diverted flights stranded us in Idaho. We ended up in a one-bedroom cabin with a woodstove burner, no TV and a deck of playing cards. I still remember snowshoeing to the general store for supplies since they had no rental cars available."

"We can relate." Dan cut into his steak, appreciating the too-hot plate and the fun memory. "On one of our road trips, our grandma stole all the condiments from the restaurant tables—the small jams, syrups, individual butters. Then we got stuck in a massive pileup on the interstate for over ten hours. Mom gave us crackers and syrup in desperation to stop us from whining about starving to death."

"I forgot about that one." Jason separated his vegetables from his pork chop.

His brother had never liked his foods co-mingling on his plate. The tension inside Dan receded—he was pleased some things hadn't changed.

Jason continued, "I was going to say every one of Dad's shortcuts. Mom would never say we were lost, only that we were having an adventure."

"We never did make it to any place that we originally set out for." Dan smiled at the wonder in his own voice. Their parents really had created the best memories for their kids. He wanted Ben to have the same.

Brooke leaned toward him. "Where did you stay?"

"We slept at campsites we stumbled upon or motels. Sometimes even the truck." Dan slid into the memory: blankets piled up past the truck windows. Jason on one side of the bench seat, Dan on the other. On those nights, Dan had stared at the stars until he'd fallen asleep, content and happy and secure. Everything he'd always wanted Ben to feel with him.

"I wonder if Dad remembers telling us that sleeping in the truck was rodeo-style camping." Jason looked at Brooke and Valerie, laughing. "Dad liked to tell us if we slept in the truck, we could get on the road early and not miss anything on our way to our next destination."

"Mom always bought something from every

little town." Dan wished their mom was there now to open a jar of honey and insist Dan sample the best thing ever. "She'd claim it was the absolute best fudge, barbecue sauce, honey or pie she'd ever tasted. Until we came upon the next town with more pies, honey and fudge, and those became the best things ever."

"I wasn't asking for your horrible vacation memories." Exasperation dimmed Valerie's smile, dismay stole the lyrical notes from her voice. Valerie waved over the waiter to refill the water glasses as if everyone needed to pause and refresh.

Brooke accepted the bread basket and Valerie's advice to dip the bread in the steak sauce for an exceptional bite. Brooke said, "These *are* good memories."

"You cannot be serious." Valerie positioned her fork and knife properly on her plate to signal she was finished eating and wanted to quit this part of their conversation. "We definitely aren't putting Ben through any of that."

"Why not?" Brooke asked. "Sometimes the unexpected is wonderful and life-changing in a good way."

"Or it is unpleasant and dreadful." Valerie pointed at Dan. "You never liked the unexpected. You always wanted everything planned out in advance, in detail."

"I still prefer that." He *still* had a job and

commitments that tied him down. Picking up and flying to any international destination *still* wasn't feasible or practical. Dan eyed Valerie. "Are you telling me that you make plans now, too?"

Jason choked on his sip of water. "Never."

"That isn't true." Valerie brushed the bread crumbs into a pile, then into her hand. "I have a very good one for Ben."

Dan frowned. When did Valerie decide to make plans for her son? Making plans for Ben sounded eerily close to a parent's job. Like Dan's job. The one he'd accepted for them both when Valerie had refused to come home and then signed the divorce papers. "That isn't your job."

Valerie set down her wineglass swiftly, but with grace. "It is if Ben is vacationing with me."

Brooke rested her hand on Dan's leg, her voice even. "What is your plan, Valerie?"

"To live life rather than endure it." Valerie's expression softened, and her inner joy returned, lighting up her face. "We could tour medieval castles in England. Watch the centuries-old changing of the guard in London. Explore the science museum in Amsterdam and bike around the historic city. Discover new Dutch foods like *stroopwafel* and *kroket*. Meet new people and learn about new cultures."

Dan searched for a snag. Ben liked bike riding and science, and would most likely enjoy an ancient castle with a torture chamber. Dan wanted to hate Valerie's plan. Instead it was the extra thought Valerie had put into vacationing with Ben that he disliked. "If you do all that now, what do you do next summer and the one after that?"

Valerie perked right up at that. "You travel to a new place. Make new memories."

"Sounds expensive and extravagant." He'd finally discovered the catch. Not everyone enjoyed a life bankrolled by a trust fund like Valerie's. Yet even that money was limited. How much longer could Valerie afford to travel the world? Her own mother had been forced to go back to work after the death of Valerie's dad to keep their home. Dan wasn't certain Luann had the extra money to continuously refill Valerie's trust fund. "There's also college to save for."

"Life is meant to be experienced now, while we can." Sadness filtered across Valerie's face.

Ten years had passed and still Valerie hadn't seemed to accept her father's passing. How long could Valerie run from it? Dan glanced at Brooke. Was she still grieving her late husband?

Valerie added, "Jason agrees with me."

"College trumps everything," Jason said. "You don't want Ben to graduate with even more debt."

"I've never even used my degree. You haven't

needed the one you never finished." Valerie adjusted the ends of her scarf as if aligning her argument. "Look at what we've done. We're both fine."

"You have the benefit of a trust fund. Normal people don't get those." Jason tossed his napkin on top of his plate, his tone defensive. "I was lucky at the poker table more than once. Again, not normal."

"You're saying we aren't normal." Valerie laughed. "Thank goodness for that."

"This lifestyle is not normal," Jason said.

"We never wanted to be like everyone else," Valerie argued.

"Well, now I'm thinking it might not be such a bad thing." Jason spoke as if to himself, not the entire table.

Yet the weariness in his brother's tone reached Dan and he wanted to help.

"This is the life I have always wanted." Valerie commanded the table's attention. She handed their plates to the waiter and accepted the dessert menus in exchange. "I won't apologize."

"No one is asking you to." Brooke took the dessert menu from Valerie. "We all have different lifestyles. Dan wants different things for Ben."

"Dan wants Ben to be just like him." Frustration pushed a blush across Valerie's face. "Ben will end up stuck in place. In a rut. Afraid to step out of his comfort zone. Afraid to take a risk. Just like his father."

"Children change things. Being a parent changes things." A headache threatened, or maybe it was the hammering of their same argument resurfacing. "If you tried being a full-time parent, then you might understand."

"I understand you're refusing to let Ben travel with his own mother." Valerie set her hands on the table and stared at Dan. "I understand we'll need to take this up with a judge in court."

The headache exploded across his temple. Dan couldn't contain the frustration. "You can't be serious."

"Very." Valerie nodded. "While we're there, I'm asking for joint custody."

"Why?" That came from Jason. Confusion bracketed the one word.

"Then I won't need Dan's permission. Just a power of attorney from a judge to get Ben a passport." Valerie stood up. "I'm not as flighty and reckless as I look."

Jason coughed and cleared his throat with a long sip of water.

But Valerie was still as impulsive as ever.

Brooke asked, "You're willing to go to court over a passport?"

The surprise in her voice comforted Dan. He wasn't the only one caught off guard.

"It's about more than that," Valerie argued. "If Dan can't see that now, maybe the judge can help him."

"This will certainly leave some lasting memories." Bitterness poured through Dan's voice, unavoidable and unstoppable.

"I'm trying to make sure Ben lives life to the fullest." Valerie swung her coat over her shoulders. "We're going to give ourselves indigestion and ruin a lovely meal if we continue this now."

Too late. Dan started to rise.

"You stay, Dan, and enjoy dessert with Brooke. You can share more childhood memories." Valerie waved him back into his seat. "Jason will cover the bill."

Jason caught up to their waiter and disappeared, leaving Dan's objection unheard. That headache rolled down Dan's neck and squeezed into his shoulders. He and Valerie had skipped court during their divorce. Surely she wouldn't want to go now.

The headache pulsed and throbbed. All Dan really knew for certain was that Valerie was still unpredictable. And seemingly absent of any doubt. The last time he'd tried to call Valerie's bluff, he'd ended up a divorced, single parent.

Dan shifted, prepared to apologize to Brooke and leave.

Brooke sat beside him, studying the dessert menu as if it was her last meal. As if Valerie's throw down of the court battle and abrupt departure hadn't given her sweet tooth a cavity.

Brooke closed the dessert menu and glanced at him. "I see no reason to pass over bread pudding with caramel-rum sauce."

"I've always preferred molten-lava cake," he said.

She never flinched. Simply ordered both desserts, then smiled at Dan. "We'll have both and try to change each other's minds."

Her smile dared Dan not to like her dessert challenge.

But Valerie's mind was the one Dan should be changing. He shouldn't be lingering over dessert with Brooke. After all, this was not some quaint date.

His ex-wife had just brought the family drama to the dinner table and spread it out like a feast for everyone to pick at. Dan hadn't stopped Valerie.

He should stop whatever it was between him and Brooke. Change their dessert orders to takeout. They could retreat to their own places with their own desserts.

Instead he picked up the extra spoon and dipped it into Brooke's bread pudding.

Challenge accepted.

CHAPTER FIFTEEN

BROOKE WALKED TOWARD the picnic-table area.
Runners, strollers and bikers crossed over the
lake bridge. Families gathered for pictures. A
painter adjusted her easel on the shore. In the
distance dogs barked and radios played. Best of
all, the park blocked the street noise.

"What am I supposed to do when Valerie
gets here?" Ben kicked off his tennis shoes and
pulled a pair of soccer cleats from his bag. "She
doesn't like sports."

"How do you know that?" Brooke shaded her
eyes and looked at the lake.

One Saturday two years into her marriage,
she and Phillip had rented a rowboat like the
ones skimming across the glassy water now.
Brooke had filled that afternoon with laughter and exercise, not business calls and budget
discussions.

Always be present in the moment, Brooke.
Another piece of advice from her therapy sessions. She'd been present that day on the lake.

Now she stood in the park again. In a new

moment. With new people. The best she could offer was to be present now. Especially for Ben.

"She never asks me about soccer." Ben rummaged around inside his bag. "She never asks me about anything, really."

Brooke kept her gaze trained on the lake. But the disappointment in Ben's voice tugged at her. She added her other hand to shade her eyes, rather than hug Ben. She'd been trained to remain impartial. To assist parties in understanding each other's sides. She couldn't *take* sides. That wouldn't bring harmony between Ben and his mother. "Maybe Valerie doesn't know what to ask you. She never got into sports or had a brother or sister growing up."

Ben stretched his legs out and tapped his shin guards. "But she had Dad and Uncle Jason. They could tell her."

"They could." Brooke shifted her gaze to the two men setting up cones for a soccer goal on the grass. Dan and Jason appeared to be tentatively trying to repair their relationship. Valerie and Dan weren't anywhere close to that.

As for Brooke and Dan, last evening they'd shared dessert, childhood stories and a closeness Brooke hadn't experienced in a long while. She'd returned to the apartment not feeling guilty about her time with Dan. Only disappointed the night had ended. She'd fallen asleep eager to see what the new day brought.

The hope and possibilities in her dreams crowded out her nightmares. She hadn't believed she'd feel like this ever again. Hadn't wanted to feel again. Reminding herself to appreciate it for what it was—only a moment with Dan—she promised to not get ahead of herself.

She pulled her gaze away from Dan and glanced at Ben. "Why don't you find common ground with your mother instead of looking for differences?"

Ben rubbed the back of his hand beneath his nose. "Like how Uncle Jason and I both like soccer a lot."

"Yes, like that." The same way she and Dan had agreed four bites of the decadent lava cake was more than enough to satisfy the most intense chocolate craving. Or that the rum sauce was the critical ingredient for the bread pudding but could've been eaten by itself. Or that butter pecan was the best flavor of ice cream.

"Okay." Ben stood up and hugged her around the waist.

Brooke had time to wrap her arms around Ben yet not hold on. Ben's embrace was tight and quick. Then he sprinted off to join Wesley, his dad and his uncle on the makeshift soccer field. And left Brooke scrambling to hold on to the unexpected affection.

Nichole stepped beside Brooke. "I knew Ben for over a year before I even got a partial hug."

"I'm his grandpa, so hugs come with the title." Rick laughed and paused on the other side of Brooke. "But he likes you, Brooke."

She liked him, too. Ben had brought her fresh bagels that morning, then extended his cheerful greeting to Luna and Cupid. He'd softened his tone for Rex yet showered the dog with even more love. The adoration was mutual between Ben and her pets. Ben was hard not to like, the same as his father. Not that she liked Dan too much. Spending time with Dan made her feel better. Made her want to enjoy life again. Nothing more. "Ben is just in an awkward place with his mom home."

"You also haven't pressured him to like her or spend time with her." Rick picked up Ben's soccer bag.

"He's old enough to make up his own mind." Just as Brooke was old enough to recognize the signs of falling in love. None of which she had. Because Dan was only a friend. "But I bet Ben will like Valerie if he gives her a chance."

"I want to not like her, but the woman makes it impossible in person." Nichole tucked a strand of her light brown hair up into her bun, which looked more like a poorly constructed bird's nest. Pieces of her hair stuck out at odd angles while others drooped against her neck, already giving up before the wind could knock her hair loose.

"Dan says that's her superpower." Brooke liked Valerie, too.

Valerie had inquired about food allergies before dinner. Attended to the table with more precision and concern than the waiters. Beyond that, Valerie was passionate about wanting to share her love of history and new cultures with Ben. Valerie was trying. She'd put thought into her ideas. Brooke couldn't fault her for that.

"One of the hardest things ever is to like a person, but hate what they're doing to your loved ones." Rick shook the ice in his stainless-steel tumbler, a wisdom in his voice only those who'd lived could achieve. "I've always adored Valerie."

Brooke nodded. She'd met quite a lot of lovely people at her job. People trapped by circumstances and situations that forced them to act in not-so-wonderful ways. They'd become the bad guy in the scene, but that wasn't who they truly were. With Brooke's assistance, those people were only the bad guys in a one-act play. She wanted the disagreement between Valerie and Dan to be only a one-act play and nothing that dragged out in family court.

"Why would Valerie come back now and want joint custody after all this time?" Nichole swapped her eyeglasses for sunglasses as if that would clarify things. "It doesn't make sense."

Brooke wanted to understand Valerie's intentions, too. Dan had given Brooke sanctuary. Brooke wanted to restore Dan's world, disrupted by his ex's arrival, then she could leave, confident she'd made a difference in Dan's life. The same way he'd made a difference in hers. Brooke glanced at Rick. "Do you think Jason knew about Valerie's intentions?"

"Valerie and Jason arrived together. And that seems to be all they planned together." Rick rubbed the back of his hand over his mouth as if to stop himself from revealing more. "Then again, that could be just an old-timer's faulty observations."

There was nothing faulty about Rick's mind. Brooke believed in a father's intuition. Her own dad's intuition had guided her more than once over the years. Not to mention her own intuition she'd relied on during her career. That voice, rusty from lack of use, whispered through her now. "I got the same impression at dinner last night."

"Dan never talks about how Valerie and Jason became a couple." Nichole stared at the soccer field, her eyebrows pinched together over her glasses. "They seem as mismatched as Dan and Valerie obviously were."

"Dan wasn't always so set in his ways and uncompromising. Jason wasn't always so remote and detached." Rick scratched his chin, yet his grin broke free. "Believe it or not, all three are quite free-spirited. The boys got that from their mother."

The spark in Rick's gaze and the chortling gave him away. The boys took after their father. "What happened?"

"Dan had a child," Rick said. "Roots became his priority."

Brooke tracked the foursome across the soccer field. Good-natured teasing and banter echoed around the group. The exaggerated boasting earned more laughs than fear in the other players. Jason placed both Wesley and Ben near the goal and demonstrated how he wanted the boys to kick the ball. Jason looked anything but distant and disengaged. Double fist bumps for each of the boys, encouraging words, then he released them to score. Goals followed along with several rounds of high-fives. "What happened that changed Jason?"

"We told the boys that Jason was adopted." Rick's pain was obvious.

"Dan never mentioned that to me." Nichole turned to face Rick. "Not once. Not even during any of those long playdates and weekly dinners of our tiny single-parent club."

"The boys are sixteen months apart. Dan only ever cared that he had a brother." Rick pulled off the lid of his tumbler and tossed the ice onto the grass as if he was already cold enough. "Jason has only ever been Dan's brother. His family."

Family was Dan's foundation. His priority. But he'd lost his brother. Then his wife and his marriage. Valerie leaving would've shattered everything Dan lived by. That wound would've been deep and intense. Brooke mused, "But the fact mattered to Jason."

"Jason dropped out of college and left to find out who he was." Rick's gaze remained on the field, the distance in his voice suggesting he was replaying a memory.

"Did he find himself?" Nichole spoke quietly as if she feared her words might carry across the field and disrupt the play.

"I think he might still be searching." Rick stuffed one of his hands inside his pocket. "I want to believe if Jason came home for a while, he might remember."

The anguish in Rick's voice wrapped around Brooke. He was a father who wanted his son home.

Brooke looked out at the field. She'd lost herself, too, after the accident. Retreated to the mountains for a new life. Yet she still wondered if she'd ever find herself again. Or if she even wanted to. What if she found herself and realized everything she wanted wasn't right? Would she have the courage to change? Perhaps Jason was in a similar place.

Or perhaps that was Brooke not wanting to be the only one lost.

No, she wasn't lost, only misplaced. Temporarily. She'd find the place she belonged soon.

The boys scored again, then rushed Dan, tackling him onto the grass. Brooke's smile came from deep inside her.

And a voice inside her—one that sounded like her mother, earnest and patient—whispered through her. *What if the place you belong is the very one you're running from?*

That had been her mother's advice after Brooke had suffered a difficult breakup in college. Brooke had wanted to transfer schools. Her parents hadn't agreed.

Her father's advice: *if you run every time, you'll never actually get anywhere.*

Brooke had stayed, completed her degree with honors and gotten multiple job offers, then met her late husband.

But was it running away if she was merely passing through to begin with?

And standing here in the park, opening up to Rick and Nichole, might feel right. Even good. But she had nothing else. This afternoon only really proved she was ready to find a new home, make new friends and move on.

Her urge to run across the field and join the ice war between Dan and the boys proved nothing more than Brooke needed more exercise.

Her phone vibrated in her pocket. She wasn't running. That was the same argument she'd used as her defense with her parents all those years ago. She pulled out her phone and studied the text message from Ann Ellis.

"You okay?" Nichole asked.

"My former in-laws have leads on two houses up north for me." And they'd thoughtfully added the details about the memorial in three weeks. Every year, they celebrated her former husband's life at one of his favorite places in the city. This year it was the beach.

She stuffed her phone away and locked her knees. That proved she wasn't running. She couldn't run, anyway. After all, she wasn't certain which direction to go.

"That's great about the houses." Uncertainty edged through Nichole's tone.

"Yeah. Really great." Brooke wasn't confident, either. But she wanted a place of her own again. Why wasn't she thrilled? Excited to get back to the life she needed? She wouldn't have to make up yet another excuse for not attending the celebration of Phillip's life. Don and Ann would understand the work involved in relocating and rebuilding.

"Are you close to your in-laws?" Nichole asked.

That was a loaded question. She'd been very close until the accident. Now it was complicated. Her therapist had labeled it survivor's guilt. Brooke called it betrayal. Look at her now.

Enjoying the day at the park with another family. This could've been her and Phillip, waiting on Ann and Don to join them for a picnic. But that wasn't her world anymore. And that guilt she expected refused to surface. "I've seen Don and Ann over the years when they've visited family and friends up north, where I was."

An excited shout grabbed their attention. Brooke turned to see Valerie, loaded down with bags, weaving her way toward them, a buoyant smile on her face.

"Valerie has enough food for two soccer teams." Nichole rushed to intercept Valerie.

"That girl never learned restraint." Rick shook his head, but his grin returned. "She was born to hostess, always keeping a crowd well-fed and entertained."

Brooke walked with Rick toward the picnic tables. Had Dan been surprised to discover he'd married a hostess, or had he known before the vows were recited? "Dan told me that he only ever wanted a marriage like his parents'."

"Didn't work out that way the first time for Dan." Rick's glance at Brooke was speculative. "Nothing says he still can't have it with someone else."

"He deserves that." Yet Brooke wasn't the someone else. She couldn't be. Sure, she wanted to enjoy life again. But being in love could be more heartbreaking than uplifting. Love wasn't for the weak. Brooke wasn't weak. She was careful. If she wasn't careful, her heart might be shattered again and possibly wouldn't heal a second time.

Rick set his hand on Brooke's arm, stalling her retreat. "After my wife died, I was quite lost. Then a dear friend told me that I have to live for those that love me. I owed them that much."

Brooke was living, wasn't she? She was fine. She'd leave love for someone else.

Nichole pointed at the table covered with take-out containers. "Valerie bought out the entire restaurant."

"I wasn't sure what everyone liked. Every entrée sounded delicious." Valerie added serving spoons to several containers. "I settled on a sample of everything."

"Taquitos and guacamole." Nichole lifted the lid on one of the containers and rubbed her stomach. "One of my favorite things."

"These you can take to your committee meeting at the school." Valerie picked up a to-go box filled with taquitos. "Do you think you need more?"

Nichole accepted the container. "This should be plenty."

"There are chips, too. I ordered extra." Valerie grabbed a bag of chips and added several containers of guacamole to the top. "Everyone's mood will improve with snacks. I guarantee no one will be able to turn you down if you ask for help."

"Thanks. This is great." Nichole adjusted the takeout, then wrapped Brooke in a one-armed hug. She whispered, "Now I really am a traitor for liking Valerie even more."

Brooke nodded.

Nichole backed away and took off her sunglasses to look at Brooke. "If they end up in court, I promise I will sit on Dan's side in the courtroom."

Court wasn't an option. Not for Brooke. She'd worked with much less likable clients in the past and succeeded. She wanted Ben to have something positive from his mother's return. And she wanted to leave knowing that she'd made a difference.

And if the thought of leaving made her heart squeeze a little? Well, that was much better than broken.

CHAPTER SIXTEEN

THREE DAYS AFTER dinner and two days after the park, Dan pulled into the school car line, fixed his gaze on the sedan in front of him and not his brother, who was beside him. The one speaking French fluently. And typing rapidly across his notepad like a seasoned business executive. That was, if the exec wore workout clothes and a black baseball cap to assist with Ben's afternoon soccer practice.

Dan self-assessed: pulse normal. Vision clear. Airways unobstructed.

Only, a deep chill seeped from his core. Had he ever really known his brother?

Jason ended the third of his business calls and shifted easily into English. "So, this is what school pickup is all about."

Deciphering the letters on the sedan's license plate was simpler than figuring out his brother. Dan spit out one word: "French."

"Spanish, too." Jason waved to an excited Ben on the sidewalk. "Some German and Mandarin."

Dan's jaw dropped, letting his racing thoughts

escape unspoken. What else didn't he know about Jason? "Why?"

"Keeps the misunderstandings to a minimum for work." Jason unlocked the doors.

Dan spoke English and misunderstood. "You're a poker player."

"That's only one of the hats I wear." Jason twisted in the seat to greet Ben.

Ben tossed his backpack on the bench seat and climbed into the truck. "Dad, did you check on Archie?"

Jason looked at Dan. "Who's Archie?"

"Archie lost his eye and part of his ear." Ben leaned between the front seats, wonder and pride in his voice. "Luna helped take out Archie's stitches, too. Because the animals knew it was infected. Isn't that awesome?"

"That's..." Jason's voice trailed off as if he struggled to find a good response.

Dan could relate. His brother spoke multiple languages. For business. Wore multiple hats—whatever that meant. And made Dan reconsider everything he'd assumed he knew.

Ben sat back and buckled his seat belt. "I need a pet like that, too, 'cause it would save me."

That was Dan's job. That much Dan knew.

"Sounds like you have quite a few smart animals at your house right now," Jason said.

"They belong to Brooke," Ben said. "Dad

keeps warning me that they'll all be leaving. Soon."

That chill turned to frostbite. Brooke. Jason. They'd all leave. And Dan wasn't certain he'd be as numb to their departures as he wanted to be.

"You want them to stay?" Jason asked.

"Definitely. Brooke let me make dog treats with her last night. And I got to hold Rex's leash by myself on our walk. Even Grandpa came with us and walked Luna, so Brooke could work on training things." Ben's backpack fell on the floor with a *thunk*. "Dad won't let the dogs use the backyard so we gotta walk them."

Ben and his grandfather didn't *have* to walk the dogs. The dogs belonged to Brooke. Dan had to work, otherwise he would've walked, too.

"Grandpa claims he likes the exercise," Ben added.

"Or the company," Jason offered.

Dan had enjoyed Brooke's company at dinner. And the next day at the park. Then he'd worked, caught up on his sleep and hadn't seen Brooke yesterday or today. Now he missed her. Not in the I-can't-live-without-you kind of way. More in the I-wish-you-were-here-so-I-could-share-a-story kind of way. The kind of way that made his day better because she was in it. The friends-only kind of way.

"Auntie Ava is gonna come over, too, so she can walk and exercise with us." Ben unwrapped a granola bar. "And Wesley's mom. She says she's too clumsy in a gym, but she thinks she can handle walking. So she's gonna walk with us, too."

It was like a walking club. With so many people walking with Brooke, how was Dan supposed to have any time with her?

"But you know what?" Ben's voice dipped into seriousness and he sat forward again. "Brooke won't walk toward the Garden District or Bayview Street. No matter how many times you ask her. Even though there's a dog park that way."

"Maybe she's worried about Rex and the other dogs," Dan suggested. Yet Brooke talked about the importance of socializing the dogs.

"Grandpa says he thinks it has something to do with the accident," Ben said.

"What accident?" Jason asked.

"I don't know." Ben rummaged in his soccer bag. "Grandpa said there was a bad car accident and her husband became an angel."

Brooke only ever mentioned the accident to Dan. She'd never given any details. Never said it had happened in the city. Then again, Dan never pried. Still, Brooke always asked about Bayview Street and State Street whenever he drove. On the way to the vet. The grocery store. Even dinner.

Was that why everyone wanted to walk with

her? Had he been forcing her to walk, even though it scared her? Surely, she would've argued more to let him use the backyard. Surely, she wouldn't believe he could be that cruel. But then, she'd have to trust Dan with her painful past. And if she trusted him, Dan would have to trust her. That was precarious territory. They were better like they were.

"Sounds like Brooke has been through a lot." Jason slipped on his sunglasses, but the concern was there in his voice.

What had his brother been through? He'd assumed it'd been one endless travel party fashioned by Valerie.

"Yeah. But you know what?" Ben asked repeatedly yet never waited for a response. "She's still really nice and happy. Except she gets sad but says she's fine. Dad can fix that."

Dan cleared his throat, swallowed. A tightness settled in. He wasn't responsible for Brooke's sadness. If he was, he'd want to hold her tight and protect her. Promise her that she wouldn't ever be sad again. Not with him. That was impractical. Impossible. No one could keep a promise like that.

"How so?" Jason asked as if he sensed Dan was struggling for a response.

Dan was struggling, period. To explain his brother. To help Brooke. What had she told him? *Let the moment be as it is.*

"That's his job, Uncle Jas." Ben's tone was direct, as if he stated what should've been obvious. "Dad says some people tell him they are fine, but he can tell by looking at them that they aren't fine. Then he helps them feel better."

"You think Brooke needs to feel better?" Jason asked.

Yes. Definitely. Dan had seen the sadness in Brooke, too. And that already pulled at places inside him that he was trying very hard to ignore.

"No one wants to be sad, Uncle Jas," Ben said. "That's not fun."

Dan had to switch the subject. Now, before Jason and Ben brainstormed ways Dan could cheer up Brooke. Dan already had a few ideas and those weren't appropriate for the friends-only zone. Things like more dates. More Friday nights around the fire pit. Sharing butter-pecan ice cream.

Dan glanced into the rearview mirror and caught Ben's gaze. "Speaking of fun and exciting things, we never talked about the picnic on Sunday."

Ben held Dan's gaze and chewed on his snack bar. "You want to know what I think about Valerie."

Dan considered correcting Ben. Valerie was his biological mother. But did that mean Ben had to call her Mom? This was new territory.

"Yes. I wanted to know what you think. How you feel."

"Well, we both like nachos and white-cheese sauce with cilantro." Ben swiped his hand under his nose. "She ate my jalapeños for me."

Dan had to smile. That wasn't exactly what he'd wanted to know about his son's feelings. "Spicy food has always been one of your mom's favorite things."

"Did you know basketball is one of Brooke's favorite sports? She played even though she isn't tall like us at all." Ben's wonder and excitement sped up his words. "In college, Brooke managed the recreation center and won basketball shoot-outs because no one thought she could play."

"Nice. A basketball shark." Jason rubbed his hands together. "Wonder if Brooke plays pool, too? We could team up and make some extra money."

Dan countered Jason's one-sided grin with a frown. This was supposed to be about Valerie—Ben's mom—not Brooke. "You're not helping."

Jason shrugged. "Brooke is hard not to like."

Jason—the man beside him—might not be too hard to like, either. But could he trust him?

As for Brooke, he already liked Brooke too much. Worse, now he considered challenging Brooke to a shoot-out in his own backyard. The bet: winner picks their next dinner destination. Because he wanted to have dinner with Brooke again. Preferably alone. If he won in a basketball shoot-out, it wouldn't be considered a date. It'd only be a bet that had to be upheld.

"Wesley and I are playing Brooke on Thursday after soccer practice." Ben peered between the front seats again. His fingers tapped an animated beat on the console. "Whoever wins gets to pick what dessert we eat for dinner."

"Can I join in?" Jason shifted to face Ben. "I'm a huge fan of dessert for dinner, too."

"Sure." Ben followed his swift agreement with a fist tap against Jason's as if that sealed the arrangement. "But you need to make all ten baskets from behind the free throw line just like Brooke."

Time to redirect the conversation. *Again.* Before Dan agreed to the shoot-out terms, too. "That sounds like fun. I can't wait to see who wins. Your mother thinks it might be fun to go on vacation."

That was Dan's attempt at easing back into the conversation of Valerie and her plans. He wanted Ben's reaction to the idea of vacationing with his mom. That would guide his strategy going into court.

"Are we going to Disney? They have a new *Star Wars* area and ride." The delight in Ben's voice bounced around the truck cab. "What about Universal? They have roller coasters, too."

"Roller coasters are the best," Jason added. "Especially the ones that go upside down."

"Definitely," Ben said. "We definitely need to go to a place with those roller coasters."

Dan pulled into the park and eyed his brother. Jason was never quite so cheery. Not even as a kid. Right now, he looked almost gleeful. Over roller coasters. Or was it that none of Valerie's vacation spots included roller coasters? Or was it simply that Valerie wasn't in the truck, claiming all the attention.

Dan stopped and cleared his throat. "Your mother was thinking something farther away, like Amsterdam. They have one of the best science museums."

"That could be cool if we get to touch things and build things like we do with my science projects." Ben pulled his soccer shoes from his bag. "Remember that volcano we built that exploded all over Grandpa on the way to the car? That was so funny."

"Your dad and I used 623 rubber bands to split a watermelon in half. It exploded in the kitchen, all over Grandpa, the kitchen cabinets and even the ceiling." Jason leaned down to retie his shoes. Yet he failed to contain his humor. "It wasn't even a science project."

Laughter surged inside Dan and spilled into the truck. That still ranked as one of their best ideas. "Grandpa refused to buy watermelon after that." Even when they promised they only wanted to eat it. Their father had complained about finding watermelon seeds a year after the explosion.

"And he forbade rubber bands in the house," Jason added.

Ben fell across the back seat in a fit of laughter. "How mad was Grandpa?"

Dan smiled at his son, his face as bright as his hair. That was how he preferred to see Ben: carefree and happy. "We were grounded for two weeks and forbidden to watch TV for one month."

"That didn't stop us." Jason glanced over his shoulder at Ben. "We moved from fruit to paint balloons."

Ben sprang up, interest widening his eyes. "What are those?"

"We filled balloons with paint instead of water," Dan explained.

"Then exploded them in the driveway in a brilliant colored burst." Jason raised his hands as if reliving the balloon drop.

Ben covered his mouth. More laughter squeezed around his fingers.

His brother left out the roof part of their brilliant plan. They'd determined they needed the extra height to ensure maximum splattering range once the balloon hit the driveway. Their dad hadn't agreed. Or even cared about maximizing the splatter range. Dan said, "We ended up getting grounded for another month."

"One of the best summers being grounded we ever had." Jason's tone was wistful, as if he missed those childhood days spent plotting and scheming and laughing until their stomachs cramped.

"That summer was definitely one of our most creative." Dan turned in his seat and pointed at Ben. "Don't get any ideas."

Ben shook his head. "Wesley already has a lot of ideas for the summer. Can he come with us to Amsterdam?"

"How many people are going with us on vacation?" Jason shrugged at Dan's confused look. "We need to consider how many hotel rooms we're going to require for this vacation."

If Valerie had her way, only one. Enough room for her, Jason and Ben. Dan didn't want Valerie to have her way.

Ben lifted up his hand and counted on his fingers. "Dad. Uncle Jas. Me. Valerie. Wesley. And we should ask Brooke and Wesley's mom, too."

"We should?" Dan's voice was tight. When had this become a group-vacation discussion? With Brooke. She'd be a welcome addition, Dan admitted. Like Nichole and Wesley, of course. Traveling with good friends was more fun.

"Of course, we should invite them. Wesley's mom really likes Brooke. She told us in the car."

Ben pulled his soccer ball from his bag and balanced it on the console. "We all had so much fun at the park on Sunday."

Simple as that. Why couldn't more things in life be just that simple?

"We forgot Grandpa." Worry rang through Ben's words as if his grandfather might have overheard. "We have to bring him. And Grandma Lulu. If they get tired, they can hang out together."

"That makes perfect sense." Jason nodded, his tone thoughtful. "I'll add them to the invite list."

And Dan could hang out with Brooke. No, that was wrong. He glanced at his son. "What if your mother wanted to go with just you?"

Ben's fingers stilled on the soccer ball and his eyebrows lowered.

Dan added, "You'd get to fly all by yourself."

"You tell me never to go anywhere alone." Ben scowled at Dan as if Dan had forgotten his own rules. "And you tell me it's better to share special times with the people I love."

Ben had him there. Dan had said all that and more. "Those are the people you love, then."

"Pretty much." Ben shrugged. "But there's also Auntie Ava and Kyle, too. I bet Kyle would like the science museum, but Auntie would like Disney."

Soon they were going to need to book an entire hotel wing. Valerie most likely didn't have this kind of vacation in mind. Although she loved entertaining large groups. "What if everyone couldn't go in the summer?"

"Then we'll have to wait until we can all go together." Ben zipped up his soccer bag as if that ended the discussion.

Would a judge accept that argument? *Your Honor, my son will only go if everyone he loves is able to join him. Since schedules cannot be aligned, I request a passport not be granted.* Dan would ask his legal team, but he doubted that constituted a valid defense. Even though it worked quite well for Dan.

"Well, everyone lives here except your mother and me," Jason said.

"You guys could just come here. Then we'd all go to Disney and ride roller coasters." Ben opened the truck door and jumped out to join his friends. His vacation preference more than clear.

"He's not wrong," Dan said. He smiled, watching Ben's teammates yell his name and wave. He'd built a good life for him and his son. He was content knowing Ben was happy. And if he sensed something was missing in his own life, well, he could find it later. After Ben grew up and headed out to start his own life.

"About Disney?" Jason asked.

"About us having fun at the park on Sunday." Dan shuddered, remembering the ice war. His dad and Brooke had even joined in to help Ben and Wesley. Dan had ended up with an entire cooler of ice dumped on him. The food had been delicious. The conversation free-flowing. The laughter unrestrained. Even Valerie had joined in for their impromptu card game.

"It was a really good afternoon." Jason's face revealed his surprise. "One of the best I've had in quite a while."

Dan leaned his head back on the headrest and confessed, "I don't want to go to court and have to fight Valerie."

"Her mind seems set," Jason said.

Dan's mind was set, too. Traveling abroad wasn't feasible. And he wasn't putting Ben on a flight by himself. Alone. Without Dan to protect him.

Even more, he wasn't going to let Ben get his hopes up only to have them crushed when Valerie changed her mind. And she would, Dan was certain of that. Wedding vows recited before family and God hadn't been enough to keep Valerie from changing her mind about marriage. Her own son hadn't been enough to clip Valerie's travel wings and anchor her to the city. Dan had recovered. But Ben—he was still a child. And the disappointment his own mother could inflict would leave a deep, possibly lasting wound.

"Valerie could've asked about the passport

over the phone." Of course, she might've anticipated Dan's refusal.

"Valerie doesn't ask," Jason said. "She just does."

"You didn't know Valerie wanted to travel with Ben?" Dan asked.

"I didn't know Valerie was coming to San Francisco until she sat down next to me on the plane." Jason's tone was resigned.

They hadn't designed their trip together. *Together* wasn't a word Dan would use to describe Valerie and his brother. He doubted pressing his brother for insight into Valerie's intentions would prove useful. But perhaps he could learn his brother's intentions. "Why are you here?"

"Business." Jason stepped onto the pavement and looked back at Dan. "And now, it seems, for soccer lessons."

Business brought Jason home. Not the family he missed.

Jason jogged onto the practice field, shook the coach's hand and high-fived every player. He demonstrated a drill, organized the players and transformed into a teacher. His brother might claim business brought him back. But Jason looked comfortable on the field with the kids surrounding him and a soccer ball at his feet.

The younger brother Dan remembered stood on the soccer field. Dan noted the differences—the ones time caused and others not so obvious.

From the scars on Jason's arms to the way he never touched the beer Valerie had ordered for him at dinner to the shadows that never quite cleared from his gaze.

Dan wasn't sure who Jason wanted to be. Dan wasn't certain who he wanted his brother to be. Accepting Jason for who he was now meant Dan also had to own up to the man he'd become. They'd both made mistakes.

Dan had kept his distance all these years. Told himself he was only doing what Jason wanted. Then Valerie had happened. And Dan had retreated completely. After all, his brother had chosen Dan's ex-wife over his own family. But life had proven to Dan that nothing was ever that cut-and-dried. Most of life was lived in the messy area in between. If he wanted to know the man his brother had become, he'd have to uncover the truth of the past few years.

And that would only happen if Jason let Dan in.

Coach Barnes motioned for Dan to join him on the sidelines. Dan climbed out of the truck and spent the rest of the hour assisting Jason and the coach with drills.

Ben gathered his soccer ball and water bottle and pointed toward Dan's truck. "I think Valerie's here."

"That's definitely your mother." Valerie's signature platinum hair was hard to miss. He handed the orange cones to Coach Barnes and walked across the field. "Maybe she wanted to watch practice."

"Not her thing." Jason shook his head and checked his phone. "It's close to dinnertime. That brought her here."

"Does she have another picnic?" Ben asked, a hint of curiosity in his voice.

"Let's find out," Dan suggested and headed toward the truck.

Valerie clapped her hands together and smiled. "I figured you'd all be hungry after practice. I thought we could go out to eat."

"Where?" Ben asked.

"I've been collecting donations for the fire victims all day and you guys are sweaty, so I was thinking The Boot Pizza," Valerie said.

Ben grinned. "Really?"

Valerie nodded. "Unless you want something fancier."

Ben scrunched up his face. "Pizza sounds great."

"Why don't you change your shoes?" Valerie said. "Then we can go."

Ben raced around to the side of the truck.

Valerie shifted her attention to Dan. "I was hoping it could be just Jason and I and Ben. It's only dinner. Not a trip to Europe."

Dan rubbed the back of his neck. "We should ask Ben what he prefers."

Valerie agreed and called Ben back. "Are you okay going to dinner with just your uncle and me?"

Dan shifted from one foot to the other. He hadn't had to share Ben ever. Surely Ben would want Dan with him, too.

Ben grabbed Dan's hand and tugged him down. Then he whispered, "Dad, I'll be okay. Uncle Jason will be with me."

Dan wasn't happy about it, he couldn't deny it. "Are you sure?"

"Yeah." Ben wrapped his arms around Dan's neck. "I'll be good. Will you?"

Dan held on to Ben. He wasn't entirely sure. "Have you checked your numbers?"

"Just now in the truck." Ben leaned back and beamed at Dan. "You didn't even have to remind me."

"Looks like I'll see you later at the house." Dan rose. His gaze collided with his brother. Jason nodded. That was all Dan needed to know. His brother would look after Ben. "Have fun, you guys."

"You, too, Dad." Ben hugged Dan around the waist, then climbed in the back seat of Jason's rental car.

Dan waited until the taillights disappeared out of the parking lot. What exactly was he supposed to do now? His afternoons and evenings were reserved for Ben's soccer practice, dinner, then homework.

He had to eat. He could update his résumé for his supervisor—a task he'd been pushing down his to-do list for the past week. But that was work-related.

And Dan had an unexpected free night. These were rare and something of a gift.

He texted his dad to see if he wanted to join him for dinner. His father responded that he was headed to the Second Winders dinner hosted by Evie.

Dan wished his dad luck. The Second Winders had started as a widow-and-widowers support group. Somehow—and Dan wasn't quite certain how—the group began playing poker. Now the Second Winders met twice a month to deal the cards and share a meal. A different group member hosted and supplied dinner each time.

Dan started his truck and dialed Ava.

She picked up on the second ring. "Hey, I'm helping Sophie and Brooke at the pet store. Everything okay?"

"Ben got invited to dinner," Dan said. *And I don't know what to do with myself.*

"Come join us," Ava said.

"What do you need?" Dan asked, even though he'd already turned in the direction of the pet store.

"Another tall person," Ava said. An ouch

quickly followed. "Sorry, Sophie hit me. Even though I said nothing about Brooke or her being short." Ava laughed into the phone, then rushed on, "I have to go. Now they're both coming at me. See you soon."

The call ended, and Dan smiled. He had something to do.

Fifteen minutes later, Dan walked into The Pampered Pooch. Sophie stood behind the checkout counter, punching a calculator. Ava and Brooke stacked dog food onto a shelf. "How can I help?"

Ava brushed her hands on her jeans and grinned. "You can go with Brooke on an errand."

Sophie's head popped up, her smile slow but full. "That's a great idea. I could really use Ava's help with a few senior cats upstairs."

"Dan doesn't need to join me." Brooke's slow nod discounted her claim.

"No. This is perfect. You can visit my customer and then go out to dinner." Sophie stuffed dog biscuits into a paw-print bag. She looked at Dan. "You haven't eaten, have you?"

"Not yet," Dan said.

"Brooke hasn't, either," Ava said. "Even though we promised to feed her."

"I can order takeout on my way home," Brooke said.

Ava grabbed the treat bag from Sophie and

shoved it into Brooke's hands. "This is better. Dan knows the best hidden places to eat."

Dan glanced between Sophie and Ava. His friends were acting strange. Then again, he wasn't going to argue. He'd wanted to have dinner with Brooke. Now he had an excuse. "Where are we going?"

"Earl Powell's house," Ava chimed.

"Why?" Dan asked. Ava and Dan had trans-ported Earl Powell more than once. But house calls were something else.

"Brooke's doing me a favor," Sophie said.

Ava ushered them toward the door. "Get going. You don't want to be late."

Dan held open the door and pointed at his prime parking space. "Lucked out."

Dan opened the passenger door for Brooke. She was up inside the cab before he could lend her a hand. He heard her deep sigh as he closed the door.

Inside the truck, she buckled her seat belt and shifted toward him. "This won't take long. Then we can get Ben for dinner."

She remembered Ben. Wanted him to join them. Pleasure, as if she'd hugged him, filled Dan. He placed his hands on the steering wheel instead of taking Brooke's. "Ben is with his uncle and Valerie."

"Wow. Really?" Concern widened her eyes.

Eyes that locked on Dan and searched. Not to judge or criticize. Rather to comfort and console.

She asked, "How do you feel about that?"

Lost. Off balance. But steadier beside you. "Ben assured me that it would be fine because his uncle was with him."

"They've become close," Brooke said. "Do you mind?"

Dan shook his head. He only minded that his brother might leave a second time—disappearing from Dan's life if Dan pushed too hard.

But it really all came down to Ben.

Jason had walked away from his family once before. Valerie had walked away from her son. Would they do that again? And if Dan couldn't trust family, who could Ben trust?

Dan pulled out into the traffic.

Ben could trust Dan and his grandfather.

As for Dan, he'd trust in himself same as he always had.

CHAPTER SEVENTEEN

BREATHE. INHALE. EXHALE. Simple and normal.

Don't look. Not so simple.

Brooke concentrated on her cell phone clutched in her hand. She pretended her emails on the screen were more than spam and store alerts for blowout sales. The heavy traffic slowed their progress, yet each block the truck rolled closer to the one place she'd avoided for five years. Surely there was a different route to Earl Powell's house.

"Everything okay?" Dan stopped at a red light.

Brooke jumped, knocked her blood pressure into overdrive and forced her fingers to release the phone. "Just checking to make sure my insurance agent didn't send any more forms."

Was it the next corner? Farther down? She'd have to check the street signs. Her heart raced. Thudded. She'd have to *look*.

"Did you finish the checklist my dad left?" Dan's voice, mild and easygoing, nudged against her distress.

"I'm still working through the inventory of

everything I lost." Still struggling to rebuild her life on paper. There was no check box for grief. No true value for heartache.

"A few years back, I went to a call at a house fire. I overheard a police officer tell a family member to use a wedding registry to recreate what the family lost." Dan pressed on the gas. "Maybe you could try that."

Change your perspective. How many times had she done that with her clients? Brooke shifted, kept her back to the window and fixed her gaze on Dan's profile. "That could be really helpful."

The truck stopped again. Brooke refused to look outside. The quiver in her voice only now evening out.

"Last light and we're getting out of this area finally." Dan smiled at her. "Took us longer to go four blocks than it will to get to Earl's place."

Brooke exhaled, long and steady. She stayed facing toward Dan. But staring at him the rest of the drive wasn't an option. Brooke checked her text messages. Two shelters she'd worked with the past few years requested her assistance. She replied, promising to help once she returned to the area. And she texted Ann and Don, thanking them for keeping her updated on the availability of the rental houses. Explained that Rex and the situation with Earl would keep her in the city longer.

All the while, she hushed that inner voice. The one whispering about changing her perspective on Dan. That Dan made her feel safe. That Dan would make everything all right.

That was only an illusion. She'd felt safe in her marriage, too.

"We're here." Dan parked in a wide driveway.

Brooke stuck her phone in her pocket and searched for the cottage tucked inside so much untamed landscape. Earl Powell had grown his own nature preserve in the midst of the urban sprawl creeping in on his land. "Are you sure?"

"I thought the same thing the first time Ava and I took a call here." Dan opened his door. "It's much better inside."

Brooke grabbed the dog-biscuit bag, followed Dan and hoped they could get inside. If Earl suspected her true intentions, she doubted he'd let her pass the front gate. She stepped over vines crisscrossing the stone pavers and rang the doorbell.

The front door cracked open. A stern voice splintered through the finger-sized gap. "I'm not interested."

"Dr. Iain Porter from The Pampered Pooch sent me." Brooke lifted the bag of dog biscuits higher. "Dr. Iain thought these homemade biscuits might help with Sherlock's digestion."

The door opened enough for Brooke to see a bald head and a pair of clear, suspicious hazel eyes. Earl Powell's stooped shoulders dropped his height closer to Brooke's.

"Do you know who made those biscuits?" Earl studied the bag.

"I made the biscuits." Brooke smiled and motioned to Dan beside her. "With help from Dan Sawyer's son."

"I know a Dan Sawyer." The door opened fully. Earl struggled to tug a pair of eyeglasses from the pocket on his gray flannel shirt.

"It's me, Earl." Dan took the eyeglasses from Earl's shaky grip and gently slid them onto the older man's face. "You look good."

"I'm standing this time." Earl's lopsided grin twitched into place. He blinked at Brooke from behind the oversize lenses. "Last time Dan saw me, I was sprawled on the kitchen floor. Not my best day."

"Ready to run some sprints now, Earl?" Dan eased inside the home, his hand sliding across the door as if holding it open. "We still need to have that race."

"Ten years ago, and you wouldn't have stood a chance against me." Earl reached for his cane on the door handle, his grip uncertain. "Maybe even five years ago."

Brooke noticed Dan's boot propped open the door. His hand was there to protect Earl. Brooke moved inside and took over door duty, freeing Dan to catch Earl if he fell. Even with the cane, the older gentleman looked like he'd benefit more from a walker.

"He's not kidding." Dan stepped beside the older man. "Earl ran his last marathon on his seventy-sixth birthday."

"That's impressive," Brooke said.

"Anyone can do that." Earl lifted his hand as if flicking away the compliment and swayed toward Dan. "Takes dedication and a commitment to yourself."

"You have to love running, too." Dan eased closer.

"No. You have to want to improve yourself. Do things that scare you. That push your limits." Earl's slow shuffle along the hallway stopped as he straightened to look at them. "That's how you know you're living life right."

Dan glanced at Brooke. "Earl's is a life very much well lived."

So many things scared Brooke. She wasn't certain she had it in her to push her limits. Those had already been pushed by accidents and nature's fury. Did that mean she was living wrong?

She followed Dan and Earl into the cottage-style house—a home well lived-in from the creak of the wood floors to the banister worn from the many hands relying on its support. If she paused and closed her eyes, she was certain she'd hear the memories collected within the walls. The timeline of framed photographs trailing along the entire hallway only hinted at Earl's well-lived life. Would she have a hallway of photographs to recapture her life in her later years? Would she consider her life well lived?

Brooke shook herself, left her introspection in the hallway with Earl's past and stepped into a welcoming kitchen. The wide window in the nook invited nature inside. The outdated appliances, polished and proud, proclaimed some things were better with age.

Dan drew a vinyl kitchen chair behind Earl, assisting the man without fuss or fanfare. Just as Dan wanted it, Brooke assumed. Earl hooked his cane on the table and pushed up his glasses. "My body might be getting lazy on me, but not my mind. You aren't here to drop off dog treats."

"These will help Sherlock's digestion." Brooke set the treat bag on the table. "But you're right."

"I wanted to check on one of my favorite patients." Dan jumped into the conversation. "And I wanted to get the end of the story about the treasure hunt. Did your great-grandfather ever find the gold?"

"Remembered that, did you?" Earl tapped his forehead with a crooked finger. "I might show you the original treasure map. But first I have to tell your friend that she can't have my dog."

"Can I make coffee or tea?" Brooke smiled

and motioned to the coffeepot on the kitchen counter.

"I like coffee in the afternoon. One cup. Black. Nothing fancy added to it." Earl picked up a cookie tin and struggled with the lid. "I get the sweet stuff from my granddaughter."

"How old is she?" Brooke poured water into the automatic coffee maker and added a filter. Everything required for coffee was set out on the counter within easy reach.

"She's twenty-two and studying to be a pastry chef." The pride in Earl's tone bolstered his gravelly voice.

"She sounds like someone we all should meet." Not that Brooke needed to meet any more people in the city. Perhaps in her new home. Brooke leaned against the counter, waited for the coffee to brew and for that inner voice to quiet down. She'd only ever intended to pass through the city. She'd overextended her one-night stay by more than a week already.

"Bakes like an angel but has a bit of the devil in her." Earl's bushy eyebrows lifted over his eyeglass frames. "Takes after her grandmother."

The twinkle in Earl's hazel eyes hinted at his own devil's streak and Brooke liked him even more. She set a mug on Earl's place mat and pushed the limits of an appropriate whisper. "Let's keep the cookies away from Dan. He doesn't know restraint."

Earl nodded and set the cookie tin on the other side, farther away from Dan.

Brooke swallowed her laugh.

"Still not listening to your partner, Dan?" Earl asked.

Dan grimaced at Brooke. "I've started walking and watching my diet."

Brooke glanced between Earl and Dan. She hadn't meant to open up anything. She'd been teasing about the cookies. "What did Dan's partner tell him?"

"Aren't we here for Earl?" Dan leaned back in the kitchen chair and crossed his arms over his chest.

Earl ignored Dan. "Ms. Ava lectured him about taking better care of himself on account of their stressful jobs. They came to transport me to my rehab hospital after my fall. My hip hurt, but not my ears."

"Sounds like wise advice." Brooke picked up the coffeepot and filled Earl's cup. "Do you think he can do it?"

"I'm right here." Dan tapped his fingers on the table.

Now it was Brooke who ignored Dan. This wasn't the approach she'd been expecting to take with Earl, but she was going with it. She'd learned to be flexible and adjust quickly at work.

Earl dunked a cookie into his coffee. "Not without help."

"Did you have help after your fall?" Brooke asked.

"Wouldn't be walking without my doctors and therapists. And my daughter Cara, of course." Earl chewed on his cookie and considered Brooke.

He wasn't wrong earlier. Time hadn't dulled or slowed Earl's mind. She saw that in his clear gaze.

Finally, Earl swallowed and said, "Now you want to help me, too."

"I don't want to take Sherlock." Brooke sat in the chair across from Earl. "But I do want to help find a good solution."

"The only solution is to stay here." Resolve etched into the lines on Earl's weathered face.

The back door in the mudroom opened and closed. A woman called out, "Dad. We're home."

A hundred-pound golden retriever ambled into the kitchen, its tail slowly sweeping back and forth. Sherlock greeted Earl, then lumbered around the table to welcome Dan. Brooke hid her grin behind her coffee cup. For a self-proclaimed no-pet guy, animals were certainly drawn to Dan.

Earl leaned forward and touched Brooke's hand. "You can help me convince my daughter to let us stay here."

"You made coffee." A woman entered the

kitchen, pulled off her hat and shook out her layered gray hair. "Dan? Is that you?"

"Hey, Cara." Dan rose, accepted Cara's hug and introduced Brooke.

Cara eyed the Pampered Pooch logo on Brooke's shirt and waved Brooke back into her seat. A small smile on her face. "I just came from the pet store. Sherlock spends several afternoons at doggy day care there. Although he slept more than played today."

"Brooke came over to tell you that Sherlock and I are perfectly fine to live here," Earl stated.

Cara kissed her dad's cheek. "Dan wouldn't have lifted you off the floor and prevented a house fire if that was true."

"People are entitled to have an accident or two in their lives," Earl countered and motioned at Dan. "That's why Dan has a job."

"We want to prevent more accidents," Dan said.

Cara handed Dan the cookie tin as if rewarding him for his support.

Earl muttered to Brooke, "She's not a good helper for Dan."

"Do you have a plan if you fall again, Earl?" Brooke asked, wanting to keep the conversation on track.

Cara opened her mouth. Brooke shook her head, the movement small and slight. Cara bit into her cookie instead.

"I'm calling Dan," Earl said.

"I'm sure Dan will be here." Brooke sipped her coffee. "But what if Dan isn't in town that day?"

"He's got coworkers," Earl argued.

"And very good ones from what I've heard," Brooke agreed. "But what about Sherlock? What if he gets injured, too?"

Earl cradled his coffee mug and frowned. "Sherlock could get hurt in a new home, too. What if no one is home to help him?"

"That's true because accidents do happen." Brooke took a cookie from the tin. "It's simple. We have to find a home where the odds are that will not happen."

"And a home that has good heat for his achy bones. No kennels because he can't move in a cage." Earl sat forward and lifted his hand. "And he needs walks—lots of them."

Brooke repeated Earl's requirements. "If I find a home with all that, will you agree to meet the family?"

Earl touched the dog-biscuit bag. A challenge threaded through his tone. "And he needs to have homemade dog biscuits for his sensitive stomach."

Again, Cara opened her mouth, caught herself, then bit into another cookie.

Brooke nodded. "Anything else?"

"It's a meeting only." Earl held Brooke's gaze.

"Agreed," Brooke said. "Nothing more than a meeting. I promise."

Earl grinned as if he doubted Brooke would find someone to meet his terms. "Until then Sherlock and I stay here."

"I'd like to be at the meeting." Cara set her hand on her father's shoulder.

Earl patted Cara's hand. "Always been a good daughter."

"I'm his favorite." Cara grinned. "Don't tell my brother and sister."

The family bond between Cara and Earl blasted through Brooke, banging around those hollow places inside her. She clutched the coffee mug to combat the sudden chill sweeping over her. The truth shook her. She missed that kind of connection with other people. That kind of bond. She missed having a family.

She straightened against another shiver. Did she miss those things enough to take such a big risk? The hurt was only greater when she'd lost someone she'd considered family. She'd vowed not to go through that again. How could she forget such crippling pain? What if she wagered her heart and lost again?

No, it was better to be alone. Better than being heartbroken.

Her gaze fastened on Dan. *Strong. Steady. Capable.* If she loved him like family, would she lose him, too? Brooke stood up, walked to the sink and searched for her balance.

"How did you get Sherlock?" Dan rubbed Sherlock behind the ears.

"Dad refused to date after Mom passed." Cara dropped into the chair beside her father.

"You kids were my priority." Earl took a dog biscuit from the bag, broke it in half and gave a piece to Dan for Sherlock. "We had a good thing."

"We definitely did." Cara squeezed her dad's arm, her voice light. "But that isn't to say we couldn't have had a good thing if you'd said yes to Paulette Conley."

Earl gave the second piece of the biscuit to the dog. "I said yes to Sherlock."

"And no to an even fuller life," Cara said.

"My life was full enough with three children, ten grandchildren and now two greats." Earl slipped another dog biscuit from the bag.

"What about your heart, Dad?" Cara stood up and poured herself a cup of coffee.

Brooke ignored her heart. That was the responsible thing to do.

Earl's grin was lopsided again. "Belonged to your mother."

Cara rolled her eyes. "You had more to give."

Even if Brooke had more to give, she couldn't. She wouldn't tempt fate. Besides, once-in-a-lifetime love was just that: *once*.

"She's always pestering me about something."

Earl cradled his coffee mug as if he held a crystal ball reflecting his past. "Been a real fine life. No regrets."

Brooke looked at Dan. She already regretted that she'd have to say goodbye to him soon.

"You don't ever think about Paulette Conley and what might've been?" Cara asked.

Brooke lived with endless what-ifs. Now she'd have even more about Dan. But her heart would be intact. That was good, wasn't it?

"Not that I'm admitting to. I'd never hear the end of it." The smile Earl aimed at Brooke shifted into his bright eyes. "Cara would probably go find the poor woman."

"It's never too late." Brooke managed a small smile to conceal her lie. Perhaps it was too late for herself, but not Earl.

"I've already climbed my hill and I'm on the back side now." Earl pointed his arthritic finger at Brooke and Dan. "It's not too late for you two, though."

"It's not like that." Dan pushed away from the table. "I'm divorced. She's a widow."

That only sparked Earl's interest. "Seems fortunate if you ask me."

"We're just friends," Brooke stammered. Her heart raced in her chest as if to remind her she still had one. "Only."

"My husband was supposed to be only a friend, too." Cara added more sugar to her coffee. "Been married forty-four years this coming November."

Earl slapped the table and laughed. "Nothing wrong with marrying your friend. That's what I did. Lasted almost twenty years."

Brooke had tried that once, too. She had three years in her memory book.

"That's the best you can do." Earl quieted. "Surround yourself with family that loves you and you love back for the time you're given."

Family. Love. Was there ever enough time?

"And have no regrets," Cara added.

"I'll have regrets if Sherlock isn't taken care of properly. Sherlock took care of me and kept me from being lonely all these years. It's only right that I do right by him now." Earl closed the bag of dog biscuits and looked at Brooke. "You understand that, don't you?"

Brooke stepped to his side. "I promise I won't let you down."

"We appreciate the help, Brooke." Cara rinsed her coffee mug in the sink. "Dad, we have to go. My granddaughter has a recital tonight."

"But Sherlock hasn't gotten any exercise," Earl said. "You said yourself he slept all day."

"We can walk him," Dan offered, then glanced at Brooke.

She forced herself to nod. *Dan will keep you safe.*

"You don't mind?" Earl asked.

"It's not a problem." Dan would be with her. She'd come to help Earl and Sherlock. Backing away wasn't the right thing to do. "Then you won't be late for the recital."

"I'll show you where the back-door key is hidden." Cara yanked her hat on her head. "Dan should know where it is in case my dad calls him."

Dan asked Cara for a pen and paper. He wrote on it and handed the paper to Earl. "This is my personal cell number. Call me whenever."

Brooke accepted Sherlock's leash from Cara, fastened it onto the dog's collar and fastened her heart back inside her chest. She wasn't someone who melted at thoughtful gestures. She wasn't someone who listened to her heart. Especially when it whispered about falling in love.

CHAPTER EIGHTEEN

"YOU COULD'VE TOLD me this was about finding Sherlock a new home." Dan didn't hide his irritation and attempted a casual wave to Cara and Earl outside Earl's cottage. Brooke didn't trust him with something minor.

"I wasn't sure Earl would even talk to me." Brooke looked up and down both sides of the street. The corner of her bottom lip disappeared between her teeth. "He's turned down all Sophie's foster families, even though he's never met them."

"Sounds like Earl. He likes things his own way." The same as Dan. And Dan wanted Brooke's trust. Now. His veins sang with tension from wanting it.

"That's fine, but Earl's health is declining." Brooke blanched.

He could've told her Bayview and State Streets—the ones she always asked about—were three miles west, past four one-way streets and six stop lights. Instead he turned in the opposite direction. As for Earl, he was at risk for a fall—one that he might not recover from. "What happens if you can't find a family that meets Earl's requirements?"

"That isn't an option."

He appreciated the resolve in Brooke's tone. Liked her determination. But sometimes that wasn't enough. He'd been determined Valerie wouldn't ever disrupt Ben's life. But Valerie already had, and his own resolve hadn't been enough to stop her. "There has to be a compromise."

"You heard Earl." Brooke's gaze darted around the street like a fly stuck in a car.

Had she always walked like that? Her extreme diligence would exhaust her by the end of the first block. He should've noticed. He was trained to notice. Perhaps if he hadn't been so caught up in his own issues. Sherlock slowed to sniff the neighbor's tree.

"Earl loves Sherlock more than anything. He'll do whatever he has to to make sure Sherlock is taken care of."

The same way Dan loved his son. The same way Dan would do anything to protect Ben. And Brooke. Had he lost his heart to her? Dan zipped up his coat, fastening his heart where it belonged. "What's the next step?"

"I'm going to revisit Sophie's list of foster families and reach out to some of my connections." Brooke shortened Sherlock's leash, guiding the dog closer to her side and allowing a family with a stroller to pass by.

The landscape shifted. Businesses and offices increased, mingling among the apartments and lofts, replacing the houses. A pair of joggers waved and sprinted past. A bike messenger swerved between cars. The city bus squealed to a stop, spurting out business suits and college students onto the sidewalk. A horn blasted.

The last had Brooke pulling up stiffly, her features strained. She edged closer to him, but not close enough.

Dan closed the distance. Certain he could protect her and his heart. "Let me know if I can help." *Let me know if I can help you.*

"You could ask around work if there's anyone who'd want to adopt a senior golden retriever." She avoided his attempts to turn the conversation into a personal one. And yet her arm brushed against his.

He could also wrap his arm around her waist, tuck her into his side and promise to take care of her. Most likely, she'd ignore that, too. It was too soon. She wasn't ready. Dan left his hand at his side, brushing his knuckles across her arm. "That I can do."

"I promised Earl." There was pain in her voice as if promises were important to her. "I can't let him down."

Dan had promised to take care of Ben. He

couldn't let his son down, either. He couldn't get distracted. Not by Brooke. Not by his messy feelings. "We can get dinner at Charlotte's Cheddar Chariot in the food-truck park to take home."

Brooke chewed on her bottom lip. "I'm not sure Sherlock has that many blocks in him."

Sherlock ambled along, tail up, tongue securely inside his mouth, his head up to greet every passerby. Dan wasn't well versed in dog, but Sherlock hardly appeared fatigued or exhausted. Brooke, on the other hand...

"I know a shortcut." Dan kept his voice mild and disinterested. Ben's words about a car accident came back to him. The farther they walked into the busier district, the closer Brooke stayed to Dan.

She continued, her words strained, "That might be too many people for Sherlock."

Or perhaps for Brooke. "It's worth it for the bacon mac and cheese at Charlotte's Cheddar Chariot. I blame Ava for introducing me to Charlotte and her food truck."

"That does sound tempting."

That was all she allowed. But she avoided looking at Dan. He said, "We could head over to the food-truck park after we take Sherlock home."

"Are you sure bacon mac and cheese is in your new diet?" Brooke asked.

"It's not the food that concerns Ava," Dan said. At Brooke's arched eyebrow, he added, "Okay. It's partially the food. But mostly it's the job."

"But she's a paramedic, too." Brooke turned a corner rather than crossing one of the busier intersections and quickened her steps.

"*Was*, and soon she'll be a physician's assistant." Dan matched her pace. "The average tenure of an EMT is five years."

"How long have you been a paramedic?" Brooke asked.

"Eleven years in February." Dan rolled his shoulders. The aches were natural and expected.

"Ava thinks you should change careers, too?"

"Ava thinks I have no work-life balance." But he balanced things fine. Maybe not perfectly. Or all the time. But his life worked.

His supervisor had once again urged Dan to turn in his résumé this morning as Dan clocked out. But the supervisor position took Dan out of fieldwork, placed him behind a desk and in a training room. He'd lose contact with patients and families. Patients like Earl. Despite the occasional rude and disrespectful patient and their family members, Dan still believed what he did mattered. His supervisor would argue that training new recruits and educating the community on illness and injury prevention and emergency skills mattered, too. But he was happy. Maybe

SINGLE DAD TO THE RESCUE

not happy, but content. He added, "Ava worries the stress is taking a toll."

Sherlock sniffed a fence. Brooke stopped and eyed Dan.

He was happy with Brooke. On a walk. At his house. His heart thumped into his throat. He zipped his coat up to his chin. This wasn't love. Love wasn't sneaky and sly, creeping up where it didn't belong. Where it wasn't invited.

"Is it?" she asked.

No, it wasn't love. His voice scratched against his own ears. "What?"

"Is the stress of your job taking a toll?"

The stress of feelings would do him in first. "This is the only job I've ever had. It's all I know. What I love." *And now there's you.* Dan shut his mouth. How had he gotten here? How did he get out? "I'm not sure what else to do."

A pop-up garden extended between two buildings, flowing onto the sidewalk. Dan stepped between the sidewalk planters. An empty bench waited, tucked against the building. He turned on the faucet and filled the cement water bowl for Sherlock. Then sat next to the Brooke on the bench, noticed the tall planters that obscured the view of the street.

Brooke stroked her hand over Sherlock's back. The motion routine as if she'd stepped into a memory and out of Dan's reach. "You should consider your options before something happens and you're forced to change."

Like Hank with his triple-bypass surgery. Like Brooke after her husband passed away. He wanted her back with him. But that wasn't fair. Maybe if he understood. Maybe then he'd know he couldn't love her. "Can I ask how your husband died?"

"A car accident." Her fingers disappeared in Sherlock's golden fur. Her words were too careful, her voice too pensive. "Here in the city."

Dan's pulse slowed. Valerie had forced a different kind of change in Dan's world. But he hadn't lost his home. Or his life with Ben and his family. "You moved up north after that?"

She sat back, her attention focused on Sherlock. "That's not exactly right."

Dan stilled. Every muscle tensed. He'd take whatever she told him. Give her whatever she needed.

Finally, she exhaled. The leash unwound along with her words. "It wasn't a car accident as in two cars colliding. It was one vehicle colliding with us. Waiting on the sidewalk for the light to change."

Dan's entire body stuttered as if the ground had cracked open. His own thoughts misfired, tripping up his composure. He scrubbed his hands over his face and searched the garden for a reset button. "You weren't in a car?"

The stillness around Brooke wasn't calm or peaceful. Dan would bet everything he owned her pupils were dilated, her mouth dry, her skin cool and damp. The fight-or-flight response gripped Brooke.

He wanted to fight, too. Fight for her.

Only the threat wasn't external. It was her memories that locked her in place.

Her pain that undid him.

She set her hand on her stomach and inhaled. Dan matched his breathing to hers. Five rounds.

It wasn't nearly enough. Not for him. Definitely not for her. Her breaths were too shallow. Her skin too pale. He shifted, started to tell her that she was safe. Wanted her to know he'd keep her safe.

But her memories spilled into the space between them.

"Five years ago, Phillip and I were in the city celebrating our anniversary at The Modern Rose. We talked about starting a family. Phillip gave me a crystal angel ornament that was the final piece of a set I collected." She curled her fingers around Sherlock's leash as if it was an anchor and stared at her lap. A breathless weariness in her voice.

Dan wanted to breathe for her. Take the hurt. Take the raw anguish. Hold her until she wasn't alone.

"I wanted to window-shop. Such a stupid, silly thing," she whispered.

Nothing was stupid or silly about her. She had to know that.

"We took our time walking to the parking lot. I stopped to peer into a shop window at the street corner. A new van ran a red light and jumped the curb. Phillip died instantly. I was injured and regained consciousness two days later in intensive care." She looked at Dan. Her cheeks dry, her pupils dilated, her gaze haunted. "It made me think it was the universe's way of telling me I shouldn't have been brave enough to believe in love."

A scream curdled inside Dan. A curse for Fate.

"After the funeral and recovery, I sold everything and relocated to the mountains." She wilted against the bench.

Alone. That was the word she left unspoken. No one like her deserved to suffer like that. Especially not alone. Dan covered her hands, rubbed her cold fingers between his. He could warm her, but the chill inside him might well be permanent. How could she love after that? How could he *not* love her?

Her strength. Her kindness. Her gentle way with Ben. She humbled him. His words came from his soul, but it'd never be enough. "I'm sorry. So sorry."

She blinked and shuddered as if shaking off the past. "You're the first person I've told the full story to aside from my therapist."

He didn't deserve her love. Better she kept it for her late husband. How could he possibly apologize enough?

"I know it's just a street corner." Her hands twisted together beneath his. "It's silly that I can't go there."

Her tremors vibrated through him, shook into his core. He knew that restaurant. Knew that area. The corner of Bayview and State. That explained her reticence. Nothing explained his selfish insensitivity. He forced her to walk alone around the city. While he had a perfectly usable dog-friendly backyard. Had he ever been a bigger jerk?

She deserved so much better. She deserved so much more. "I know routes through the city a lifelong local doesn't."

"Am I even more silly for being grateful for that?" Her hands stayed twined with his.

"There are a bunch of places in town that still get to me." He tightened his grip, sealing their hands together. "It's been years and yet some accident scenes are burned into me."

"What do you do?"

"Don't blink and hold my breath as I pass by," he said. "Take a different route if I can."

"And if you can't?" Her voice lowered.

"I face it." He held her gaze, searched for that glimmer of hope, however faint, still inside her. He never wanted her to lose that. "Replace the darkness with the light."

"You counter the bad with something good." The barest hint of a smile whispered across her mouth.

It was enough. For now. "Should we take Sherlock back and head home?"

Brooke nodded.

Dan held her hand in his and headed back to Earl's. He held on to Brooke for the drive to his house and during the short walk to the rental apartment. Rex and Luna surrounded her at the front door. He said, "The dogs can have full run of the backyard."

"That's not—"

He interrupted her. "It's not enough, but it's a start."

"Thanks." Brooke's smile flashed into her eyes, flowed across her entire face and filled Dan.

"In an effort to find that work-life balance, I'm going to turn on the fire pit, sit outside and enjoy the evening." Dan rubbed his chest. His heart shouldn't be racing. Or his nerves firing. "You're welcome to join me."

"I'd like that," Brooke said. "Let me get a sweatshirt."

Dan exhaled as if he'd been holding his

breath, willing her to say yes. The truth was something stronger. Something deeper. He didn't want to be alone. Even more, he didn't want Brooke to be alone.

He called Luna with him and turned back. "Don't forget to leave the door open for Rex."

Tomorrow he'd bury his feelings.

Tomorrow he'd remind himself of the reasons content was enough.

Tonight he'd replace the loneliness he so often ignored with something good—someone good.

CHAPTER NINETEEN

BROOKE WAITED FOR the cabdriver to stop at the curb outside The Pampered Pooch. Across the street, a pair of college students sampled each other's food at a table outside Bits and Bites Pantry.

Last night, she and Dan had had the same dinner: vegetables from her place and steak from his refrigerator. They'd talked and discovered even more things they shared: a similar love of camping. A joy for skiing, even though they were both bad. How much they both still missed their moms. And how they still talked to their moms, seeking advice.

Brooke pulled out her money, paid the driver and picked up her boxes of croissants from her favorite patisserie. On the sidewalk, she paused and stared at the departing taxi. That was the first cab ride where she'd kept her eyes open. Not only were her eyes open, but she'd also looked out the window and took in the city around her: the cable cars, the policeman patrolling from a horse and the rhythm of the tourists weaving through the locals along the sidewalks.

Not out of fear that she'd see her past, instead she'd seen the city as it was now. In the present.

That had led to her asking the cabdriver to pull over in front of Beaux Arts Bakery for an impromptu stop. Terror hadn't seized her on the sidewalk or back inside the cab.

Brooke opened the door to The Pampered Pooch, a lightness inside her she hadn't experienced in far too long. A familiar musical laugh and lilting voice filled the store. Brooke moved along the center aisle, following the voice like a beacon. She rounded the endcap and had no time to prepare for the embrace that muffled her greeting.

"Sophie told me you'd be here soon." Valerie squeezed Brooke and released her.

Brooke adjusted the croissant bag and her voice. "Valerie. What are you doing here?"

"Ben and Wesley told me at the park that Sophie was the one to talk to about how to organize the donations for victims of the wildfires." Valerie raised her hands. "So here I am."

Sophie grinned, clearly appreciative of Valerie's efforts. "Valerie is putting together a small event to raise money and collect donations for both families and animals affected by the fires."

Brooke was impressed. Valerie stood behind her words. She hadn't been exaggerating about her charitable work. "That's incredible. And a lot of effort."

"I'm tapping into my mom's network of friends and business associates." Valerie shrugged one shoulder. "I've discovered that people want to help, but sometimes they don't know how. I figure out ways to supply the how."

That was no small feat. Once again, Brooke softened toward Valerie. "I'm sure the families and animals will appreciate it."

"I know the rescue organizations I work with will." Sophie brushed her hair out of her eyes, unable to remove the exhaustion, too. "Everyone is really overextended right now."

"Then it's a good thing I brought chocolate and other treats." Brooke set the bakery boxes on the counter.

"I'm so pleased Beaux Arts is still open. One of the best on the West Coast." Valerie set her joined hands under her chin. "Although I have to admit, there's this small village in southern France, nestled among the vineyards and farmland. Lovely place. Their patisserie is the best I've tasted in the world."

"Sounds simply charming." Sophie opened a container and sighed.

"Brooke, do you think Ben would like to visit a village like that?" Valerie handed napkins to Sophie and Brooke.

Sophie paused midbite. "Ben is going to Europe?"

"I'd like him to," Valerie said. "There's a few

small details Dan and I need to work out first, though."

Dan's refusal was more than a small detail. And threatening legal action and a courtroom showdown wasn't minor, either. "We should let Ben sample one of these croissants. If he likes it, you can ask him about France."

"That's a good idea." Valerie toyed with the corner of her napkin. "I'm also leaning toward the soccer idea after watching Ben at the park with Dan and Jason."

Brooke refused to be moved again by Valerie. Yet Valerie had been paying attention. She was trying to put Ben into her plans. Brooke would test her. Maybe if Valerie failed, Brooke could like her a little less. "What do you have planned?"

"That football-stadium tour of sorts could be fun." Valerie's fingers tapped against the napkin as if she was unsure of her idea. "Ben could list the soccer stadiums he wants to visit. Then he can check off the places we go to. Sort of like Americans do with baseball and the football stadiums in the States."

Brooke reached for a chocolate-filled croissant and forced herself not to frown. Valerie's ideas were not allowing Brooke to like the woman any less. Valerie had come up with something Ben would love.

"That sounds like a trip I want to take." Sophie winced and shrugged at Brooke as if she

277 CARI LYNN WEBB

couldn't help herself from joining Valerie's travel train.

Brooke understood the feeling. She bit into the croissant, relishing the rich chocolate flavor, and convinced herself this was a good thing. Valerie was taking Ben's likes into consideration. Funny, Brooke wasn't convinced Dan would appreciate that.

A woman stepped up to the counter, holding one of the plush, higher-end dog beds. "Are these beds really worth the price?"

Sophie set down her croissant and brushed a napkin over her mouth.

"What kind of dog do you have?" Valerie reached over and ran her fingers over the heavy-duty stitching on the dog bed.

The woman's tender smile gentled her voice. "We've adopted a greyhound named Marley."

"My friend rescued two greyhounds from being euthanized in Australia last year. Such sweet and precious dogs. They shouldn't have to suffer so much for people to profit." Valerie straightened and smiled at the woman. "But you've saved Marley. He won't starve anymore or be forced to live in a cage two sizes too small. He'll have freedom and love."

"I'll take this one." The woman set the bed on the counter and looked at Sophie. "Marley has earned a little pampering."

She added, "Give me one minute. I need to grab a few more things."

"Take your time," Sophie told the woman. Then shifted her smile to Valerie and mouthed the words *thank you*.

"My pleasure." Valerie tucked her hair behind her ear and stuffed a notepad into her purse. "I better not linger any longer. I need to get busy on those donations."

Brooke understood right then that Valerie's donation to the fire victims wouldn't be small or inconsequential. Not after she aimed her full-wattage smile at potential givers and persuaded them to help a good cause. More charities could use people like Valerie on their teams.

"Sophie, I'll be in touch later this week." Valerie wrapped a croissant in a napkin. "Thanks for this, Brooke. I needed a pick-me-up."

"You can take more than one," Brooke offered.

"Then I'll just be overindulging." Valerie laughed and hugged Brooke. "If you could tell Dan I changed my mind about traveling for soccer, maybe he'll reconsider his own travel ban for Ben."

"You should probably tell him that," Brooke suggested. She stepped to the side of the counter to give Marley's owner room to set chew toys and a blanket on top of the plush bed.

The woman laughed and touched the plush

snowman and the stuffed squirrel. "I couldn't decide which one he'd like better."

"Always good to have options." Sophie picked up the cash-register scanner. "You can rotate the toys, then he won't get bored."

"You don't think Ben would be bored traveling with me, do you?" Valerie muttered as if unsure.

Brooke doubted she would be bored traveling with Valerie. "That's not Dan's concern."

"He doesn't trust me to take care of Ben." Valerie adjusted her purse on her shoulder and tipped up her chin. "But Ben is my son."

It sounded as if she'd asked a question, not made a claim. As if she doubted herself. Valerie brushed her platinum blond hair away from her eyes as if everything about her was suddenly out of place. "Maybe you should show Dan that you can take of Ben while you're here."

Valerie's hand stilled. "Dan did let Ben go to dinner with Jason and me last night."

And that had allowed Brooke to spend the evening alone with Dan. Once again, she wanted to thank the woman. Or she would thank Valerie if she was someone different. If she was someone who listened to their heart and took risks.

"Maybe Ben would want to stay at the hotel and swim in the indoor pool." Valerie's voice strengthened, and her hand dropped to her waist as if the fidgeting never happened.

Then Brooke could spend another evening with Dan. But this wasn't about her and Dan. This was about Valerie and Dan finding common ground for Ben's sake. This was about avoiding a courtroom brawl—one that forced Ben to pick a side and where no one won. And everyone ended up hurt. "You won't know until you ask."

"I'll text Ben right now," Valerie said.

"He's in school," Brooke reminded her.

"Right. I'll do that later." Valerie walked down the aisle and turned around. "When does school get out?"

"Three-oh-five p.m." Brooke glanced at Sophie to confirm her answer.

"Correct. Evie is on car pool duty today." Sophie finished putting Marley's new supplies into a bag and thanked Marley's owner for her purchase.

"I'll walk with you to your car." Valerie took the bag of toys and treats from Marley's owner. "You don't want to drop the new bed on the sidewalk."

The pair walked outside. The door chimes marked their departure.

Brooke turned toward the counter and took in a confused Sophie.

"I seriously tried not to like her. I really, really tried." Sophie lifted both hands and smoothed out her ponytail. "I mean, who leaves their husband and child to travel the world? A selfish, self-centered woman, right?"

Brooke took a large bite of her croissant, letting Sophie ramble.

Sophie picked up the credit-card receipt and shoved it in the drawer. "Not a woman who organizes a donation drive for a city she doesn't live in. Then convinces a stranger to spend over three hundred dollars on dog supplies in a pet store that isn't hers."

Sophie wasn't the first person conflicted over Valerie. Even Dan had yet to utter a negative thing or bad word about Valerie, since she'd arrived. Dan—more than anyone—had every reason not to like his ex-wife. Yet Brooke doubted Dan's ability to dislike anyone.

She'd heard stories about first responders and hard-to-deal-with patients and families. Dan hadn't denied that patients could get combative, physically and verbally. He hadn't denied that even family members insulted him and his coworkers. Yet he had proclaimed that his work still mattered, perhaps even more in those moments. Dan had been called to help other people—he accepted every part of his job just as he accepted Valerie for who she was.

Just as he accepted Brooke, the woman too scared by her past to walk within two blocks of a street corner. The woman who couldn't say no to any animal in need. Valerie might have a gift for optimism, but Dan's gift of acceptance was greater.

How accepting would Dan be when he learned Brooke suggested Ben spend the night with Valerie? "I think Dan is going to be mad at me."

Sophie opened the second box of croissants and sighed. "You bought the berry galettes, too?"

"I couldn't resist." She also couldn't resist trying to help Valerie and Dan.

Sophie closed the box and eyed Brooke. "What did you do?"

"Encouraged Valerie to host Ben for a sleepover at the hotel," Brooke said.

"Okay." Sophie opened the box and took out a berry-and-cream-filled galette.

"She wants Dan to trust her." Brooke held out her hand and waited for Sophie to put a pastry on her palm.

"How could Dan trust her after what she did to him and Ben?" Sophie asked between bites.

"That's the problem." Brooke peeked behind the counter. "Now would be a good time for Evie's Irish coffee."

"Yes, it would." Sophie nodded, slowly and deliberately.

"But Dan and Valerie can't go to court," Brooke argued. "Imagine what that would do to Ben."

"And if Valerie wins joint custody, it won't matter if Dan trusts her or not." Sophie frowned and plucked a raspberry from the center of the pastry.

"I should tell Valerie it was a bad idea," Brooke said.

Sophie straightened. "Or you could have Dan come up with the idea on his own."

"What?" Brooke asked.

"No. It's brilliant." Sophie wiped her hands on her jeans. "Convince Dan that Ben should spend the night with Valerie, but make it seem like Dan came up with the idea himself."

Brooke set her forehead on the counter. "How am I supposed to do that?"

Sophie said, "You'll figure it out. You're good at this type of thing."

Her thing wasn't manipulating people. More specifically, manipulating Dan. "I'm not sure what my thing is."

"Well, you got Earl to agree to meet a family," Sophie said. "That was beyond genius."

"I haven't found a family or solved Earl's problem yet." Not that she'd given up. She hadn't exhausted all her contacts yet.

"But you will. I have faith." Sophie touched Brooke's shoulder, drawing Brooke's gaze to her. "Your heart is in the right place with Dan, Ben and Valerie."

"Do you think that will be enough for Dan

not to be mad about the sleepover?" Brooke asked.

"I think it will be enough to guide you," Sophie said.

When was the last time Brooke had followed her heart? She was more practical than that. "That's very whimsical and fairy godmother–like of you."

Sophie shrugged. "Sometimes our hearts know what we need before we do."

"I need to work off these croissants." Brooke touched her stomach. "I'm going to the play yard. Then I'm going to look through your list of foster families again."

There had to be a solution for Earl and Sherlock. Brooke just wasn't seeing it. Just like there was a compromise for Valerie and Dan. She just had to uncover it.

CHAPTER TWENTY

BROOKE STOOD OUTSIDE the apartment and closed her jacket up under her chin. The day would eventually warm enough to shed several of her layers. But for now, she needed the extra warmth. The excited thumps of the dogs' tails against the walkway drew Brooke's attention. She looked over and her own excitement sparked. Dan walked across the backyard, his uniform replaced with a sweatshirt and workout pants.

Brooke waved. "You just missed Ben. Nichole picked him up. Your dad left to meet up with Jason."

Dan nodded.

Up close, the deep shadows under his eyes and the gloomy cast to his gaze drew Brooke closer. "Are you okay?"

"Very long night." Dan leaned over to greet the dogs.

The misery in his words and etched into the lines around his eyes was heartbreaking. Brooke wanted to hug him. Hold on until whatever ate away inside him ceased its assault. "Is there anything I can do?"

Dan scrubbed his hands in his hair, disrupting the wavy strands as if that would disrupt whatever haunted him. "Sometimes there are calls that hit hard, like a ten-ton brick dragging you under."

"Does it help to talk?" She hadn't believed a conversation could have such an impact for her, but she'd been wrong. She'd shared her dark past with Dan and shed a shroud from herself in the process. A shroud that shaded her view of the world around her.

Dan kicked at a pebble. "A twelve-year-old girl suffered a severe asthma attack at her grandparents' house."

She failed to mute her gasp. Ben was only a few years younger than that poor child.

"She'll be fine," Dan assured her. His touch on her shoulder soothed. "We wheeled her into the ER. Her frantic parents barreled into us. Her mother, hysterical, kept yelling her daughter's name, her high heels slipping on her gown and the floor."

"I imagine I'd have been the same." Brooke picked up a tennis ball and tossed it into the yard. Both dogs raced off to claim it. "Is it Ben? That Valerie wouldn't be there for him?" Brooke considered that. Hated it for Ben. Wanted very badly for Valerie to prove her wrong.

"Valerie." Confusion pulled his mouth into a frown. "It's not about her. It's me."

Brooke faced Dan. The ashen cast of his cheeks tipped worry through her. "You told me the little girl was fine."

"Her father was in a tuxedo, his tie smashed and partly undone. Terror in his eyes." Dan fisted his hands at his sides, dropped his head back and drew in a shaky breath. "'Did she suffer?' That's all he kept repeating."

Brooke, horrified, snared another gasp.

"He thought his daughter had died. Thought he hadn't been there with her." Dan wiped at his tears. "I stared into his eyes. Father to father, Brooke. Looked right into my own greatest…"

Fear. Brooke launched herself into his arms. Held on. Tighter and tighter. Until he curved his arms around her and squeezed. She stayed in his arms, waited for his breaths to even out. Waited for her own heart to slow. Minutes. Maybe longer. Time didn't matter. Only Dan.

The tennis ball rolled against her foot. She peered down at Rex. He leaned against Dan's legs as if offering his own encouragement.

"I'm too restless to sleep." He pulled away and tucked her hair behind her ear. "Would you want to walk with me?"

"Let me get the leashes." Brooke slipped inside, returned and handed him Rex's harness.

A fragment of a smile drifted across his face. "I'll let you lead the way."

Brooke walked down the driveway, Luna be-

SINGLE DAD TO THE RESCUE

side her, and paused. Dan had looked directly into the face of his darkest fear—could she do the same? *Have no regrets.* What would she regret more: confronting her fear or always wondering about a life well lived? "Ben tells me there's a larger park in the opposite direction. Do you know the way?"

Dan tilted his head and eyed her. His earlier anguish replaced with concern. For her. "You're sure you don't want to go the usual route?"

No, she wasn't sure. Not at all. But the dog park wasn't the accident site. She might be walking in the same direction. But no one was forcing her to go there. Not today or any day. *Push your limits.* "I thought the dogs might like a change."

He nodded, then lifted his chin toward her. "I like the new clothes. The bright colors suit you."

"Thanks." Brooke's smile was tenuous. Most of her new wardrobe had finally arrived. Was that the reason she wanted to try a different route? New clothes, new attitude. True, she felt different: lighter and freer. Still, it wasn't the clothes exactly. She suspected it was more likely due to the man beside her. The man with fears as stifling and consuming as her own.

She fell into step next to Dan. Silence extended between them.

Around them, the city moved at its own pace. Runners clocking one more mile before that midmorning conference call. Mothers pushing strollers and relying on each other for support. Cars returning from the school drop-off line. People piling into the last express bus heading to the financial district.

Inside her, those old jitters surfaced. She accepted the nerves, allowed herself to fidget. And kept on walking.

At the park, Dan glanced at her. The anguish muted in his gaze. "This might be the balance that Ava has been lecturing me about."

"Feeling better?" Brooke checked in on herself, too. She was better.

"More settled," Dan admitted and pointed to a curved stone-and-grass path. "The dog play area is over there. Down that trail."

Perhaps the fear would always be there, always willing to cast its shroud. Perhaps the challenge was to find the brightness within the dim gloom. The dogs. The park. Dan. This was the good. The dogs released to roam and smell, Dan and Brooke sat on a bench.

Dan stretched out his legs, stacked one ankle over the other and glanced at Brooke. "Valerie called to ask if Ben could spend the night at her hotel."

No wonder he wasn't completely settled. Brooke shifted on the metal bench—she'd forgotten all about her and Sophie's plan regarding the sleepover. "I'm sorry. I talked to Valerie yesterday at the pet store. She might've gotten the idea from me."

"Might have?" Dan asked.

Brooke unzipped her jacket. Had that warm weather already rolled in? "Valerie really wants you to trust her. I know that's asking a lot, given your history."

Dan rubbed his chin. "And a sleepover is going to fix that?"

"It's a start," Brooke hedged. "A chance to prove she can look after Ben." Except the little girl with asthma had been with her grandparents and certainly, they'd looked after her. Yet she'd ended up in the hospital. Dread crept beside Brooke, offering its cloak. She swatted it away. The little girl was going to be fine. Ben would be fine, too.

"I told her I thought it was a good idea." Dan studied the sky.

Brooke pulled back, unable to keep the surprise and skepticism out of her voice. "Really?"

"Yes." Dan glanced over at her. Small shadows lingered under his eyes. Caution leveled the conviction in his tone. "Really."

Brooke envied his control and ability to rein in his deepest fears. He was scared but wanted to do what was right for Ben. Could she dare to?

"I need to know if Ben is comfortable with Valerie. Going to dinner or spending the afternoon in the park is one thing." He smoothed his hands over his hair. Uncertainty lingered. "An overnight is a whole different scenario."

What-ifs prowled inside Brooke. She refused to drag them both under. Nothing was ever solved with pessimism—her often repeated words to her clients. "Ben could enjoy himself."

"I'm still not sending him out of the country for a vacation." Dan's voice was matter-of-fact and firm. International vacations were not up for debate.

Brooke agreed. That could be one step too far. If something happened to Ben overseas, Dan wouldn't forgive himself. "What if Valerie agreed to travel in the US?"

"If they're going to Disneyland, I want to go." Dan's grin lifted his eyebrows, lightened those shadows.

Not a definitive answer. But Dan hadn't shot down her suggestion. Brooke kept her request to join them to herself. "It's something to consider."

"And I will." Dan shifted his legs to let Rex scoot under the bench. "Did you find any foster families at the pet store that matched Earl's requirements?"

"Not one family. It's so frustrating." Brooke shifted and leaned against the bench. "I expanded the search across the bay."

Dan urged Rex out from under the bench and pet his head. "I'd be concerned about the stress of a long-distance move on a dog Sherlock's age."

Sherlock wasn't even Dan's. The man who didn't want pets now worried about other people's animals. That slipped inside, adding more good. She had to be careful. Dan was taking up more and more space inside her heart. "I put distance as another consideration. I don't think Earl would agree, either."

"So, what can we do?" Dan met her gaze.

We. Brooke liked that. *Too much.* Her chest expanded. She'd forgotten how much she liked working through a problem, even a minor one, with someone. Someone she trusted and… "I'm not sure."

"What if the family doesn't meet his specific requirements? But they can offer something Earl didn't think of in exchange," Dan suggested.

Could that be the solution? Brooke faced Dan. Ideas rushed through her, boosting her resolve. "Maybe I could find a family who would bring Sherlock to the nursing home to visit Earl."

"That could work." Dan ran his hand through his hair. "Does the assisted-living center allow that? I know Ava and Sophie visit hospitals and nursing homes with the therapy dogs."

"But Sherlock isn't a therapy dog." This was only a small roadblock, Brooke told herself. "I'll visit the assisted-living center that Cara wants to move Earl into and find out."

"It's the best place to start," Dan said.

Brooke gathered her confidence. She had to start someplace, too. "We should probably get more steps in. Then you can tell Ava you walked off your stress."

"I liked sitting here in the park." Dan reached his arms over his head and stretched. "Can all our walks include a break on a park bench?"

Brooke just wanted every walk to include Dan. She quieted the whispers inside her heart. Her heart was safe as things were. Wasn't that all that mattered?

Dogs clipped to their leashes, Dan and Brooke strolled along the path. At the entrance, Brooke stopped. Left took her back to Dan's house. Right took her back to her past.

Earl's gravelly voice echoed through her. *How do you know you're living life right?*

Her feet flexed, wanting to turn toward Dan's house. Run away.

But had she run so far and so fast there was no place left to run? A different voice whispered through her. Telling her it was time. Time to live again.

Brooke zipped her jacket and the shiver inside her. Then turned right.

Dan set his hand on her arm. "You don't have to go there."

"What did Earl tell us?" Brooke tipped her chin up, strengthening her voice as if inspiring her resolve. "We have to push our limits. Do what scares us."

"He's an eighty-six-year-old man." Dan closed the distance between them, his voice a mix of concern and affection. "What does he know?"

Earl knew loss. Grief. And living through the good and the very worst. Earl understood the richness of a life without regrets. Brooke locked her gaze on Dan's. "You'll come with me."

"I'll be right beside you." Dan slid his hand down her arm and his fingers linked with hers. "Whether you turn back or go all the way, I'll be right here."

"I think I have to do this." Brooke tightened her grip on Dan's hand, using his assurance and composure to reinforce her spine. "Does that sound weird?"

Dan touched her chin and lifted her face up. His gaze, serious and intent, centered on her as if she had to see him to hear him. "It sounds brave."

Brave. How she wanted to be that. Her voice hushed as indecisive as a last lingering patch of fog. "Can you be brave and terrified at the same time?"

"That's the definition of courage." Dan touched her cheek. One quick caress… "Being willing to face what scares you despite your fear."

"Tell me something weird you're afraid of."

"Snakes."

"You like to camp and hike." She considered jogging, setting off into a brisk run. Then she'd have an explanation for the burning in her chest.

"As much as I can." Dan tapped his shoulder against hers. "But don't think I'm not on hyperalert, scanning for snakes everywhere. On the trails. In the trees. In my tent. Inside my sleeping bag."

"Do you have a snake plan?" Brooke had no plan. The burn seared as if she'd hiked past the clouds to a mountaintop, not walked one block.

"Simple. Outrun the people I'm with." His voice was bland, neutral against her winded nerves.

Brooke paused, concentrated on Dan like that buoy in a storm-tossed sea. "That's not a plan the people with you will appreciate."

Dan shrugged. "Then they should've trained harder."

She appreciated Dan even more. For giving her a moment to collect herself. Could he feel the tremor in her fingers? See her pulse straining in her neck. "People with shorter legs are at a disadvantage next to gazelles like you."

"I've never been compared to a gazelle," Dan said. "Clearly you haven't seen me run."

"Lack grace and coordination." Her lungs no longer lacked oxygen.

"Exactly," he said. "Which gives you an advantage."

"I'll take that into consideration on our next hike."

Dan's gaze trailed over her face. One side of his mouth tilted upward, slipping satisfaction into his voice. "That sounds like you want to spend more time with me."

Her pulse skipped again—the good kind. The kind that led to joy and hope. That was exactly what she wanted—more time with Dan. But she had a past to face. And a heart she'd sworn not to open. "Or I just want to beat you at a race."

"Accepted." Dan sobered and stepped fully into her space.

Into the pulse racing, any closer and they'd touch with the barest of shifts, space. The space that blocked the world out. That belonged to only them.

"Seriously, though." Dan brushed her hair off her face as if he couldn't see her. "I'm afraid every single day of failing Ben."

"You're a great father. The best. Dedicated. Involved." Loving. Brooke placed her hand over his heart. How could he doubt himself?

"Thanks," Dan said. "When Ben was younger, I realized I got to wake up every morning and choose what kind of father I'd be. I still make that choice every day. Same as I choose to put my patients first at work and my fears second. Some days I'm more successful than others. But each day is another chance to try again."

He was telling Brooke that she had a choice, too. That even if she turned around now, she could make a different choice tomorrow. The volume increased on her inner voice. *How much longer could she keep running? How much longer could she avoid living?* "I want to keep going."

Dan moved to her side, tucked her hand back in his and let Brooke set the pace.

One block later and Brooke wanted to punch whatever it was that propelled her forward.

The pain and grief surged inside her, pummeling her. Trying to root her in place. Trying to seal her leaden feet to the cement. When had the sidewalk become quicksand?

Dan and the dogs slowed with her. The last block stretched like a time warp.

One step at a time. Would she ever want to run to something and not away?

The air dissolved around her as if extracted by the phantoms from her past. One foot in front of the other.

Until finally, she stood at the intersection of Bayview and State Streets. The site of the accident on the opposite side—diagonally across from her.

Emptiness stole inside her.

The night replayed in her mind. Glimpses of time frozen and framed: dinner tucked inside a quaint booth. Laughing after finally shaking off the workday stress. Being present together without cell phones or distractions. The plump miniature apple pie piled high with homemade vanilla ice cream. Splitting the last bite.

Window-shopping. Senseless. Fun. Devastating. A shudder built from her feet as if the ground shook, not her knees.

Brooke braced her legs, blinked and focused on the shops wrapping around the busy corner. The stores had changed. Or perhaps not. That hadn't ever been the important part.

The part worth remembering had been holding hands. Having a connection with another person. A connection that linked two hearts.

Brooke glanced down at her hand tucked safely inside Dan's. A different hand. As it should be. It was a different time. Yet his grip was protective, too, perhaps even more.

The connection was there. In the warmth. In the strength. In the not wanting to let go. And the linking-two-hearts part—that could definitely be there.

If she dared. If she dared to do what scared her.

But that was for later.

First, she had to face a different sort of fear. The fear of letting go. Allowing the past to rest a little easier, a little quieter inside her. Balancing the memories. Finding comfort in the good rather than focusing only on the bad. Carving out a piece of her heart for the past—for what was. All that she once had. But there was room. Room for more.

Brooke stood silent for another five minutes. Ten. The dogs sat patiently beside her as if they, too, understood the importance of the moment. Dan never flinched. Never urged her to leave. Never released her hand.

Finally, Brooke said, "I'm ready."

Dan released her and brushed the tears off her cheeks with his thumbs. His tone was tender. His voice was raw as if her tears—*her pain*—was his own. "Only if you're sure."

Brooke closed her eyes, leaned against him. His warm caress seeped deep inside to those cold places and exhaled. "I'm sure."

Dan touched her cheeks one last time. Wiped the last of her tears away and searched her face.

He nodded then and pressed a soft kiss on her forehead.

And Brooke's heart burst open. Open and unguarded. The truth clamoring to be heard.

She wasn't falling in love. She was already in love. With Dan.

CHAPTER TWENTY-ONE

BROOKE OPENED THE jewelry box on the mantel and ran her fingers over the Bubble Wrap–covered angels nestled inside. She'd never unpacked the angels in her cabin in the mountains. Fearful an errant tail or paw would knock the angels off a shelf, shattering them on the floor. But tonight, she reached for one in particular: *Joy.*

She removed the packaging. A crystal angel holding a bouquet of flowers smiled back at her. *Laughter shines from your soul and heals your heart.* Her mother's advice.

Dan had given her laughter yesterday. After he'd stood beside her and wiped her tears away at the site of her accident. He'd been the first person she'd opened up to. The first person to hear the truth. She'd trusted him. Trusted him not to judge her. After all, if she hadn't wanted to window-shop that night, the van might've missed Phillip and her. She'd trusted that Dan would hold her together if she fell apart. Instead he'd held her hand the entire walk home.

Then he'd brought her dinner and butter-pecan ice cream for dessert. Invited her to spend the evening with him outside under the stars. Entertained her with his antics as a boy. Listened to her dating mishaps and awkward teenage moments. Added his own versions. This time, the tears, when they arrived, came from the laughter.

The knock on the door woke the dogs. Brooke set the angel in the center of the mantel, closed the jewelry box and walked to the front door.

Dan stood on the patio, his hands tucked in the pockets of his dress pants and his button-down shirt ironed and wrinkle-free. "I've been given strict instructions to bring you to the coed bash for Mia and Wyatt tonight."

"And if I decline?" she asked.

"Ava told me I'm not allowed to take no for an answer," he countered. "It'll be easier if you just agree to come with me."

"I'm not really dressed for a party." Brooke pointed to her flannel pants and the EMT sweat-shirt.

Dan ran his hand over his mouth. "You don't have to get dressed up. They'll be happy to have you there just as you are."

Would he be happy to have her just as she was? Brooke twisted the door handle, noting the worry in Dan's gaze.

"I told Ava you might not have ordered fancy

clothes." Dan frowned. "And now I've put you on the spot."

And he disliked that. His worry was for her. Brooke released the door handle. "I need to walk the dogs, then I can change."

"You'll go?"

She nodded. "If you don't mind waiting for me to get ready."

Dan grinned. "Why don't I walk the dogs while you change?"

"Are you sure? You're not dressed for a dog walk." He was dressed for an evening out. And Brooke wanted to be beside him. She wanted another night of laughter.

He motioned to the backyard. "I'll walk them out here."

"You'll need to coax Rex out with you and Luna." Brooke opened the door and motioned him inside. "I won't be too long."

He followed her inside. Brooke rushed into the bedroom, pulled a dress from the closet—she'd ordered several on a whim—and hurried into the bathroom. She left Dan and the dogs to take care of their own business.

Thirty minutes later, Brooke buckled the straps of her high heel around her ankle and stepped out into the family room. She paused in the doorway and gaped at Dan holding Cupid.

Dan was built like a professional football player. His size was better suited to a Great

Dane than an eight-pound cat. Still, his hold on Cupid was tender, his soft expression and attempt at a stern voice endearing.

"Look, Cupid, you have three legs, but that doesn't make you better than everyone else." Dan lifted the cat up until the two were eye to eye. "However, we're going to need you to hold down the fort tonight."

Cupid licked Dan's nose. Dan's eyebrows lifted along with his grin. "I think we understand each other."

"Are you sure you don't like pets?" Brooke asked. *Could you like me as much as I like you?*

"It's difficult not to like Cupid with his three legs and superior attitude." Dan shifted Cupid and held him against his chest as if he'd been a longtime cat lover. "Besides, I never said I didn't like cats. I just don't have any."

"You're good with animals," Brooke said. He was good with her, too.

But his training taught him to be compassionate, helpful and patient. All the things he'd been with her. Brooke was like an emergency call he took during one of his work shifts. Only she was living in his rental unit temporarily. She repeated the word: *temporary*. He was helping her enjoy the world around her again. Helping her rediscover her laughter.

Dan turned toward her. Surprise curved

across his face, his mouth opened in a startled yet charming O.

Brooke smoothed a hand down her sheath dress. "Will this work?"

"You're stunning."

And Brooke wanted to start to dream again. To take the greatest risk of all again. With Dan.

Brooke climbed into the truck, determined to keep the conversation light and easy and away from the risk her heart wanted to take. Dan obliged, giving her a detailed layout of Kyle's game room and the strengths and weaknesses of every guest at the party. She needed to avoid playing Skee-Ball with Ava, unless she was on her team. Pinball was a no go if Wyatt was playing. And Sophie could clear the pool table faster than a professional. Kyle crashed a lot on the racetrack games, while Mia pretended not to know what she was doing and always finished the race courses first.

Brooke followed Dan into the lobby and together they listed the games they could potentially take high score. The elevator up button blinked and Brooke stepped inside, ready for another evening of fun.

Dan stepped off the elevator, checked his phone and frowned. "Earl is being taken to the hospital."

Brooke froze. "What happened?"

"Another fall." Dan rubbed the back of his neck. "On the stairs."

"Is he going to be okay?"

"We'll know more in a few hours." Dan stuck his phone in his pants pocket. "Cara texted that she'll stay in touch."

The worry in his voice underscored the lines around his eyes. She said, "But it's not good."

"Let's not jump ahead." Dan opened the suite door. "We'll enjoy the party and wait until Cara texts us an update."

Brooke nodded and stepped inside. Laughter, cheers and a buzz of celebration circled Brooke, challenging the unease within her.

Dan took her coat and her hand. "Earl wouldn't want us to miss a good party."

"You can't walk into a party looking like you've arrived at a funeral," Evie scolded Brooke and Dan.

Rick stepped beside Evie, blocking Brooke's view of the partygoers. "No one passed away, right?"

"Not exactly," Dan said.

Evie and Rick shared an alarmed look. Evie recovered first. "Then we can fix this."

She guided Brooke and Dan to a large seating area.

Two sleek leather couches and two sets of chairs framed a steel-and-glass coffee table. Sequined throw pillows in every color of the rainbow splashed an inviting welcome on the dark leather. Brooke sat on the end of a couch across from Rick. Evie perched in the chair beside her. Dan dropped onto the couch next to Brooke.

Rick adjusted the ends of his silver-and-white sash embroidered with the words *King of the Groom Squad* and set his hands on his knees. "Couples argue. It's how you resolve your differences that gives you staying power."

Evie sipped from her champagne glass and nodded sagely.

Couple. She'd only just lectured her heart to stand down. "We aren't…"

Dan set his hand over hers, distracting her. He whispered, "They're just warming up."

"What does that mean?" Brooke whispered back.

"We wait until they've gotten out what they feel they have to say." Dan shifted his attention to Evie and his father.

"My late husband and I always ended every disagreement with a kiss, even if we hadn't resolved anything." Evie smoothed her fingers over her silver-and-white *Queen of the Bride Squad* sash. "A nice kiss makes it hard for both of you to hold on to your irritation."

Rick and Evie eyed Brooke and Dan. Rick said, "You should try that."

Brooke's mouth dropped open. They wanted her to kiss Dan. Now. Just like that. She hadn't kissed anyone since Phillip. Not like that. She hadn't wanted to kiss anyone. Not like that. *Until now.*

"Okay. Stop." Dan motioned between Brooke and himself. "We're fine."

But would they be better if they kissed? Cheers and hollers erupted from the arcade area, as if encouraging Brooke to kiss Dan. She stared at Evie's champagne glass. Maybe a drink would help.

"You don't look fine." Evie wiped a napkin over her glasses, not bothering to remove them. "I've only had half a glass of champagne."

"It's not the champagne," Rick said. "Evie, your eyesight is as good as ever."

Evie crinkled the napkin and toasted Rick. "That's a relief."

Dan leaned forward. "Look. It's about Earl Powell. He fell again and is being admitted to the hospital right now."

Brooke scooted closer to the edge of the couch. "We don't want to tell Sophie and ruin her night. She'll worry about Sherlock."

"Who is watching Sherlock?" Evie asked.

"His daughter for now," Dan said.

"We'll walk and feed him, too," Brooke said. "Whatever she needs."

"The problem is that I don't think they'll discharge Earl back home this time," Dan said.

And that was what she'd seen in Dan's face

outside the suite. Concern for both the older gentleman and his dog. "Time is now up to find Sherlock a new family."

"This is a somber group." An elegant older woman pushed a wheelchair with another woman between the two chairs.

Evie offered quick introductions. The women's silver-and-white sashes proclaimed them friends of Dan's. Helen's sash read: *Mom of the Groom Squad.* Helen indicated Brooke should move over, closer to Dan, and sat down.

Karen's sash proclaimed: *MOB in Training.* She explained that stood for *Mother of the Bride-to-Be* and pointed at Ava with a wide smile.

"Now, really, who died?" Helen dropped a pink-and-gold sequined pillow on her lap as if she needed the cheer.

"No one passed away." Karen swatted Helen's knee. "Can't you see that Dan and Brooke are having a quarrel?"

Helen tsked. "Seriously, one good kiss and you'll win every argument." She waved to Mia and Wyatt at the Ping-Pong table. "Already gave that advice to Mia to use on Wyatt. My poor son won't ever win, but he'll be happy about it every time."

Evie clapped her hands. "That was exactly the advice I gave them."

"We really should put together an advice

column." Helen drew a heart in the sequined pillow.

"Just in the Prime Timers crew alone we've got over a century of marriage experience," Karen added. "That's quite impressive."

"When we need marriage advice, we'll come to you." Dan ran his hands over his dress pants.

A collective sigh passed through the Prime Timers as if they were disappointed there wouldn't be a kiss. Brooke caught herself and her sigh before it escaped. She wasn't disappointed about not kissing Dan. Although she was interested to know if their advice really worked.

She said, "We're desperate to find a home for an eleven-year-old golden retriever. Special considerations attached."

"Ava and I have a pair of senior foster cats with us or we'd take the dog," Karen offered.

Brooke smiled at Ava's mom. "Thanks. We'll figure something out. I don't want any of you to worry."

Dan nudged Brooke's shoulder. "Getting overly involved is their form of fun."

"Dan is right." Helen set her hands on the pillow as if she was in court, preparing to swear on the Bible. "We're going to figure this out together."

"It's what we do. Ask the kids." Karen patted her curls into place and looked at Brooke. "Now, tell us what you've done. No sense repeating the hard work you've already put in."

Brooke shifted her gaze around the group. Their expressions thoughtful, eager and sincere. Everyone wanted to help. The collective support wrapped around her like a bear hug. And she jumped in, unable to resist, detailing the last few days of her search.

Twenty minutes later, one cheese platter and more than thirty potential families discarded, Helen tapped her palm on the pillow. "Which assisted-living center does Charlene Leonard volunteer at?"

"Charlene is at Golden Sunrise Manor." Evie pointed at her friends. "It's one of the nicer facilities, but I'm not moving in there. Neither are any of you."

"No one is moving anywhere." Helen laughed and shook her head. "Charlene mentioned she wanted to adopt a pet at our most recent Second Winders gathering."

Dan leaned into Brooke. "It's supposed to be a group for widows and widowers. Except it's really a poker night with appetizers, Evie's Irish coffee and cash bets."

Brooke wanted to join that widows club. She grinned. "How do I get an invite?"

"I'm sure they'll take you." He teased, "You've already admitted you aren't good at poker."

"Is that a requirement?"

Dan nodded. "Levels the playing field or so they claim."

She definitely wanted to spend an evening or two playing poker with them. "Count me in."

"That wasn't Charlene you're thinking of, Helen." Karen wiped a napkin across her mouth, her words slow, as if she was running through a guest list in her head. "I believe it was Teresa Knowles."

"Teresa missed our last gathering." Evie built a cheese-and-cracker appetizer on a napkin and passed it over to Karen.

"That's right." Rick tapped his hand on his knee. "Teresa had to work late last week and couldn't make it."

"I remember now." Helen snapped her fingers as if focusing her memory. "Charlene's children want her to travel more. But the poor dear is scared to death to fly."

"Her children only need to get more creative. A train ride or cruise ship or RV could be options," Karen said. "But it was Teresa's kids that want to buy her a puppy."

"Teresa doesn't want a puppy and the work involved raising one. Says she already raised enough kids." Helen glanced at Brooke. "Not that I blame Teresa, given her work schedule."

"Teresa works at Bright Heart Sanctuary,"

Karen added. "She manages housekeeping and the kitchen for the entire center."

That was the same assisted-living center Cara wanted Earl to move into. Excitement bounced around inside Brooke. She set her hand on Dan's leg, stopping herself from jumping up to celebrate. Teresa Knowles could be the solution. She swallowed hard, reminding herself not to get too far ahead. "Would Teresa possibly consider a senior dog already housebroken and well trained?"

"We could ask her," Karen said.

"What if the senior dog belongs to a patient that was going to become a new resident of Bright Heart Sanctuary?" Dan asked. "Would that help sway Teresa?"

"Earl Powell is moving into Bright Heart?" Evie clapped. "It's almost too perfect."

That made Brooke pause, not party.

Karen drummed her fingers on the armrest of her wheelchair. "Well, Teresa is quite darling with her contagious laugh and Midwestern accent."

"She never wins. Not one hand." Rick lifted his gaze toward the cheers erupting from the pinball machines. "Still, Teresa smiles and laughs the entire evening."

Those were wonderful qualities for anyone. But Sherlock required more than that. Brooke asked, "But does Teresa want a dog?"

"There's always this pause after one of Teresa's deep laughs, as if she's reaching for more laughter to keep the loneliness away." Evie's mouth turned down as if she hurt for the dear woman, too.

"I agree with her children." Karen nodded. "A dog would give Teresa a companion."

"Teresa needs a dog for the nights the laughter is hard to find." Helen's voice was pensive.

A collective hum of agreement flowed through the group. They all understood. They'd all been there. They all knew exactly how Teresa felt. Brooke knew, too. "I'm not sure what I would've done without my pets."

Brooke glanced at Dan and Rick. Now she wondered what she would've done without the Sawyers after the wildfire.

"Now you have us." Evie lifted her champagne glass toward Brooke. "Best of all, you don't have to wait for a Second Winders gathering if you need us."

"We're right across the backyard," Rick offered.

Dan was right across the backyard. She could walk onto his porch, kiss him good-night and run into her apartment before he could react. Brooke touched her mouth. She wasn't running onto any porches. She wasn't kissing anyone. "I'm more grateful than I can ever say."

"That's enough business for tonight." Karen waved at Dan and Brooke. "You two need to get over there and join in. You're missing out on some really good prizes."

"Let us talk to Teresa in the next day or so." Evie shooed them away. "Go have fun. There's nothing more we can do for the moment."

Rick grinned at Evie. "We can show these youngsters how to properly play Ping-Pong, Evie."

"We can definitely do that." Evie stood up and arranged her sash as if she'd just been announced the winner of a beauty pageant and awaited her crown. "We'll give you two ten minutes to warm up and strategize."

Dan held his hand out to Brooke. "Ready for this?"

She was ready to jump into the fun and games. Discover her laughter. The kissing—well, she'd bury that back inside her. She set her hand inside Dan's and let him pull her off the couch. "Definitely."

CHAPTER TWENTY-TWO

DAN STEPPED OFF the elevator on the third floor of Bay Water Medical, silenced his phone and tucked it in the leg pocket on his pants. He'd worked overtime two nights in a row. Then filled in on the day shift. His body wasn't certain whether to sleep or accept the exhaustion as its new normal.

He hadn't seen Brooke since their three-game losing streak on the Ping-Pong tables to his dad and Evie, followed by their indisputable victory on the basketball free throw game. Brooke had written their names in bold on the chalkboard standings wall and accepted their award at the trophy ceremony: his-and-hers fuzzy socks, chocolates with Wyatt's and Mia's initials and handkerchiefs embroidered with No Ugly Crying.

Brooke and Dan had sampled the chocolates on the drive home. He'd left her with both pairs of fuzzy socks, then grudgingly accepted his hankie and that his night with Brooke was over.

Dan waved to the nurses behind the desk,

continued to Room 324 and discovered his first smile. Brooke waved to him outside Earl Powell's hospital room. She'd texted him earlier to ask if he'd meet her there to talk to Earl about Sherlock.

Dan would've met Brooke even if Sherlock and Earl weren't the topic. He just wanted to see her. He just wanted to be with her. Dan slowed and shoved his hands in his pockets. Otherwise he would've reached for Brooke and hugged her as if he'd always greeted her that way.

"Thanks for coming," Brooke studied him. "You're tired. You should've said no."

Not likely. And he was less tired now standing there beside her. He opened the hospital-room door and motioned her inside. "I'm good. Let's talk to Earl."

Earl called out a greeting to Brooke and Dan, then pressed a button to raise the headboard. "Come in. Come in. I'd get up, but the nurses yell at me."

Dan shook Earl's hand. "You look good."

"And you look exhausted," Earl countered.

Brooke frowned at Dan, then hugged Earl. "It's good to see you, Earl."

Earl told them to sit and launched right to the point. "Cara brought Teresa Knowles over here during lunch today. Did you know Teresa told me that she'd only agree to take Sherlock if I gave her permission?"

Brooke smiled. "She was lovely to speak with over the phone."

Earl shook his finger at Brooke. "I know you introduced Sherlock and Teresa."

Dan leaned over and whispered, "You've been busy."

"Just introductions." Brooke's voice barely lifted above the hum of the blood-pressure machine. She stepped closer to the hospital bed. "I hope you understand, Earl. If Sherlock and Teresa weren't compatible, I wasn't going to suggest that you meet her."

What Brooke didn't add was that time wasn't on their side. Dan had talked to Cara that morning. A room would be available the day after next for Earl at Bright Heart Sanctuary. Willing or not, Earl would be discharged from the hospital to his new home. Without Sherlock.

"Well." Earl's bushy eyebrows lowered over his blue gaze. "You've got to tell me about their meeting."

Dan moved the two chairs closer to the bed. This wasn't going to be a short story. From the firm set of Earl's wrinkles, he expected Brooke to give him every detail from the beginning to the end of the meeting.

"I walked Sherlock from The Pampered Pooch to Bits and Bites Pantry. It's across the street from the pet store. Teresa and I planned to meet there." Brooke leaned forward and touched Earl's arm as if sharing a really good secret. "Sherlock was more than happy to escape the doggy day care. The Australian shepherd brothers, Lewis and Coop, were more rambunctious than usual. And every doggy in day care seems to believe Sherlock wants to play."

"Sherlock used to fetch the ball a lot and run beside me, carrying a stick." Earl grinned and tapped his forehead. "Now our minds want to play, and our bodies tell us no. Sherlock will nose a tennis ball around the house. Be sure to tell Teresa that."

Brooke glanced at Dan. A smile wavered across her face, dancing through her gaze, before she turned toward Earl. "We were early so Sherlock and I ordered broccoli-cheddar soup and cookies. Then retreated to the last table on the patio. The one tucked behind the planters that hides the patrons but grants an excellent view to people watch."

"Sherlock enjoys sitting at the park bench and watching the world pass by almost as much as his walks." Earl dropped back on his pillow and eyed Brooke. "You'll need to remember to pass that along, too."

Brooke never reacted. Dan barely refrained from nodding himself. Only then did he realize that Earl hadn't actually given his permission to Teresa Knowles. He'd said "if he gave his permission" earlier. Clearly Brooke had caught on to that one key phrase much sooner than Dan.

"Teresa arrived. She brought treats for Sherlock," Brooke said. "The dog biscuits were homemade by one of her kitchen staff who bakes for her own dogs. I've already requested the recipe for myself. Ben and I plan to make them together for the dogs."

That phrase Dan caught. His son and Brooke had plans. *Future plans.* But Dan and Brooke hadn't discussed her future plans. Or made plans for themselves. She'd mentioned that her in-laws had found her a rental home up north. She was waiting on availability. Dan studied her profile. Could she be waiting on something else? Or someone else? Specifically, Dan. But discussing the future was significant. It transformed whatever was between them into something much more serious.

Dan was already committed to Ben. How could he help Ben flourish, if he was committed to something else? To someone else. To Brooke. What if he failed them both?

Earl rubbed his chin. "Did Sherlock like the biscuits as much as your treats?"

"I think even more." Brooke shook her head as if disappointed. Yet the delight was there in her tone.

Would she be disappointed or delighted when she moved up north? Dan refused to consider what he'd be. He stretched in the chair. When had the hospital chairs become so hard and un-comfortable?

"You should definitely get that recipe." Earl smoothed his finger over the tape covering his IV port. "Always good to give the dogs options."

"I like to think so," Brooke said. "Sherlock sat between Teresa and I while we ate. He edged closer and closer to Teresa throughout the meal and finally put his head on her lap."

Dan figured the dog wanted a second bis-cuit. If the biscuits were that good, who could blame him?

"But she hadn't given him the biscuit yet," Earl mused.

"No, we saved those for the end of lunch." Brooke grinned. "I think Sherlock sensed her loneliness. Teresa became a widow less than a year ago."

"Sherlock always had a keen sense of emo-tions." Pride was there in Earl's gravelly voice. "Always right beside me before I knew I needed him."

Like Brooke. She'd been right beside Dan, starting with Valerie's unexpected arrival. She'd been there even when Dan hadn't known he'd needed her. What was he supposed to do when she wasn't there? When she returned north to her own life? He rolled his shoulders as if that would smooth the uneasiness away.

"Teresa welcomed his attention and lavished Sherlock with her own affection," Brooke said.

"Do you think they bonded?" Earl asked.

Brooke nodded. "Even better, I think they understood each other."

"Looks like I'm moving out of here and into Bright Heart Sanctuary." Earl adjusted the pillow behind his head. A peaceful smile overtook his weathered face. "And Sherlock is moving, too."

"Then you're going to give Teresa your permission to take Sherlock home?" Brooke stood up and sat on the side of Earl's bed.

"I'll call Cara and tell her as soon as you leave," Earl said.

"I know this is hard." Brooke wrapped Earl's hand inside hers. "But it really is for the best."

What was for the best with Brooke? To stay in the city or leave. If she stayed in the city, would she expect more from Dan than he could give? She had her once-in-a-lifetime love. Surely, she wasn't looking for that again. But she deserved that, didn't she? Dan rubbed his chest and moved the chairs back against the wall.

"It's easier now that Sherlock has a special place to spend the rest of his days, too," Earl said.

"And Teresa told me she'd bring you pictures of Sherlock." Brooke patted Earl's hand.

"Don't be telling anyone on account that you

might get Teresa in trouble." Earl checked the doorway, then motioned Brooke closer. "But Teresa promised me that she'd bring Sherlock to work and let him visit me."

"That's wonderful." Brooke's voice sounded watery.

Like she swallowed her tears. Would she cry when she left the city? Would she cry when she said goodbye to Dan? Would he? *No.* After all, they weren't anything like that. He cleared his throat.

Earl set his other hand on top of Brooke's. "I'll be expecting to see you now and again, too."

Dan wanted to see Brooke more than now and again.

"You can count on it." Brooke hugged Earl and wished him a good-night.

Could Dan count on Brooke to stay? Dan pushed his errant thoughts away and shook Earl's hand, promising to stop in to see Earl after his shift ended in the morning. That was something he could count on: his job.

"Remember, it's black coffee," Earl called out. "No sugar and none of those fancy flavored creams."

"Got it." Dan grinned. "Still want the fancy-shaped pastry?"

"The one with the cinnamon-apple filling?" Earl's eyebrows lifted, widening his eyes.

"That's the one," Dan said.

"Have to admit, I'd like to sample that one again." Earl patted his stomach.

"See you tomorrow," Dan said. "For another sample."

An elevator ride later, Dan walked outside the hospital and touched his stomach. "Talking about apple turnovers made me hungry. That and the success with Earl and Sherlock."

"I'm not sure there's anything that doesn't make you hungry." Brooke bumped into him, laughter in her tone.

"Liver pâté," Dan said.

"Excuse me."

"I don't like liver pâté." Dan shuddered, drawing her laughter and his own smile. "Looking at it reminds me of cat food. Tasting it ruins my appetite."

"That is very good information to have."

Brooke's joy surrounded him. He wanted more time with her like this. "Almost sunset and that means suppertime."

Brooke bit the corner of her lip and looked at him. "How hungry are you?"

"You just told me that I'm always hungry."

She shifted, set her hand on his chest and stopped him. "Can you maybe wait to eat until after sunset?"

"Maybe." Dan forgot about eating. He wanted to wrap his arm around her waist and draw her closer. He wanted to feel more than her hand on his chest. "What do you have in mind?"

"We're less than four blocks away from the Lyon Street Steps." Her gaze dropped to his mouth. Her fingers tensed on his chest. She blinked, dropped her hand and rushed on, "If we hurry, we can climb the stairs before the sun goes down."

Dan wanted to say no. He had a good life with Ben. She'd had the perfect marriage. What could they give each other? They lived in different worlds—he liked the fast-paced city, she preferred the mountains. He had a son. She had her animals. She made him better. He made her... "There's over 275 stairs."

"That are perfect for working up a really good appetite." Her plea was wrapped inside her encouraging voice.

Dan set his hands on his hips, rather than on her waist. "You're serious?"

"It's one of my favorite places in the city." Brooke blushed with her confession. Her enthusiasm dimmed, lowering her voice. "I haven't been up there since before my marriage. Phillip and I always talked about hiking the stairs to watch the sunset, but we never did. Something always came up. Usually work meetings or after-hours business calls."

Dan could give her this. A new memory in

the city. *With him.* He held out his hand. "Let's start climbing."

"Really?" Excitement rushed through her voice.

Absolutely. When she left the city, she'd have this moment to take with her.

Four blocks and 188 stairs later, Dan stopped counting, content to follow Brooke and listen to her commentary about the possible owners of the mansions lining either side of the stairs. Her speculation on how many generations of the same family roamed the manicured lawns. The history of weddings and birthdays celebrated on the extensive patios. The tiered garden fountains and wrought-iron benches keeping their own secrets.

Dan had his own secrets. His own wishes. Impractical. Impossible. That was the problem with matters of the heart.

Yet at the top of the stairs, the sun burned the sky and greeted the evening. Maybe it was the sunset casting the city in a golden haze. Or maybe it was the glint of gold in Brooke's gaze. Or the awe in her face. Or the pure joy in her touch.

She took his hand. He pulled her to him.

And somewhere inside that sunset, their lips found each other. Their hearts connected.

Seconds slowed the minutes as if even time recognized the significance.

Dan held on to Brooke and the happiness inside him.

And for that instance, he believed in magic. In wishes. And the impossible.

CHAPTER TWENTY-THREE

Two NIGHTS AGO, Brooke had shared a heart-flipping, butterfly-inducing kiss with Dan. After she'd made a positive difference in Earl Powell's life. She'd accomplished something with Earl and Sherlock that gave her satisfaction. Her therapist would commend her for rejoining the world.

Her feet were back underneath her. The ground more stable. She couldn't have gotten there without Dan. He'd helped her rediscover her confidence—a confidence that allowed her to enjoy life again. A confidence that allowed her to hope.

Brooke opened the jewelry box and unwrapped another angel. The Hope angel held a dove, its wings spread and ready to fly. Her phone rang in her pocket. She set the Hope angel next to the Joy one.

She answered her phone, hoped it was Dan, calling to tell her he'd gotten the night off.

"Brooke." A weak voice drifted across the phone line.

Concern replaced her disappointment. "Ben. What's wrong?"

"Can you come. And get me?" His plea was disjointed, as if he spoke through tears he refused to shed.

Brooke switched the phone to her other ear and forced herself to listen through the rush of blood in her head. "Where are you?"

"The movie theater in the Bay District." He hiccupped.

"Where's Valerie?" Brooke tugged on her boots. Grabbed her jacket. Searched for her purse.

"Watchin' the movie." Ben's voice drifted. The connection scratchy, as if he was moving. "Brooke. I don't feel so good."

His words lodged like a knife between her ribs. "When did you last check your numbers?"

"I don't know."

The silence twisted the knife, drove it deeper. "When did you eat last?"

"I don't know." More shuffling. More static. His voice more diluted. "Valerie said we could eat after the movie."

Brooke rushed outside, slammed her front door and raced through the side gate.

"Brooke?"

"I'm here. Ben. I'm here." Brooke scanned the empty street. Taxis wouldn't wait on this street.

She had to go to the city center. Into the traffic. That was the only way to get to Ben.

"Brooke." He whispered, "I'm scared."

The crack in his voice clipped her knees as if she'd face-planted into the cement. "I'm coming. Ben. I'm coming."

"Okay."

"Ben!"

Silence. She stared at her phone. The screen went blank. The call ended.

Brooke ran. Waved her arms for a cab. Ran another block. Shouted and lunged into a cab before it stopped. She clicked on Dan's name in her contact list. Clutched her phone.

Chanted, *Pick up. Pick up. Pick up.*

Voice mail picked up. Dan's recorded voice greeted her.

On the third attempt, she hung up before the voice mail greeting and called Nichole. Asked her to meet her at the movie theater.

Sprinting into the theater, Brooke dialed Rick. He'd gone back up north to help with the fire recovery. Rick picked up on the second ring. Brooke's words tumbled into the speaker.

"Brooke." Rick's steady voice swirled around her. "Slow. Down. Breathe."

Brooke explained the situation and scanned the movie-theater lobby. She found the familiar redhead sitting on the floor outside the arcade.

Brooke raced across the checkered carpet and skidded onto the floor beside Ben.

"You came." Ben collapsed toward her.

She dropped her phone to catch Ben. "We have to check your numbers."

"Valerie went to get my stuff from the car." Sweat matted his hair against his forehead.

Brooke scanned the lobby. Where was she? How could Valerie leave Ben like this? What had Brooke done leaving Ben with her? Brooke drew Ben closer.

Valerie hurried inside and rushed over to them. Her eyes wide. Her bright lipstick worn to a pale smear.

Brooke grabbed the backpack and dug through it, searching for the kit Rick told her Ben always carried. She unzipped the leather superhero bag, set the meter beside her, kept the syringes at hand.

"You're doing that here?" Valerie set her hands in her coat pockets and rocked back on her booted heels. Her lipstick completely gone, her lips colorless. "Right now?"

Brooke muffled her shriek. Wanted to scream at the woman to get over it. But she didn't have time to waste on Valerie. Her reply was no less bitter. No less curt. "Yes. Right now."

"I'll go wait outside for Nichole." Valerie held up her hands toward the main entrance and backed away. "Ben told me they were coming."

Brooke shooed the woman away.

"It's not her fault. She really doesn't like needles. They make her sick." Ben rubbed his nose. "Her face is green, like moldy broccoli."

That wasn't Brooke's problem. Or her concern. This was all Brooke's fault, anyway. She'd wanted to believe in Valerie. She handed Ben the lancet and vial of test strips, and her fingers shook. "Can you do this part?"

"You don't like needles, either?" Ben eyed her. His skin too gray.

"I don't like seeing you hurting." He wouldn't be sick and hurting if she'd listened to Dan. If she'd trusted Dan to know what was best for his own son. If she hadn't meddled, where she wasn't invited. This wasn't the harmony she'd wanted for Dan and Ben.

"It's gonna be okay." Ben scooted into her side. "You know why?"

Brooke watched him. Wanted to believe. Wanted his confidence.

"Because you're here." Ben pricked his finger. "Now I won't have to go to the hospital."

Brooke wrapped her arm around his shoulders and Ben walked her through the process: where to put the test strip, how the unit powered on with the test strip inserted, where the batteries went and where the extras were.

Wesley sprinted toward them and plopped down on Ben's other side.

Brooke tossed her cell phone to Nichole. "Can you call Rick back?"

Brooke called out the readings. Nichole repeated the numbers to Rick and listened for his instructions. Nichole ordered Valerie, still hovering in the periphery, to buy a soda and pretzels from the concession stand. Brooke ordered the woman to hurry up.

Brooke set her alarm on her phone for a ten-minute recheck. Another test strip. Another reading. Still too low. Rick added a granola bar and cookies to the concession purchases.

After thirty minutes, which felt like days later, Brooke stuffed the superhero kit into Ben's backpack, helped Ben stand and repeated Rick's instructions about a small balanced meal for Ben. She hugged Ben's backpack in one arm and held Ben's hand with her other.

Outside the movie theater, Brooke confronted Valerie. "I'm taking Ben home with me. Dan will want to see him as soon as he can."

"Thanks." Valerie nodded and buttoned her fitted jacket as if putting herself back together. As if she'd been the one suffering a health scare. Then hugged Brooke, tightly like a dear friend.

Valerie released Brooke and squeezed Ben's shoulder. "I'm glad you're better."

Ben wrinkled his nose. "Sorry about the movie."

Brooke glared at the sidewalk, frustration

rolling through her, her love for the sweet boy soaring. Valerie should be apologizing to her son.

"We'll watch it another time." Valerie waved to Nichole and Wesley, then walked away.

The foursome headed to the parking garage and climbed into Nichole's car. The boys played a video game in the back seat, their heads together. Suggestions for moves and cheers over better levels filtered out.

At a red light, Nichole took off her glasses and rubbed her eyes. Exhaustion leaked into her voice. "I don't know how Dan does it. Working nights. Volunteering for everything. And keeping up with Ben's diabetes."

"He loves Ben and what he does." Brooke glanced over the seat at Ben. His color was returning. His hair no longer damp.

"I love Wesley and don't mind anything if it's for him," Nichole admitted. "But my data entry work is a different thing completely."

"Yet you're working to provide for Wesley."

"Exactly." Nichole pushed her glasses onto the top of her head to pin back her hair. "Unless I can figure out who has my super secret trust fund and why they haven't told me about it yet."

"Valerie is the only person I've ever met with a trust fund large enough to live on for the rest of her life." Brooke leaned back on the headrest.

"It's interesting that Valerie has this trust fund while her mom had to go back to work," Nichole said.

Brooke straightened. "What do you mean?"

"I don't know the details." Nichole tapped her fingers on the steering wheel. "So I could have it wrong. But Ben talks about how his Grandma Lulu retired late. Now she's traveling so much to catch up with her friends and their adventures."

"So she worked late into her life to support Valerie's travels?" That sounded backward to Brooke. Valerie should've been working to support her mother in her retirement. Then again, Valerie should've been aware of how to handle Ben's diabetes, as well.

Nichole shrugged. "Grandma Lulu has often talked about the value of hard work. And praised Dan and I for setting good examples for the boys."

Dan was everything a father should be.

"I've helped Grandma Lulu more than once with her computers," Nichole said. "She's a fascinating lady."

"Like her daughter." *Fascinating* was one word Brooke could use to describe Valerie. There were others, some kind and some not so kind. "Can you believe Valerie wanted to take Ben on tours of the soccer stadiums in Europe? That's not going to happen now."

"Wow," Nichole said. "I'm sure he would've loved that. It sounds really expensive."

"Now you sound like Dan." A quick grin passed over Brooke. But she wasn't ready to smile yet. Brooke checked the back seat again. "I can't believe how careless she was."

"She's not a full-time or even part-time parent." Nichole pulled into Dan's driveway.

Neither was Brooke. Ben was going to be with her now. And she didn't know how long. What if she was as careless as Valerie? "Can you keep your phone close tonight?"

"Sure," Nichole said. "I'm a light sleeper, anyway. Call or text anytime. Dan still hasn't replied?"

Brooke checked her voice mails and texts again. "Nothing."

"Must be a bad night at work." Nichole opened her car door.

Could it be worse than Ben's scare? Brooke touched her stomach, willed it to stop churning. How did Dan manage his work and his life? He'd kept his humor and his lightness. Ben and Wesley spilled out of the car together, twin grins on their faces. Excitement lit up both their gazes. Ben looked no worse for his episode. Brooke envied his resilience.

The boys wanted a sleepover—they'd been plotting in the back seat. Brooke promised a basketball shoot-out, walking the dogs and s'mores at the fire pit tomorrow afternoon, if they could wait.

Nichole agreed. Then added another condition. "This only happens if Brooke and I get to play, too."

The boys shared a look, then nodded in unison.

Nichole pointed her finger at them. "I saw that look. You don't believe we can win."

Ben stifled his laugh with his hands. Wesley patted his mom's arm. "It's okay not to win, Mom. It only matters that you have fun."

"Oh. Now it's on." Nichole rubbed her hands together. "You both better get lots of sleep and be prepared to lose. Because tomorrow it's on."

Nichole pulled both boys into the same bear hug. Made Brooke promise to call no matter the time. Then helped Wesley back into the car.

Brooke shut the door of her apartment and looked at Ben on the couch. Archie was curled up on his lap. Cupid rested on the back of the couch behind Ben's head, his tail draping around Ben's neck. Luna and Rex framed Ben on either couch cushion.

The muscles in Brooke's shoulders relaxed. It hadn't taken Ben long at all to make himself at home.

Ben grinned at her. "Can I sleep here tonight?"

"You want to sleep on the couch and not

in your own bed?" Brooke sat in the recliner. Ben looked fine. Acted fine. Still, she worried something else could happen. She glanced at his backpack on the kitchen stool. She should get the test kit out.

"Definitely." Ben curved his palm over Archie's back. "I've never slept with cats and dogs before."

"I'm sure they will love to have you," Brooke said.

Ben giggled, pushing Cupid's tail away from his mouth.

His laughter unknotted more of those kinks in her body.

Ben's hand stilled on Archie, his bottom lip disappeared. "You're not mad I called you, are you?"

"No." She slowed her words into an easygoing rhythm, the same way she rocked in the recliner. "Not at all."

Ben played with Cupid's tail and avoided looking at her. "I wanted to stay with you instead of Valerie."

"Why?"

Ben shrugged. "I just feel safer with you."

That heart Brooke kept trying to restrain flipped over again. For Dan's son. Brooke sank back into the recliner. She could relate to Ben. She knew the power in feeling safe. She felt the same way with Dan.

DAN RUSHED INTO the backyard and hung up from the pediatric ward at Bay Water Medical.

Ben hadn't been admitted. Where was his son?

Where was his family? No one answered his calls.

Where was Ben?

Terror ricocheted inside him, bouncing against his ribs, up into his throat. He'd been more calm facing an armed family than he was now.

The shift had started out routine, then tripped into anything but, with a standoff with a patient's armed family. Dan had been forced to remain in a bedroom with a gunshot victim until the police had arrived. Between the standoff and the paperwork, he hadn't looked at his phone until he'd climbed into his truck hours later to drive home.

The list of missed calls choked him. Valerie's voice mail about an incident meant he hadn't listened to any other messages. He'd started calling for answers.

Dan lifted his fist, ready to pound on Brooke's door. Someone was going to tell him where his son was. *Now.*

The door swung open and Brooke shoved him in the chest.

Dan never budged, opened his mouth to demand answers.

Brooke steamrolled over him. "Wake up Ben and I'll kick you."

Dan's mind stuttered. He tilted like a tree in a strong wind. But he had to know. Had to know he'd heard her right. "Ben is here?"

"You never read our texts," she accused. "Never listened to my voice mails."

"I…" He'd panicked. Straight-up panicked like he'd been trained not to do. Like the father of the little girl with asthma in the ER.

Brooke's gaze softened. She recapped the evening, starting with Ben's call, then the events at the movie theater and Nichole's assistance.

"Where's Jason?" he asked.

"On a plane to New York for business." Brooke rubbed her hands together. "He probably hasn't landed yet."

"Why didn't Valerie answer her phone?"

Brooke scowled. "She probably turned it off, so she wouldn't have her sleep disturbed."

Dan massaged the back of his neck. That sounded like Valerie. She'd have assumed Brooke had everything handled.

"You should know I was not nice to her." Brooke shifted from one foot to the other in her fuzzy socks. "I'm not apologizing, either."

Dan liked Brooke as she was: determined and protective of Ben. And him. "I'm not asking you to."

"Ben was up rather late. That's my fault. He

had to call his grandpa. Ben wanted Rick to tell me that Ben didn't need to check his blood through the night."

Dan stared at Brooke. "You checked his blood."

"Absolutely. I would've done it every hour all night to be sure. I don't trust those machines. My dad had one and it never seemed to register his counts correctly. Or maybe it was that my dad liked to visit with the friendly nurse at the lab." Brooke waved her hands around her as if scratching that story from the air. "It doesn't matter. Rick and Ben convinced me that Ben was good. Sorry I made him test so much."

But it did matter. *A lot.* Brooke had tested his blood without flinching. Never stuttered. Never called to tell Dan to come home and take care of his son. Or maybe she had—he hadn't listened to the voice mails. But somehow, standing there, he doubted it. "Where did you say my brother is?"

"Jason had to fly to New York for a business meeting. Ben told me that he felt safer with me rather than with his mom." Broke walked over to the door, peered inside her apartment, then softly closed the door again. "Are you sure your brother is a professional gambler? He has a lot of business meetings."

Dan wasn't sure of anything. "What did you say?"

Brooke blinked. "Are you sure your brother is a gambler?"

"No, about Ben."

"He felt safer here." Brooke brushed the hair out of her face. "I'm sorry. We should've kept calling. I fell asleep in the recliner."

Dan understood exactly why Ben wanted to be with Brooke. Dan grabbed her hands and pulled her attention to him. "Stop apologizing."

"But…" she said.

He squeezed her hands until she quieted. "Thank you."

She tipped her head and watched him. "I was the one who encouraged you to do the sleepover."

Dan shook his head. He was speechless, humbled, grateful. And he was desperately trying to catch his heart before it fell completely for such an incredible woman. But he kept fumbling and falling harder.

Brooke stepped away and opened the front door. She waved Dan closer. "Look how precious they are."

Dan peered inside. Ben lay stretched out on the couch. One arm thrown above his head. Cupid slept, curled up on his stomach. Archie shared Ben's pillow, snuggled against his head. Luna had flopped down on the floor in front of the couch. Even Rex snuggled on the couch near Ben's feet.

"I don't know how you sleep," Brooke whispered and shut the door. "I've checked on Ben every hour."

Dan tugged Brooke into his arms and dropped a soft kiss on her forehead. "Thank you."

Thank you for taking care of Ben. Thank you for being here. With me.

CHAPTER TWENTY-FOUR

SEVERAL HOURS LATER, Dan and Ben debated the merits of zucchini as noodles at the farmers market. Brooke shook her head and added several plump zucchini to her basket. "You're going to love them. I promise."

"I don't know." Ben's face scrunched up, then relaxed into a grin. "But I do love real pasta noodles with extra cheese."

Brooke ruffled his hair. "Then we'll add extra cheese to the list."

"Cool." Ben squinted at an heirloom tomato and pointed out its pumpkin shape. "Brooke, are you going to be looking at the vegetables much longer?"

Brooke glanced up and took in Dan's and Ben's miserable expressions. "There are two more rows of vegetables and fruits waiting for us."

Ben slapped his hand on his forehead. Dan rolled his shoulders as if preparing to take on the task. Brooke burst out laughing. "You don't have to stay with me. There's homemade fudge and cookies over there."

"Really?" Ben spun around and scanned the large market covering more than two blocks.

Dan touched Brooke's cheek and lifted her gaze to his. "Do you mind if we head over there?"

"Only if you don't mind sampling every vegetable I buy," she said.

He leaned down, pressed his lips against hers. "Deal."

Ben made a gagging noise that tempted Dan to kiss Brooke again. Brooke grinned at Dan. "This isn't going to distract me from buying brussels sprouts."

"Are you sure?" he asked. "Maybe we should try again."

Brooke pushed him away. "Take Ben and pick out the cookies with the most chocolate chips."

"Yes, ma'am." He traced his finger along her cheek and his gaze over her face as if memorizing the moment. Then he disappeared down the aisle, hurrying to keep pace with his eager son.

Brooke tracked their progress, thankful for Dan's height. She touched her lips, held on to the kiss and hummed along the next aisle.

Fifteen minutes later, Ben's excited voice reached her. He lifted a bag of cookies and waved.

She never heard what he said.

The screams and shouts stripped his words from the very air.

A car had overshot the curb and sent people scrambling. The next thing she knew Ben was falling forward. Dan blocked a wooden crate with his arm, stumbled.

Brooke, too, staggered, dumping her produce on the ground.

She was too late. Ben hit the pavement. Dan beside him.

And Brooke's world flatlined.

Sirens splintered in the air.

Dan pushed himself up, crawled to Ben. Brooke skidded on her knees beside the boy.

Dan touched her cheek. "Are you okay?"

Brooke nodded. That was the correct response, wasn't it?

"Can you stay with him?" Dan asked. "I need to find help. I need to help."

Brooke nodded again. Her head heavy on her neck. Her body rocking. Ben groaned, drawing her focus. Ben needed her. She pressed her shirt against the gash on his forehead, held him close and held back her panic.

Police officers moved around her. Paramedics swooped in. Secured Ben to a gurney. Escorted her to the ambulance. Confused, she searched the crowd. "Dan? Where's Dan?"

The paramedic guided her into the ambulance. "He's fine. He's okay. He's following in another rig."

Again, Brooke nodded. Her head pounded.

Ben called her name. That centered her. She scooted closer to the gurney, grabbed his hand and held on as her world tipped over itself.

Nurses and a doctor met the gurney, wheeled Ben inside. Spoke to her about running tests and stitches and contusions. Then they were gone. Taking Ben away and her focus.

Brooke clutched her head and wandered into the waiting area.

The past and present stumbled over each other. The street corner on Bayview. The shop windows. Ben falling. Brooke too far away. Squeals. Shouts. Screams. The shattering of glass. The crunch of metal. Of her heart.

She ached. Everywhere.

Gentle hands gripped hers. A strong voice. A familiar face. Her heart knew him. "Dan."

"I need you to focus on me, Brooke," he ordered.

No. There was no place safe to look. Especially not at the man she loved. The man she almost lost… Brooke squeezed her eyes closed.

Her chest hurt as if the world had collapsed on it. Her voice raw and stabbing. "I can't do this. I can't be here."

Dan eased her into a chair and knelt in front of her. "Brooke. Please, listen to me. You need to breathe. Inhale. Exhale."

Didn't he understand? It hurt to breathe. It hurt so much more to love.

Dan falling. Ben crashing beside him. Helpless. She'd been helpless. Like before. Like now.

A doctor in navy scrubs joined Dan and touched his shoulder. Wyatt. The groom. Did he know how much love hurt?

Wyatt told Dan that Ben wanted him. Brooke latched onto Dan's arm. "You need to go."

She needed to go.

"Brooke. Stay here. Don't move. I'll be right back." Dan clasped her hands. "Wyatt is getting someone to help you."

No one could help. She had to move. She had to run from so much pain. That was the only way.

Dan released her to go to Ben. As it should be. That was his life. A shudder swept through her, leaving a deep chill in its wake. She was not Dan's life. She couldn't be.

The ache returned and squeezed her heart. She'd known better than to love again.

Brooke shoved herself out of the chair. Stumbled past Rick and Valerie. Ignored Jason calling her name.

She lunged for the door. Escaped outside. And ran.

CHAPTER TWENTY-FIVE

"SOMEONE NEEDS TO sit with Brooke," Dan said to Wyatt. Her hands had been too cold. Her eyes too glassy. Her skin too pale. He'd hated to leave her. Hated to walk away. But Ben needed him.

His name echoed into the hall. Dan and Wyatt turned. A frantic Valerie rushed toward them. His dad and his brother close behind. Dan searched the waiting area. Brooke's chair was empty.

A scream built inside him. He wanted to call out Brooke's name.

Valerie launched herself into Dan's arms. But he wanted Brooke. In his arms. Beside him. With him.

His dad would find her. Jason, too. Dan started toward his brother.

A hand landed on his arm. A nurse smiled at him. "Mr. Sawyer, your son is asking for you."

Ben. Dan had to get to his son. Ben was his priority. Always.

Dan knew then that Brooke was gone. As it should be. He only had room for one.

He'd had to choose. It was Ben. Every time. Dan turned to follow the nurse.

Wyatt stepped in front of Valerie. "Just his father for now. We don't want too many visitors at once to add additional stress."

Valerie lifted her chin. "I'm his mother."

And yet like Dan, Ben preferred Brooke.

"And you'll have a chance to see him." Wyatt asked a nurse to show the family to the waiting area.

Dan scrubbed his hands over his face.

Wyatt squeezed his shoulder. "The doctors want Ben to stay the night. Make sure numbers are stable. And watch his head."

Dan glanced at Wyatt. "Did he really ask only for me?"

Wyatt shook his head. "Ben wanted you and Brooke."

That resonated with Dan. He wanted Brooke, too. "Does Ben know his mom is here?"

Wyatt nodded. "Said he could hear her in the hall."

Dan wiped his hands over his face again. His son was safe, but things were not right in his world. Would Ben hurt, too, when he found out Brooke was gone? "You're sure Ben is good?"

"It's only protocol. A twenty-four-hour watch for any concussions." Wyatt opened the door to Ben's room. "And yes, he's going to be fine."

"I'll stay with him," Dan said.

"Never doubted it." Wyatt adjusted the stethoscope around his neck. "They're getting a room ready now. I'll be up to check on you guys after my shift ends."

Wyatt walked away and called back to Dan, "I'll check on Brooke, too."

Dan only nodded. Wyatt couldn't help her. He'd realize that soon enough. Dan wanted someone to bring Brooke up to Ben's room. To bring them back together. But he knew deep inside his cracked heart that it wasn't going to happen. Only Dan could get Brooke back. But he'd made his choice. He'd had to. Ben came first.

Dan stepped into the room, sat on Ben's bed and wrapped his son in his arms. His love for Ben seeped through those cracks in his heart.

Ben flopped on the bed and crossed his arms over his chest. "Dr. Wyatt says I need to stay tonight."

"You hit your head pretty hard." Dan set his hand on Ben's chin and tipped his head to scan Ben's forehead for the contusion. A bandage already covered the stitches. And blackness started settling into the skin around his eye.

Ben scowled but let Dan gently move his head around. "You always tell me that I have a hard head."

"Fortunately, your head was a challenge for

the cement." Dan leaned away to look at Ben. "But the pavement still won."

Ben turned the plastic medical band around his wrist. "It's only one night, right?"

"That's the plan, but—" Dan began.

"But we have to listen to the doctor," Ben interrupted and let out a long and profound sigh. The kind of sigh any well-seasoned ten-year-old perfected to inform their parents of their true feelings. "I know. Can we at least get ice cream?"

"I'll see if Grandpa can get some for us." Dan arranged the blankets over Ben's legs.

"Then you're staying the night, too."

"Absolutely." Dan never wanted Ben to doubt that. To doubt that he wouldn't be there for him.

Ben's shoulders relaxed into the bed and stretched his legs out. "What about Brooke?"

Dan had lost her. Maybe he never had her. Maybe this was for the better. Why didn't he feel better, though? Why did he feel like that car had stolen something from him? "Brooke had to go and check on the animals."

"Rex is probably pacing around, waiting to use the bathroom, and Cupid is biting Rex's tail as he paces by the couch." Ben grinned. "Rex can't stop pacing until he goes. And we've been gone a really long time."

Brooke would be gone even longer. Indefinitely. Dan shoved aside that thought. Tonight was about Ben. His son and his family. "Your grandpa, uncle and Valerie are waiting to see you. Grandma Lulu is on her way, too."

"Grandma Lulu is home?" Ben cheered up.

Finally. Luann had texted while they were at the farmers market. Just before the accident. He'd texted her on his way to the hospital to tell her about Ben. She'd replied: On my way.

Dan's support team would surround him and Ben. But who was going to support Brooke? Who was going to take care of her? Dan stood up. "Can I let your mom and the others in?"

Ben nodded.

Ten minutes later, Dan slipped out to the waiting area and let Ben soak up the attention from his grandpa and uncle.

"Dan."

The familiar voice turned him around. He opened his arms and welcomed Luann Bennett's hug.

Luann rubbed his back, then wiped at her eyes. "Ben is good? You're good?"

Dan nodded. He would be, but that was for later. "Ben is detailing the accident to my dad and brother."

Luann touched the gold necklace around her neck. Dan had never seen her without it. "Valerie is here, too?"

"Hello, Mother." Valerie stepped into the waiting area.

And for the first time since he'd known both women, they skipped over the welcoming embrace. Dan shifted his gaze from one to the other.

"Should I welcome you back home or wish you well on your upcoming travels?" Luann asked. Her fingers remained on her necklace as if the gold gave her strength.

"Have you reconsidered your intentions?" Valerie countered.

Luann's smile was slight. "I'm assuming you explained to Dan why you came home."

"To spend time with my son," Valerie said.

"And challenge for partial custody," Dan added. He wanted to know what was really going on with Valerie. Now that Luann was here, he wanted answers. If those had to come out in the hospital waiting area, so be it.

"That's a bold move, Valerie." Luann set her purse on a chair. "What did you hope to prove to me?"

To Luann? Partial custody was about proving to Dan that she wanted to get to know Ben. That she wanted him in her life. That she could be trusted to take care of her own son. Except she'd dropped the ball with him the one night she could've proven she'd changed.

"That should be obvious." Valerie set her hands on her hips.

"Why don't you explain it?" Dan said. His

brother stepped into the room behind Valerie and crossed his arms over his chest.

"It's a family matter," Valerie countered.

"We're all family here." Jason stepped around a chair and faced her.

"I made some changes to my will," Luann said. "Valerie doesn't approve."

"I'm your only heir." Valerie closed the distance. Her voice low. "I should inherit what my father built."

Luann unfastened her gold necklace and handed it to Valerie. "This is what your father left behind in the estate. You can have it."

Valerie refused to take the necklace. "There was more."

"Debt. And more debt," Luann said. "Why do you think I worked for twenty years? Why do you think I extended my retirement more than once?"

"I had a trust fund," Valerie said.

"That I never touched." Luann spoke with pride in her voice. "Not one penny. Your father left that for you. Now I'm leaving my estate and my assets to my grandson."

Dan's mouth dropped open. *Ben.* Ben was Luann's heir.

"What am I supposed to do?" Valerie asked.

"You have a trust fund." Jason tipped his head at her.

"Had." Valerie's hands fisted at her sides.

"You spent all of your trust fund?" Dan asked. How was that possible?

"She's been relying on my goodwill and my bank account." Jason rubbed his hand over his mouth as if to remove a bad taste. "Now it makes sense. We never made sense. But this does."

"Everything would've been fine if mother made me an executor." Valerie reached for Jason.

He stepped away, his tone appalled. "You were going to steal from your own son?"

Who does that? Dan noticed the desperation in Valerie's wide gaze. "Is that why you wanted partial custody?"

"I think I get it." Luann set her hand on Dan's arm. "If you trusted Valerie with partial custody of Ben, then I would have to trust her as the executor."

"Except I never agreed to partial custody," Dan said. Nor would he ever. He'd take that battle to court every time.

"And I never removed you as the executor of my will," Luann said.

Dan looked at her. "Me?"

"If you agree." Luann smiled at him. "But now I want to see my grandson for myself."

"What am I supposed to do?" Valerie stopped her mother as she walked by.

"Do what we—Dan, Jason and myself—all

had to do." Luann straightened and cupped her daughter's cheek. "Get a job and become an adult."

Luann walked down the hall and disappeared around the corner.

Valerie adjusted her purse on her shoulder and eyed Dan and Jason. "I always hated hospitals."

With that she strode toward the elevators and left. *Again.*

Dan nodded to Jason. Together, the brothers returned to Ben's room and their family.

CHAPTER TWENTY-SIX

THREE DAYS LATER, Dan parked his truck in the driveway and climbed out. He was on car pool duty for school. He'd dropped Ben and Wesley off early so they could meet Ella to help her with her science project. Now he had seven hours to avoid the empty rental apartment and his feelings.

He'd returned from the hospital Sunday afternoon. Got Ben settled in with a movie, then walked out to the apartment. He'd already known Brooke wouldn't be there. The apartment looked colder and emptier without her. Like he felt.

But that would ease. Broken hearts repaired themselves. Healed with time. He'd recovered after Valerie left. He just needed time.

He stuffed his keys in his pocket and glanced at the front porch. A woman waited, leaning against the railing. But she wasn't the dark-haired one who had stolen his heart. She wasn't the one he wanted.

He walked up the steps and paused at the top. "Valerie."

She was alone this time. The dimmer switch pressed on her smile. No food or presents waited near her feet.

"You were right." She tucked her hair behind her ear, her fingers trembling. "I did return for the money."

Dan frowned. "Is this supposed to help?"

"I returned for the money." Valerie twisted her hands together. "And then I met Ben. Then I started to like Ben."

Dan nodded and smiled. "He's easy to like."

"It's more than that." Valerie tapped her chest, above her heart. "There's a spot only for him in here. Can you believe that?"

He would've said no. But he had a spot in his heart for Ben. And now one for Brooke, too. How could he love two people so much? How could he not? "What now?"

"I need to figure out my life." Valerie waved her hands in the air. "I've never been good at adulting."

"You could stay in the city," Dan suggested. "Be close to Ben." And people who would help her learn to be an adult.

"I've never been good at staying." Valerie pointed at her heeled boots. "My feet are too restless."

"But you'll come back to visit?" Dan joined her, leaning on the railing, and crossed one ankle over the other. "Ben will want to see you on US soil."

"Ben and I can have fun wherever we are." Something tender shifted through her smile and into her voice. "Even if it's at my mother's house."

"Or maybe Disneyland," Dan offered. "Although there's a list of people who plan to join you."

"I could organize that group. That's my specialty." Valerie laughed, then sobered. "You know it was never about you, don't you?"

Dan tipped his head and eyed her. This wasn't about Ben or traveling. This was about the past. This was that conversation they'd never had. Maybe it was all for the better. He wouldn't have listened. She wouldn't have explained. Maybe it was all about becoming an adult.

"I was never meant to be a mom," Valerie continued. "The more I pretended the more bitter I became. I resented you."

Dan understood. He could've said the feeling had been mutual. But like she said, this wasn't about him.

"You fell into being a father and a dad so easily and confidently. You were a natural. I was not."

"It was never easy," Dan allowed.

But Valerie continued, rushing on as if she feared he'd stop listening, "When I started to resent our beautiful, precious baby boy. That's when I knew I couldn't come home."

Dan swallowed and swayed on the railing.

Grief and distress blended into her voice, silencing the lyrical tone. "If I'd come home, that resentment would've turned into hate."

"You don't hate," Dan countered. Valerie was many things, but she wasn't someone who hated. Cruel and unkind weren't in her makeup.

"Exactly. I couldn't take the risk. I couldn't damage Ben's life like that." Valerie picked up her purse. "One day I hope he can understand. I hope he can forgive me."

First, Valerie needed to understand herself. Forgive herself. But that wasn't for Dan to do. That was something Valerie had to do herself. Thanks to Brooke, he'd forgiven Valerie. There was peace in that. He hadn't needed Valerie's explanation. But he was glad she'd shared the truth however uncomfortable it was.

"I'll be in touch when I figure out some things." Valerie smiled, touched his arm and walked down the stairs.

Dan watched her get into her car and pull away from the curb, then he went inside. Too restless to stay in his house, he stepped into the backyard, pulled his keys out of his pockets and opened the apartment door.

No four-legged friends greeted him, tails wagging and tongues hanging out. Cupid didn't stretch on the couch, rolling over onto his back, inviting Dan to meet him. And Brooke wasn't there to tease him or kiss him. Dan stepped into the bedroom.

The four-poster queen bed was made, the throw pillows arranged neatly on top. The towels were folded and hanging on the towel rack as if waiting for the next visitor. Everything was clean, put together and ready.

Except Dan wasn't put together. He was out of sorts and unsure how to fix it. He feared the only person who could help him was the one person he'd chased away.

Back in the living room, his heart clenched as he spotted the mantel, where two crystal angels waited. Dan picked up the Hope and Joy angels—the very things Brooke had given him. They belonged to Brooke and were part of a set she'd gotten from her late husband. One was missing, like that piece of his heart.

The front door opened. His father and brother entered. His dad motioned to the lights. "We saw the lights on in here and figured this was where you were."

Dan set the angels on the mantel. "You just missed Valerie."

"We already said our goodbyes." Jason opened and closed cabinets in the kitchen. "This place is fully furnished."

"Yeah," Dan said. "You'll recognize most of it as Mom and Dad's old stuff."

"It's not old," Rick said. "It's vintage, like me."

Dan smiled. "Nothing wrong with old or vintage."

"Are you going to get a new tenant?" Jason asked.

The last tenant opened his heart, then took it with her. Dan shook his head. "I'm not sure I want the stress of another stranger."

"How about a brother?" Jason asked.

Dan rocked back on his heels. "You want to move in here?"

"Yes, if you'll let me." Jason faced Dan, his tone serious. His words careful. "I want to be close to my family again."

Family. That was all Dan ever wanted. "What about Valerie and your travels?"

"I've been building a global transportation company the past few years," Jason said. "It grew faster than I expected. I've started opening more offices."

"And you're putting one here in the city," Dan said, guessing.

"I came back for the business," Jason said. "But it's my family that's keeping me here."

Dan hugged his brother, adding a slap on his back. "What about Valerie?"

"It was never right between us," Jason said. "But it was easier than being alone."

Dan nodded. He wasn't sure how he was going to handle being alone now.

"Enough about me." Jason punched him in the shoulder. "When are you bringing Brooke back home?"

Rick stepped toward them. "We all miss her."

"I miss her, too." Dan paced into the family room. "But she's a widow. I'm a single dad."

His dad and brother stared at him as if they didn't understand.

Dan threw his hands up in the air. "She's no ordinary widow."

"No widow is," Rick countered.

Dan scratched his fingers over his cheeks. "Dad, did you ever hear Hank Decker tell the story about the scene that almost ended his career?"

"Yeah. A hit-and-run. Vehicle jumped a curb, hit a couple and then rammed into a building." His father's head shook as if he'd witnessed the scene and was replaying it in his mind. But his dad had witnessed enough other horrifying scenes to fill in the details easily enough.

"Brooke and her husband were that couple," Dan said.

"You can't be serious." His dad frowned at him.

"She told me about the accident that took her husband's life. It sounded so familiar. I checked with Hank. Then checked the news reports."

"She lost her husband on the scene," his dad added.

Dan nodded. Brooke had confided in him.

"That's why she never wanted to walk toward Bayview," Jason said.

But it wasn't about walking.

"They were the perfect couple. He was an attorney on the fast track to becoming a partner. She was a mediator at a law firm. Both successful, up-and-coming in their fields and ready to start a family. That's how it's supposed to be." Dan shoved his hands in his hair and pulled. "Until a drunk driver took the dream away."

"It doesn't mean there can't be a new dream," his father said.

"Dreams are for the naive." Dan dropped his hands. "I'll leave the dreams to the kids like Ben."

"Do you think Ben dreamed of Valerie returning like this?" his dad asked.

"I know he's dreamed of a mom." Dan paced around the room. "Sophie and I have both heard Ella and Ben over the years."

Jason grimaced. "I doubt Valerie was a part of that dream."

"What could I offer Brooke?" Dan asked.

"Your love," his father said.

"It's not that simple," Dan argued.

"It should be." Jason followed their father to the door. "It should be just that simple."

The soft click hardly disturbed the air. Yet a sense of loneliness vibrated through Dan, weakening his knees and his certainty.

Dan walked to the mantel, stared at the angels. Hope and Joy grinned back at him. All that was missing was Love.

Dan smacked his palm on the bricks lining the fireplace. Love was missing.

And he was going to get her back.

CHAPTER TWENTY-SEVEN

BROOKE WIPED AT her eyes and stared at her fire-ravaged land. The soot and ash had barely settled, the air barely cleared. The loss rocked her no less hard the second time viewing it.

The claims adjuster from her insurance agency handed her a tissue and an apology, as if assuming her tears were for the land and home she'd lost. But her tears weren't only for the destruction the wildfire had caused to her neighbors on the mountain. The bulk of her tears were for all that Brooke had left behind in the city five days ago.

"Can I give you a ride someplace?" the adjuster asked.

Not unless you're driving to San Francisco. Brooke shook her head. "That's my rental car across the street."

The insurance agent promised to be in touch later in the week and left for his next appointment. Brooke surveyed her land one last time, got into her car and drove down the mountain.

The animal shelter was desperate for volunteers. And Brooke was desperate to keep busy. To do something outside her rental house. Only a month ago, she'd been content to remain inside her mountain cabin and keep to herself.

Now the blank walls pressed in on her. The silence irritated and forced her outside. Forced her off the property and out into the world. The dogs watched the front door as if waiting for Ben to burst inside to play or Dan to greet them with a belly rub. The dogs watched the door as if waiting for their world to come back.

But that wasn't going to happen. Brooke gripped the steering wheel. This was her world now. Five days ago, she'd left the hospital and Dan behind. She'd rented a car, loaded up her pets and few things, then called her in-laws. Ann and Don had met her at the rental house with keys and open arms.

But the arms Brooke wanted to step into were Dan's. The keys she wanted were the ones to his heart. Yet to have Dan's love, she had to open her own heart. She had to love in return. She had to love despite the fear.

At the animal shelter, Brooke urged a Lab mix back into his kennel and shut the door. Four hours walking the shelter dogs should've been enough to walk off her melancholy. Four hours should've been enough to shake off her loneliness.

Instead, Brooke got into her car, feeling more

dismal and alone than ever. She checked her phone messages.

Ava had texted to remind Brooke that she'd promised to help her shoe shop for her bridesmaid's outfit this weekend.

Cara texted to let Brooke know that Earl was settled into his new rooms and eager for visitors. And apple-cinnamon turnovers.

Teresa forwarded pictures of Sherlock sleeping on the couch with their newest addition, a senior cat named Beau, courtesy of Sophie at The Pampered Pooch. Then invited her to come meet him.

Nichole texted asking about a basketball rematch with the boys. Her place this time.

Sophie texted a picture of chocolate croissants and labeled it: bribery. Then added: to get you to come back where you belong.

Evie forwarded the invite for the Second Winders upcoming gathering the following week, and that there was a two-dollar minimum. And added: Helen says you forgot her advice and wanted to remind you—it's all about the kiss. Nothing else matters.

Broke swiped at her face, brushing the tears from her cheeks the entire drive back to her rental house. She was alone again. While a group of people wanted to be with her in the city. A group of friends wanted to support her.

Wanted to be there for her. And she wanted to be there for them.

Brooke pulled into the driveway and dropped her head on the steering wheel. She'd built a support system, then abandoned it. Her therapist would be disappointed in her choices. Brooke was disappointed in herself, too.

How many times had her clients reminded her to cherish what she had while she had it? The wildfires and the accident were personal examples of how precious time was.

Do things that scare you. Earl's words circled through her. *She was always scared.*

Brooke got out of the car and hurried inside. Perhaps that was the catch. She was *always* scared. Would *always* be scared. But Dan had called her brave.

And she wanted to be brave now. She wanted to have courage for the people she loved. Brooke picked up her phone and scrolled through her contact list. She pressed the phone number and waited for the call to connect.

Several hours later, the doorbell rang. And Brooke jolted. She picked up her garbage bag of personal items—she really needed to buy luggage—and rushed to the door. Her greeting dwindled, and the garbage bag sagged onto the floor beside her feet.

"Don't say anything," Dan said quickly. "Just listen."

She couldn't speak if she wanted to, her heart raced so fast. *Dan*. Dan was here. On her doorstep.

"If you're choosing to be alone, I'll walk away and leave you to it." Dan drew a deep breath and focused on her.

Alone. She didn't want to be alone.

"But if you're settling for being alone because you're scared. Or worried. Or too afraid. Then I want to change your mind." He held his hands out at his sides. "I'm scared, too. I'm worried that I'll lose you. That I won't ever love you like you deserve. That I'll fail you."

She'd already failed him. She'd walked away. She reached for him.

He shook his head. "I have to get this out. I have to tell you that I love you. Not the young kind of love that burns hot and fast. Rather, the kind that doesn't need to be proven to the world or put on display for it to matter. It's the kind of love that sticks." Dan pressed his fist over his heart. "That sticks in your heart for a lifetime."

Brooke covered her mouth with her hand. She knew that kind of love. She felt that kind of love in her heart, too. For Dan. She started to speak…

Ben squeezed in front of Dan. "Is it my turn now?"

Brooke sobbed. She couldn't stop it this time.

Dan set his hands on Ben's shoulders yet kept his gaze locked on Brooke. "It's your turn, Ben."

"Brooke, you have to come home. Dad doesn't smile anymore, and his vegetables don't taste so good." Ben chewed on his bottom lip. "And I think your pets miss me because I *really* miss them."

Ben couldn't miss her pets more than Brooke had missed this sweet precious boy or his dad.

"But mostly, you gotta come home because I miss you." Ben lifted his chin and looked at her. "My heart always wished for a mom and then I got you."

Both of Brooke's hands weren't enough to capture her tears.

Ben glanced up at his dad. "Is she okay?"

Brooke brushed at her cheeks, unable to stop crying. "I'm going to be."

Dan pointed at the garbage bag near her feet. "Were you about to leave for somewhere?"

"Yes." Brooke used her sweater sleeve to dry her face. "As a matter of fact, I was waiting for my ride to arrive."

Ben's eyebrows pulled together. "When is your ride getting here?"

Brooke tipped her head and studied Dan. "Your dad didn't tell you?"

"Tell us what?" Dan looked at Ben.

Ben shrugged and shook his bangs out of his eyes.

"I called your dad to ask if he'd come and pick me up." Brooke stepped out onto the front porch.

"Why?" Dan watched her. A smile lifted one corner of his mouth. And love and hope curled through his gaze.

"I wanted to come home. I wanted to be with my family and friends." Brooke opened her arms. "But even more, I wanted to be with the people I love."

"Yes," Ben shouted and wrapped his arms around her waist. He pulled back enough to look up at her. "Can I get the animals ready?"

Brooke stepped to the side to let Ben rush ahead. His greeting for the dogs bounced off the walls.

Dan held back. "Are you sure?"

"I'm sure I'm scared. I'm sure I'll always worry." Brooke closed the distance. "But I'm even more sure in our love. Certain that I can face anything with you beside me."

Dan framed her face with his hands. "And if something happens?"

Brooke set her hands over his and locked her gaze on his. "Then I'll know I lived and loved without regrets. And I'll look back on a life well lived."

"I love you." Dan leaned toward her, covered her mouth with his.

And Brooke put everything in her heart into that one kiss. She didn't know what the future would bring. But for right now, she loved.

And in loving, she lived.

EPILOGUE

One week later

"BROOKE, WE'RE SO happy you came." Ann Ellis hugged her warmly. Brooke noticed Ann studying her intently, her gaze calm and peaceful. Then she nodded as if she'd found what she had been looking for. "And you brought company?"

Brooke motioned Dan and Ben over for introductions.

Her mother-in-law wrapped both Sawyers in her warm embrace. Stepping back, the kind woman held on to Dan's hand. "You're the one who has put the light back into Brooke's world."

Dan smiled. "Brooke has done the same for me."

Ann grabbed Brooke's hand and linked their hands together. "That's all we can ask for. A life that shines with love for as long as we have it to hold on to."

"I never expected…" Brooke started.

"That's the challenge, isn't it? To keep living." Ann squeezed her hand. "Phillip would never have wanted us to stop living."

"I believe that now." Brooke glanced at Dan, grateful for his strength and support. Even more so for his steady love.

Don arrived and greeted them. "Well, believe this, too," he said, "Phillip would approve. He'd want this for you."

"Thank you." Brooke hugged him. "Thank you for loving me."

"Always." Ann whispered, "That never changed."

Brooke wiped her eyes. "I think I forgot for a while."

"Please be happy," she said.

"I will," Brooke promised.

"If you walk to the end of the beach, you'll have a perfect view of the sunset." She pointed down the shoreline.

Dan took Brooke's hand in his. "Shall we?"

"Definitely." Brooke reached for Ben's hand.

Together they walked along the beach, smiling, looking ahead to their future.

* * * * *

Don't miss more great heartfelt romances from acclaimed author Cari Lynn Webb, available today at www.Harlequin.com!

Get 4 FREE REWARDS!

We'll send you 2 FREE Books plus 2 FREE Mystery Gifts.

Love Inspired® books feature contemporary inspirational romances with Christian characters facing the challenges of life and love.

FREE
Value Over
$20

YES! Please send me 2 FREE Love Inspired® Romance novels and my 2 FREE mystery gifts (gifts are worth about $10 retail). After receiving them, if I don't wish to receive any more books, I can return the shipping statement marked "cancel." If I don't cancel, I will receive 6 brand-new novels every month and be billed just $5.24 for the regular-print edition or $5.99 each for the larger-print edition in the U.S., or $5.74 each for the regular-print edition or $6.24 each for the larger-print edition in Canada. That's a savings of at least 13% off the cover price. It's quite a bargain! Shipping and handling is just 50¢ per book in the U.S. and $1.25 per book in Canada.* I understand that accepting the 2 free books and gifts places me under no obligation to buy anything. I can always return a shipment and cancel at any time. The free books and gifts are mine to keep no matter what I decide.

Choose one: ☐ **Love Inspired® Romance Regular-Print** (105/305 IDN GNWC) ☐ **Love Inspired® Romance Larger-Print** (122/322 IDN GNWC)

Name (please print)

Address   Apt. #

City   State/Province   Zip/Postal Code

Mail to the **Reader Service:**
IN U.S.A.: P.O. Box 1341, Buffalo, NY 14240-8531
IN CANADA: P.O. Box 603, Fort Erie, Ontario L2A 5X3

Want to try 2 free books from another series? Call 1-800-873-8635 or visit www.ReaderService.com.

---

*Terms and prices subject to change without notice. Prices do not include sales taxes, which will be charged (if applicable) based on your state or country of residence. Canadian residents will be charged applicable taxes. Offer not valid in Quebec. This offer is limited to one order per household. Books received may not be as shown. Not valid for current subscribers to Love Inspired Romance books. All orders subject to approval. Credit or debit balances in a customer's account(s) may be offset by any other outstanding balance owed by or to the customer. Please allow 4 to 6 weeks for delivery. Offer available while quantities last.

Your Privacy—The Reader Service is committed to protecting your privacy. Our Privacy Policy is available online at www.ReaderService.com or upon request from the Reader Service. We make a portion of our mailing list available to reputable third parties that offer products we believe may interest you. If you prefer that we not exchange your name with third parties, or if you wish to clarify or modify your communication preferences, please visit us at www.ReaderService.com/consumerschoice or write to us at Reader Service Preference Service, P.O. Box 9062, Buffalo, NY 14240-9062. Include your complete name and address.

LI19R3

Get 4 FREE REWARDS!

We'll send you 2 FREE Books plus 2 FREE Mystery Gifts.

Love Inspired® Suspense books feature Christian characters facing challenges to their faith... and lives.

FREE Value Over $20

YES! Please send me 2 FREE Love Inspired® Suspense novels and my 2 FREE mystery gifts (gifts are worth about $10 retail). After receiving them, if I don't wish to receive any more books, I can return the shipping statement marked "cancel." If I don't cancel, I will receive 6 brand-new novels every month and be billed just $5.24 each for the regular-print edition or $5.99 each for the larger-print edition in the U.S., or $5.74 each for the regular-print edition or $6.24 each for the larger-print edition in Canada. That's a savings of at least 13% off the cover price. It's quite a bargain! Shipping and handling is just 50¢ per book in the U.S. and $1.25 per book in Canada.* I understand that accepting the 2 free books and gifts places me under no obligation to buy anything. I can always return a shipment and cancel at any time. The free books and gifts are mine to keep no matter what I decide.

Choose one: ☐ **Love Inspired® Suspense Regular-Print** (153/353 IDN GNWN)   ☐ **Love Inspired® Suspense Larger-Print** (107/307 IDN GNWN)

Name (please print)

Address   Apt. #

City   State/Province   Zip/Postal Code

Mail to the **Reader Service**:
IN U.S.A.: P.O. Box 1341, Buffalo, NY 14240-8531
IN CANADA: P.O. Box 603, Fort Erie, Ontario L2A 5X3

Want to try 2 free books from another series! Call 1-800-873-8635 or visit www.ReaderService.com.

*Terms and prices subject to change without notice. Prices do not include sales taxes, which will be charged (if applicable) based on your state or country of residence. Canadian residents will be charged applicable taxes. Offer not valid in Quebec. This offer is limited to one order per household. Books received may not be as shown. Not valid for current subscribers to Love Inspired Suspense books. All orders subject to approval. Credit or debit balances in a customer's account(s) may be offset by any other outstanding balance owed by or to the customer. Please allow 4 to 6 weeks for delivery. Offer available while quantities last.

Your Privacy—The Reader Service is committed to protecting your privacy. Our Privacy Policy is available online at www.ReaderService.com or upon request from the Reader Service. We make a portion of our mailing list available to reputable third parties that offer products we believe may interest you. If you prefer that we not exchange your name with third parties, or if you wish to clarify or modify your communication preferences, please visit us at www.ReaderService.com/consumerschoice or write to us at Reader Service Preference Service, P.O. Box 9062, Buffalo, NY 14240-9062. Include your complete name and address.

LIS19R3

THE FORTUNES OF TEXAS COLLECTION!

18 FREE BOOKS in all!

Treat yourself to the rich legacy of the Fortune and Mendoza clans in this remarkable 50-book collection. This collection is packed with cowboys, tycoons and Texas-sized romances!

YES! Please send me **The Fortunes of Texas Collection** in Larger Print. This collection begins with 3 FREE books and 2 FREE gifts in the first shipment. Along with my 3 free books, I'll also get the next 4 books from The Fortunes of Texas Collection, in LARGER PRINT, which I may either return and owe nothing, or keep for the low price of $5.24 U.S./$5.89 CDN each plus $2.99 for shipping and handling per shipment*. If I decide to continue, about once a month for 8 months I will get 6 or 7 more books but will only need to pay for 4. That means 2 or 3 books in every shipment will be FREE! If I decide to keep the entire collection, I'll have paid for only 32 books because 18 books are FREE! I understand that accepting the 3 free books and gifts places me under no obligation to buy anything. I can always return a shipment and cancel at any time. My free books and gifts are mine to keep no matter what I decide.

☐ 269 HCN 4622   ☐ 469 HCN 4622

Name (please print)

Address   Apt. #

City   State/Province   Zip/Postal Code

Mail to the **Reader Service:**
IN U.S.A.: P.O Box 1341, Buffalo, N.Y. 14240-8531
IN CANADA: P.O. Box 603, Fort Erie, Ontario L2A 5X3

*Terms and prices subject to change without notice. Prices do not include sales taxes, which will be charged (if applicable) based on your state or country of residence. Canadian residents will be charged applicable taxes. Offer not valid in Quebec. All orders subject to approval. Credit or debit balances in a customer's account(s) may be offset by any other outstanding balance owed by or to the customer. Please allow three to four weeks for delivery. Offer available while quantities last. © 2018 Harlequin Enterprises Limited. ® and ™ are trademarks owned and used by the trademark owner and/or its licensee.

Your Privacy—The Reader Service is committed to protecting your privacy. Our Privacy Policy is available online at www.ReaderService.com or upon request from the Reader Service. We make a portion of our mailing list available to reputable third parties that offer products we believe may interest you. If you prefer that we not exchange your name with third parties, or if you wish to clarify or modify your communication preferences, please visit us at www.ReaderService.com/consumerschoice or write to us at Reader Service Preference Service, P.O. Box 9049, Buffalo, NY 14269-9049. Include your name and address.

50BFT19R

Get 4 FREE REWARDS!

We'll send you 2 FREE Books plus 2 FREE Mystery Gifts.

FREE
Value Over
$20

Both the **Romance** and **Suspense** collections feature compelling novels written by many of today's best-selling authors.

YES! Please send me 2 FREE novels from the Essential Romance or Essential Suspense Collection and my 2 FREE gifts (gifts are worth about $10 retail). After receiving them, if I don't wish to receive any more books, I can return the shipping statement marked "cancel." If I don't cancel, I will receive 4 brand-new novels every month and be billed just $6.99 each in the U.S. or $7.24 each in Canada. That's a savings of at least 13% off the cover price. It's quite a bargain! Shipping and handling is just 50¢ per book in the U.S. and $1.25 per book in Canada.* I understand that accepting the 2 free books and gifts places me under no obligation to buy anything. I can always return a shipment and cancel at any time. The free books and gifts are mine to keep no matter what I decide.

Choose one: ☐ **Essential Romance**   ☐ **Essential Suspense**
                 (194/394 MDN GNNP)   (191/391 MDN GNNP)

Name (please print)

Address   Apt. #

City   State/Province   Zip/Postal Code

Mail to the **Reader Service**:
IN U.S.A.: P.O. Box 1341, Buffalo, NY 14240-8531
IN CANADA: P.O. Box 603, Fort Erie, Ontario L2A 5X3

Want to try 2 free books from another series? Call 1-800-873-8635 or visit www.ReaderService.com.

*Terms and prices subject to change without notice. Prices do not include sales taxes, which will be charged (if applicable) based on your state or country of residence. Canadian residents will be charged applicable taxes. Offer not valid in Quebec. This offer is limited to one order per household. Books received may not be as shown. Not valid for current subscribers to the Essential Romance or Essential Suspense Collection. All orders subject to approval. Credit or debit balances in a customer's account(s) may be offset by any other outstanding balance owed by or to the customer. Please allow 4 to 6 weeks for delivery. Offer available while quantities last.

Your Privacy—The Reader Service is committed to protecting your privacy. Our Privacy Policy is available online at www.ReaderService.com or upon request from the Reader Service. We make a portion of our mailing list available to reputable third parties that offer products we believe may interest you. If you prefer that we not exchange your name with third parties, or if you wish to clarify or modify your communication preferences, please visit us at www.ReaderService.com/consumerschoice or write to us at Reader Service Preference Service, P.O. Box 9062, Buffalo, NY 14240-9062. Include your complete name and address.

STRS19R3

READERSERVICE.COM

Manage your account online!

- Review your order history
- Manage your payments
- Update your address

> *We've designed the
> Reader Service website
> just for you.*

Enjoy all the features!

- Discover new series available to you, and read excerpts from any series.
- Respond to mailings and special monthly offers.
- Browse the Bonus Bucks catalog and online-only exculsives.
- Share your feedback.

Visit us at:

ReaderService.com

RS16R

COMING NEXT MONTH FROM

⊕ HARLEQUIN®

HEARTWARMING™

Available September 3, 2019

#295 AFTER THE RODEO
Heroes of Shelter Creek • by Claire McEwen

Former bull rider Jace Hendricks needs biologist Vivian Reed off his ranch, fast—or he risks losing custody of his nieces and nephew. So why is Vivian's optimism winning over the kids...and Jace?

#296 THE RANCHER'S FAMILY
The Hitching Post Hotel • by Barbara White Daille

Wes Daniels is fine on his own. He has his ranch and his children—he doesn't need anything else. But the local matchmaker has other plans! Now Wes is suspicious about why Cara Leonetti keeps calling on him...

#297 SAFE IN HIS ARMS
Butterfly Harbor Stories • by Anna J. Stewart

Army vet Kendall Davidson has found the peace she's been searching for until loud newcomers Hunter MacBride and his niece arrive with love and laughter to share, making her question what kind of life she's truly looking for.

#298 THEIR FOREVER HOME
by Syndi Powell

Can a popular home reno contest allow Cassie Lowman and John Robison their chance to shine and fall for each other with so much—personally and professionally—on the line?

———————

YOU CAN FIND MORE INFORMATION ON UPCOMING
HARLEQUIN® TITLES, FREE EXCERPTS AND MORE AT
WWW.HARLEQUIN.COM.

HWCNMR0819